THANKS TO ROBERT GOLDSBOROUGH "NERO WOLFE HAS NEVER BEEN IN BETTER FORM!"*

FADE TO BLACK

"Goldsborough knows the advertising game through and through, and his treatment of agency rivalry, the idiosyncrasies that afflict account executives, and his detailing of the office decor of agency overlords makes sparkling copy."

—CHICAGO SUN-TIMES

SILVER SPIRE

"Mystery fans can revel in this superb revival."

—ST. LOUIS POST-DISPATCH

THE LAST COINCIDENCE

"I report with glee that Nero lives through the brilliant writing of Robert Goldsborough. . . . I double-dare you to put it down. Triple-dare you."

—LARRY KING, USA TODAY

* ALFRED HITCHCOCK MYSTERY MAGAZINE

THE BLOODIED IVY

"A classic Wolfe mystery—Goldsborough has the style down thoroughly—with a few cute twists."
—CHICAGO TRIBUNE

DEATH ON DEADLINE

"Robert Goldsborough does a first-rate job in re-creating Rex Stout's . . . Nero Wolfe. . . . A worthy successor."
—FORBES

MURDER IN E MINOR

"Mr. Goldsborough has all of the late writer's stylistic mannerisms down pat. . . . And Wolfe is as insufferably omniscient as ever."
—THE NEW YORK TIMES

· A NERO WOLFE MYSTERY ·

THE
MISSING CHAPTER

Robert Goldsborough

BANTAM BOOKS

NEW YORK · TORONTO · LONDON · SYDNEY · AUCKLAND

This edition contains the complete text
of the original hardcover edition.
NOT ONE WORD HAS BEEN OMITTED.

THE MISSING CHAPTER
A Bantam Book

PUBLISHING HISTORY
Bantam hardcover edition / January 1994
Bantam paperback edition / December 1994

ISBN 0-553-56874-4

Published simultaneously in the United States and Canada

Bantam Books are published by Bantam Books, a division of Bantam Doubleday Dell
Publishing Group, Inc. Its trademark, consisting of the words "Bantam Books" and
the portrayal of a rooster, is Registered in U.S. Patent and Trademark Office and in
other countries. Marca Registrada. Bantam Books, 1540 Broadway, New York, New
York. 10036.

PRINTED IN THE UNITED STATES OF AMERICA

RAD 0 9 8 7 6 5 4 3 2 1

To
MARY MCLAUGHLIN
AND
FIORA SCAFFI

"He's over this way, Sergeant." Mogoven led Orville Barnstable through knee-high grass and weeds to a gully about two hundred yards north of the sway-backed barn. The man wore denim coveralls and a red plaid shirt. He lay face down, the lower half of his body partially submerged in the shallow, slow-moving water.

"Whoever stabbed him really ran that knife in deep," the patrolman announced solemnly as Barnstable knelt beside the corpse. "There was a powerful lot of force behind it."

"It's old Lightning Greaves," Barnstable pronounced. "Although, shoot, he hasn't been called 'Lightning' for close on forty-five years now. Christian name's Edgar, of course. Got tagged with that when we were at Reed's Grove High. He was one slick basketball player—made All-State twice and took the team farther'n it ever got before or since. I was on that same team, son, keepin' the bench warm. Too durn slow, which is why Lightning here stuck me with the name 'Snail.' That's okay, though: When they passed out medals for winnin' the district tournament, mine was the same size as his."

The sergeant took off his battered felt hat as he got to his feet. "Poor fella. In the years since high school, this man's life's been rougher'n a burlap sack on a baby's bottom. Lost his spread to the bank, then Arla left him. They say the Lord has a plan for us all, but dog-gone if I can fathom what his plan could have been for Lightning."

From *Death in the North Meadow*
by Charles Childress

THE
MISSING CHAPTER

ONE

"**Y**ou're almost fifteen minutes early," I told the elegant-looking visitor who stood erect on our front stoop. "We don't deny admission on a technicality like that, though. And I've seen your picture in the newspapers—more than once. Come on in."

"Thank you," Horace Vinson said with a smile, smoothing well-tended salt-and-pepper hair that had been ruffled by rude April winds. "I thought the cab ride down here would take a lot longer. You, of course, are Archie Goodwin. I, too, have seen your picture in the papers. And I recognize your voice from yesterday."

I grinned back and held out a paw. "Guilty as charged. He won't be down until eleven, but there's no reason you can't park yourself in his office. I'll even keep you company at no extra charge," I said as I hung his expensive Burberry on a peg and led him down the hall.

Vinson squinted cornflower-blue eyes as he stood in the doorway to the largest room in the house and nodded approvingly. "Just as I pictured it. Arguably the most famous work space in Manhattan. And from a quick look, very possibly the most comfortable, too.''

"Unless you are a murderer Nero Wolfe is about to finger. Have a seat. Can I get you coffee?"

Vinson said yes, heavy on the cream, as he settled into the red leather chair in front of the desk. I went to the kitchen, where Fritz Brenner, chef *extraordinaire,* keeps a pot warm all morning. Fritz looked at me anxiously as I filled a cup with java and the cow's finest. "Too early to tell," I responded to his unspoken question. "Of course Mr. Wolfe hasn't even seen him yet, let alone heard him out. If something of interest develops, you'll be the fourth to know."

Fritz sighed and turned back to building the cassoulet Castelnaudary that Wolfe and I would be devouring in the dining room in a little more than two hours. He frets when Wolfe isn't working, which means he almost always frets. Fritz figures we're constantly on the brink of bankruptcy, and nothing I ever tell him to the contrary seems to help.

Actually, this time I was more than a little worried myself. We hadn't done any work in months, unless you count the child's play in which we—make that I—collared the Fifth Avenue jewelry store clerk who made a cute little game of substituting passable imitations for the expensive ice in his employer's display cases and carting the genuine articles away. It took all of three days before I doped out which of eight employees in the pricey store was making the switches. I caught the poor wretch in the act, and our reward was enough to keep Wolfe in beer, books, and bouillabaisse for a couple of moons.

Not that we hadn't had other recent opportunities for gainful employment, as in a pair of potential cases, each of which would have given the bank balance a healthy transfusion. But both times, Wolfe found excuses for taking a pass. The real reason he turned thumbs down—and I told him so—was downright laziness, combined with a contrary streak as wide as his back.

I should correct myself. *Lazy* is not a word to be strictly applied to Nero Wolfe. Stubborn, yes, but not lazy. He allots four hours every day—nine to eleven in the morning and four to six in the afternoon—to nurturing the ten thousand orchids in the plant rooms on the roof of the brownstone. Most of the rest of his waking hours are spent either in the dining room devouring Fritz's superb lunches and dinners, or in his office, where he devours anywhere from five to ten books a week, sometimes juggling three at a time. Okay, the guy's not doing push-ups, but his mind is in high gear, so scratch the lazy comment.

My roles in the operation are varied. I handle Wolfe's correspondence, balance the books, work with our live-in orchid nurse, Theodore Horstmann, to keep the germination records up to date, and serve as so-called man of action when the two of us are working at being private detectives—duly licensed by the Sovereign State of New York. I also function as a burr under Wolfe's saddle when he doesn't feel like working. Obviously, I hadn't been a real good burr of late, and I'd been indulging in mopery on that April Tuesday morning when the phone rang.

"Nero Wolfe's office, Archie Goodwin speaking."

"Mr. Goodwin, my name is Horace Vinson. I am

in the publishing business, and I would like to engage Nero Wolfe to investigate a murder."

The good old direct approach; that's a guaranteed way to get my attention. Another is name recognition, and I immediately recognized Vinson's name. "Who got murdered?" I asked, poising a pencil above my stenographer's pad.

"Charles Childress. He was shot a week ago."

"The writer," I said. "Found in his apartment in Greenwich Village last Tuesday, an apparent suicide. Three paragraphs in the *Gazette* the next day, somewhere back around page thirteen."

The response was a snort. "Suicide, hell! Charles was killed. Those idiots who masquerade as police in this town don't think so, but I know so. Are you interested or not?"

I told Horace Vinson I'd take it up with Wolfe, which I did when he descended from the plant rooms. That brought the glare I was expecting, so I got up and walked all of three paces from my desk to his, placing a computer printout on his blotter. "That," I told Wolfe, "is the result of your consistent refusal to reenter the work force. You may recognize those figures as our bank balance. Note how the last nine entries have been withdrawals. Note also that if we continue at the current pace, we will be forced to file for bankruptcy after another fourteen withdrawals."

"Your mathematics are suspect, as usual," Wolfe said with an air of unconcern.

"Okay, maybe you've got some other funds tucked away, a fortune you've never told me about. Even so, given our monthly expenses, you'd need at least—"

"Archie, shut up!"

"Yes, sir."

Wolfe closed his eyes, presumably because looking at me was more than he could bear. He stayed that way for over a minute, then awoke and favored me with another glare. "Confound it, call Mr. Vinson, tell him to be here tomorrow at eleven."

Which is why I was sitting in the office chatting with Horace Vinson, editor-in-chief of Monarch Press, at eleven the next morning when the groan of the elevator announced Wolfe's descent from the plant rooms. The lord of the manor paused at the office door, dipped his head a fraction of an inch in our guest's direction, then detoured around his desk, placing a raceme of orchids in a vase on the blotter before settling into the chair that was expressly constructed to support his seventh of a ton. "Mr. Vinson," he said. His version of an effusive greeting.

"Mr. Wolfe, good to meet you. My God, those flowers are stunning."

"*Doritaenopsis,* a crossing of *Phalaenopsis* and *Doritis,*" Wolfe replied. Vinson may not have known it, but he had said precisely the right thing; Nero Wolfe loves to have his orchids gushed over.

"Would you like more coffee or something else to drink?" he asked Vinson. "I am going to have beer."

"Not just yet. Mr. Goodwin told you why I am here?"

"The death of a writer. Mr. Childress. One of your authors, I believe."

Vinson shifted in the red leather chair and studied his pearl cufflink. "Yes, one of my authors," he said huskily. "He was shot last week—eight days ago now—in his apartment in the Village."

Wolfe paused to pour beer from one of two chilled bottles Fritz had just brought in. "I read the newspaper accounts." He frowned at the foam in his glass. "The police have labeled it a suicide."

"Nonsense! Charles had everything to live for. He was a relatively successful writer, he had a terrific future, and he was about to be married to a beautiful woman whom he loved and doted on."

"He was shot with his own gun, and when Mr. Goodwin telephoned the police yesterday at my direction, he was informed by Sergeant Stebbins of Homicide that the only fingerprints on the weapon were his own," Wolfe said evenly.

Vinson leaned forward and placed his palms on his knees. "Mr. Wolfe, surely you have seen enough murders to realize that killers know how to make their handiwork seem like something else."

"I have," Wolfe said, drinking beer and dabbing his lips with a handkerchief. "Tell me why someone would want to kill Mr. Childress."

Vinson's well-tailored shoulders sagged, and he dropped back into the chair with a sigh. "All right. First off, Charles was, well, not the most pleasant person you'd ever be likely to run into. Some people found him boastful and arrogant, to say the least."

"Do you agree with that assessment?"

"Mr. Wolfe, Charles Childress was a talented writer—not brilliant, but with an ability that I felt was soon to come to full flower, if you'll pardon the hyperbole. And he possessed a well-developed sense of self. He knew what his strengths were. And he wasn't the least bit reticent about proclaiming them."

"Fanfaronade is not a trait conducive to the development of friendships, but rarely is it the primary stimulus for murder," Wolfe observed. Yep, I was there. He really said it.

"Fanfaronade, as you term it, was only a part of Charles's problem," Vinson replied without missing a beat, forming a chapel with his long, bony fingers. "He also was contentious, combative, and exceedingly vengeful. Does the name Wilbur Hobbs mean anything to you?"

Wolfe grunted. "He attempts to review books for the *Gazette*."

That brought a slight smile to the editor's angular face. "Well said. As you probably know, Charles was the continuator of the long and extremely popular series of detective novels, the Sergeant Barnstable stories, which were originated by Darius Sawyer in the forties."

"I learned as much from the newspaper reports on Mr. Childress's death," Wolfe replied dryly. "My current schedule does not allow for the reading of detective fiction, let alone its so-called continuation by a second author."

Vinson shrugged and let his eyes travel over Wolfe's bookshelves. "Actually, some detective stories qualify as solid literature, better certainly than a lot of the non-genre work being turned out today. And I happen to think Charles did a fine job of capturing the spirit and flavor of Sawyer's writing. Of course, my opinion could be termed suspect, as I am the one who picked Charles to be the series continuator after Sawyer died. I had read the books he'd done previously, for another publisher, and I felt he had potential to ultimately go beyond writing mysteries. Anyway,

Wilbur Hobbs has been rough on all three of Charles's Barnstable books, and he was particularly savage in reviewing the last one, which we published about six weeks ago."

Wolfe drained his glass. He refilled it from the second bottle. "I read the review. How have other critics treated Mr. Childress's work?"

"Mixed," Vinson said. "Most range from mildly favorable to mildly negative, but nothing like Hobbs, who is a nasty, vituperative little man. As you know, his *Gazette* review of the most recent Barnstable book, *Death in the North Meadow,* was incredibly mean-spirited. Among other things, he called it a 'towering exercise in mimicry' and said that 'Any self-respecting lover of mysteries should treat this volume as if it were a radioactive cobalt isotope.' "

Vinson exhaled. "Charles never took criticism particularly well, and Hobbs's piece—it occupied all of page three in the *Gazette*'s Sunday book review section—really lit his wick. He fired off an article to the *Manhattan Literary Times* blasting Hobbs. I tried to talk him out of submitting the piece—there's almost never anything to be gained by lashing back at a critic—but he was adamant. Are you familiar with the *MLT*?"

Wolfe said no, and Vinson went on. "It's a self-styled avant-garde weekly tabloid that thrives on controversy. Of course they printed Charles's article, in which he attacked Hobbs as 'a preening poseur, a peacock, a dandified and self-important satrap who is trying desperately, yea, pitifully, to become an arbiter of public taste, which is roughly equivalent to John Travolta trying to fit into Astaire's white tie and tails.' Quite a sentence, eh? But that wasn't the worst of it.

Charles all but accused Hobbs of being on the take, of accepting gifts—financial and otherwise—from authors and publishers whose works he praises in print."

"Is there substance to that charge?"

Vinson set his jaw, then nodded reluctantly. "Possibly. It has been rumored in the publishing community for years, but nobody had ever come out and said anything publicly before. There's no question about Hobbs having his favorites—both among writers and publishing houses. You can pretty well predict how he's going to react to a book—with fawning praise or fiery vitriol—depending on who the writer and publisher are. Hobbs doesn't like Monarch, never has, despite our having had two Pulitzer Prize winners and five National Book Awards in the last six years. Why doesn't he like us?" Vinson asked, anticipating Wolfe's question. "Because nobody in our house, from me on down to the lowest editorial assistant, will kowtow to the little viper. We've never made any secret of our feelings about the man, and I've even written to the publisher of the *Gazette* complaining about the obvious bias in Hobbs's reviews. And he certainly didn't like Charles Childress. After the *MLT* piece came out, almost a month ago, Hobbs phoned me in a fury. He made loud noises about a lawsuit, but that's the last I heard about it."

Wolfe leaned back and scowled. "Has Mr. Hobbs ever approached anyone at your company soliciting money or other favors?"

"A few years ago, two editors on our staff mentioned he tossed out some veiled hints to them that he was open to 'offers,' is how I think he termed it," Vinson responded sourly. "Both editors assured me they pretended they didn't understand what he was talking about. Apparently, Hobbs did not press the issue with either of them, but soon after those episodes, we started getting execrable reviews from him on virtually every one of our books."

"Is it commonplace for book reviewers to accept *cadeaux* from publishers?"

"It is *not*. God knows I've been angry at reviewers through the years, but always because I disagreed with their literary opinions. Then Wilbur Hobbs came along. With him, I question the motives *for* those opinions."

"And you suggest that Mr. Hobbs committed murder in retaliation for the scathing indictment Mr. Childress had penned about him?"

"I see that as a distinct possibility," Vinson responded with a scowl of his own. "Although it is by no means the only possibility."

"Indeed?" Wolfe raised his eyebrows.

Vinson nodded grimly. "I can think of two other people who might also take satisfaction in helping to end Charles Childress's life."

Wolfe's eyebrows stayed up. "Sir, I confess amazement that book publishing holds such potential for violence."

"I wish I could honestly tell you I was amazed myself," Vinson replied earnestly. "But I've been in this business for forty years, and there's damn little that can surprise me anymore."

I could tell that Wolfe was still amazed, but he pulled himself together long enough to finish the beer in his glass.

TWO

I refilled Vinson's cup, and he took two sips before going on. "I thought about all of this for a long time before calling you," he told Wolfe, rubbing a palm along his well-defined jaw. "As I said earlier, Charles Childress was contentious. And if anything, that's an understatement. In the last few months, Charles had fought—quite publicly—with both his editor at Monarch and with his agent, Franklin Ott. Charles and the editor, Keith Billings, who oversaw our mystery line, didn't get along from the start, and I'm sorry to say their relationship had deteriorated through Charles's three Barnstable books. He felt Billings over-edited him and made capricious changes. Keith, for his part, claimed the books' plots were both weak and slipshod and badly needed shoring up."

Vinson sighed. "Both of them were to some degree correct, and it seemed that every time I turned around I was mediating one of their battles. Finally, Frank Ott called and told me Charles wouldn't write for Monarch anymore unless he got assigned a new editor. I gave in and tabbed someone else to work with him on his next book. Billings quit in a rage, feeling, perhaps with some justification, that his authority had been undercut. He now is working for another publisher—Westman & Lane—I'm sorry to say."

"You valued the writer more than the editor," Wolfe remarked.

Vinson stirred his coffee, then looked up. "I have always been referred to as 'a writer's man,' " he said, turning a palm up. "Maybe in this case, I tried too hard to live up to that tag. Anyway, at the same time he was mixing it up with Billings, Charles was sniping at Frank Ott, and he eventually fired him. He was angry because, among other things, Ott didn't cut a better deal with us on his new Barnstable contract."

"Did you feel Mr. Ott adequately represented his client?"

"I've known Ott for years, and he has always been a top-drawer agent, honest, hard-working, and plenty tough," Vinson replied. "You should be aware that there were two factors at work here: First, Charles's Barnstable books have sold okay, but not great; and second, I don't have to tell you that these aren't exactly the best of times anywhere, especially in the publishing world. I was a great supporter of Charles—hell, I'm the one who brought him in to continue the Sawyer series, and then I sided with him against a damn good editor, losing the editor in the process. But when Ott came at me three months ago looking for an eighty-percent increase on a new two-book contract, I dug in my heels. I knew Frank was being pressured by Charles, because he—Frank, that is—was realistic enough to know that such a demand was ludicrous. *Eighty percent,* for God's sake, for books that don't have a prayer of making the best-seller lists!"

Vinson realized his voice had been rising and checked himself. "So then what happens?" he said in more moderate tones. "First Charles fires Frank Ott, telling him something to the effect that 'You're supposed to be such a damn close buddy of Vinson's, but you can't get me a decent deal.' Then he writes an article, one of those 'It's my turn to speak out' things, for *Book Business*, our weekly trade magazine, in which he blasts both literary agents and editors. He calls agents 'lazy and reactive,' among other things, and he whacks editors as being 'dictatorial, closed-minded meddlers and stiflers of creativity.' Charles didn't mention names, but he didn't have to; most of the people who read the magazine, at least here in New York, knew exactly whom he was targeting in both cases."

"Mr. Childress had a penchant for diatribe," Wolfe observed. "When did the article about agents and editors appear?"

"Three weeks ago, and within minutes after the issue was on the street, you'd better believe I heard from both Billings and Ott," Vinson answered, his voice rising again. "Keith already was well established at his new job, but he was really hot. He swore that if he ever ran into Charles again, he'd do some major-league stifling of his own. But his anger was nothing compared to Frank's. He told me—I remember the phrasing precisely—that I'd better 'put the lid on that smart-mouthed, marginally talented, egomaniacal bastard or I'll sue his ass from here to Trenton. Hell, I may sue his ass anyway, and yours, too, while I'm at it.' I've known Frank Ott for more than twenty years, and I've never, ever heard him talk like that, to me or to anyone else. I think he felt that his reputation had been damaged beyond repair."

"Do others in the publishing community agree?"

Horace Vinson wrinkled his brow for several seconds before responding. "It's . . . a little soon to tell, but, yes, that article probably did hurt Ott to some extent, even though a lot of people know that Charles had a penchant, to use your word, for shooting off his mouth."

"You apparently feel that given the consecution you have described, either Mr. Billings or Mr. Ott is capable of murder, along with Wilbur Hobbs."

Vinson shook his head mournfully, looking like he'd just missed the last night train to Poughkeepsie. "Mr. Wolfe, I like and respect two of those men very much. But yes, I'm convinced that Charles was killed by one of the three."

"Have you discussed this with the authorities?"

"Huh! If you want to call it that. I went and saw a man at NYPD. Homicide—not that fellow Stebbins you mentioned earlier—and it took me less than fifteen seconds to realize I was wasting my time. This cretin, I forget his name, but he's tall and has bulging eyes, he acted—"

"Lieutenant Rowcliff," I put in.

"Yeah, that's the one, George Rowcliff. He acted like my sole purpose was to ruin his day. He *did* listen, but his expression made it clear that the idiot was humoring me. About the only piece of information I got from him was that nobody in Charles's apartment building even heard a shot that day, and he was damn grudging about giving me even that. I haven't been patronized like that since one of my daughter's elementary school teachers explained why she—my daughter, that is—was having trouble learning her multiplication tables.''

Wolfe moved his head up and down a fraction of an inch, which for him is the equivalent of a vigorous nod. "Lieutenant Rowcliff has never mastered the art of interacting civilly with other human beings." He laced his fingers over his center mound.

"And obviously he never will," Vinson huffed. "Mr. Wolfe, book publishing has been extremely good to me. I've always worked hard, so I don't apologize for whatever success I've attained, but I have also been well rewarded for my efforts. By most standards, I'm a wealthy man. I dislike seeing anything happen that reflects badly on the publishing business, to say nothing of my extreme dislike of violence. I know that you don't come cheap, nor should you, given your record. But I feel confident that I can afford your rates. I want you to find out who killed Charles Childress."

Wolfe considered him through narrowed eyes. "Sir, you say you dislike that which reflects badly upon your profession. It is likely that were Mr. Goodwin and I to undertake the investigation you propose, a substantial amount of negative publicity would accrue to that profession, or at least to substantial segments of it. You may want to heed one of Mr. Dickens's passages and let sleeping dogs lie."

Vinson's jaw dropped. "I must tell you that I'm shocked," he snapped. "Here a murder has been committed, and you, who have solved so many killings through the years, suggest that I merely look the other way!"

"At the risk of incurring your displeasure, I remain unconvinced that a murder *has* been committed," Wolfe replied evenly. "The police are not total lackwits, with the possible exception of the man you encountered at headquarters. And even Lieutenant Rowcliff is possessed of a brain, albeit one not always fully operational. You appear to be the only person of the opinion that Mr. Childress did not take his own life."

Vinson's aristocratic face flushed. "Not so! I should have mentioned this earlier, but I talked to Charles's fiancée yesterday. She absolutely agrees with me that it's inconceivable he committed suicide."

"Indeed?"

"Her name is Debra Mitchell. A stunning woman, absolutely lovely." Vinson stopped to take a deep breath. "They were to be married at the end of the summer, in September."

Wolfe raised his shoulders a fraction of an inch and let them drop. "One's betrothed would hardly be likely to concede the possibility that her suitor committed suicide. Let me approach the matter from the opposite direction: Why are the authorities so unshakable in their conviction that Mr. Childress killed himself?"

Vinson was clearly angry, but he struggled to compose himself. "Charles was subject to pronounced mood swings," he said tensely. "I had seen him at both extremes; the highs were . . . well, very high, and the troughs were canyons."

"Was he manic-depressive?"

"I'm no psychiatrist, Mr. Wolfe, so I don't know the precise clinical definition of that affliction, although Charles certainly showed what I think of as symptoms. But suicide—absolutely not, regardless of what the police say."

"Why did Mr. Childress possess a handgun?"

"Oh—I should have mentioned that earlier," the publisher said apologetically. "There had been several break-ins on his block in the last year or so, one of them an armed robbery in which a man and his wife both were beaten quite badly by the intruders. Charles had a first-floor front apartment, and that kind of thing made him jittery. He mentioned three or four months ago that he had bought a pistol."

"Did others know he had the gun?"

"I can't answer that, although I knew—because he told me—that he kept it in a drawer in the nightstand next to his bed."

I've been around Wolfe long enough to tell when his mind begins to wander, and it was straying now, undoubtedly in the direction of the cassoulet Castelnaudary that he would be demolishing before long. "Mr. Vinson, I am not yet prepared to accept a commission from you," he said, rising. "Mr. Goodwin will inform you of my decision."

"When?" Vinson rasped, turning in his chair to follow Wolfe's progress out the door.

I was left to supply the answer to one very angry and frustrated editor-in-chief. "You'll be hearing from me later today," I said with more confidence than I felt. "I know he sometimes seems rude, but then, he's a genius, and things are bouncing around in his cranium that you and I can't begin to fathom." It was part of my standard "He's-tough-to-figure-out-but-he-means-well speech." It did not play well with Vinson.

"He sure as hell *does* seem rude," he snapped, standing and squaring his shoulders. Then the lines in his face softened. "But . . . I've worked with a lot of authors who thought they were geniuses—a few actually were—and most of them kept whatever manners they possessed well hidden. I've made all sorts of allowances for them, and of course I'm willing to make damn near any allowance if Mr. Wolfe does go to work on this awful business. Is there anything else I should be doing to persuade him—and you, too—that Charles was murdered?"

"You don't have to persuade me. As for Mr. Wolfe, I can't think of anything at the moment. He's going to have to come around to that opinion on his own, but there's no law that says I can't give him a push in the right direction," I said as we headed for the front hall.

"Push away," Vinson answered, smiling tightly. Giving me a thumbs-up, he stepped into the wind and went down the steps in search of a taxi.

THREE

Wolfe considers any discussion whatever of business—or potential business—at the dining room table as bordering on heresy. There have been a handful of times when, for various reasons, I have ignored the house rules and persisted in talking about some revenue-producing venture during a meal. This, however, was not such an occasion. For the moment, I was content to get my choppers into the cassoulet Castelnaudary, which I sometimes refer to as boiled beans, although to call it that hardly does the dish justice. For the record, it's got white beans, but also pork, carrots, mutton, onions, and a batch of other wonderful stuff that only Fritz knows for sure. Wolfe thinks he can list every ingredient, too, but I happen to have evidence—Fritz's word—to the contrary.

Anyway, Wolfe and I ate with respectful gusto, and he held forth on the relative merits of limiting the terms of members of Congress. I can't say that his monologue nudged me toward one camp or the other, because he was equally persuasive in his arguments on each side. When I asked where he stood, he said nothing, but the folds in his cheeks deepened, which for him is a smile.

Back in the office with our coffee, we busied ourselves—Wolfe by signing checks and correspondence I had typed from his dictation, and me by entering orchid germination records into the personal computer. We both knew I was about to raise the subject of Horace Vinson's request.

"Well?" I said, swinging around in my chair to face Wolfe, who had picked up his latest book, *Churchill*, by Martin Gilbert.

"Well, what?" he replied with a glower, keeping his eyes stubbornly on the pages.

I grinned. "You just signed checks totaling slightly more than thirty-seven hundred dollars, checks that I will hand-carry to the main post office later this afternoon. Would you care to know what the impact of these checks is on the bottom line?"

"I abhor that term."

" 'Bottom line'? Yes, I know you do, and I promise never to use it again in your presence if you turn loose with some instructions—instructions relating to Mr. Vinson's visit, that is."

Wolfe expelled a bushel of air and set his book down deliberately. "Very well. I could ignore your ululations, but you would continue to badger me until the atmosphere in this room became oppressive. Your notebook."

"Yes, sir." This time, I kept my grin to myself. Lily Rowan more than once has told me that smugness does not become me.

"Telephone Mr. Cohen," Wolfe said curtly. "Better yet, visit him. Learn everything you can about Mr.

Childress, Mr. Ott, Mr. Billings, Mr. Hobbs, and Mr. Vinson. And Mr. Childress's fiancée."

"Do I also call Vinson and ask him to open his checkbook and start writing?"

"Not yet. Let him wait. He has no viable alternative." Wolfe picked up his book and hid behind it, signifying that his order-giving had ended.

A word or three about Lon Cohen: He has been on the payroll of the *New York Gazette* for so long that I tell him he can remember when they set type by hand —and by the light of kerosene lamps. If he has a title, I don't know what it is, but he's got an office on the twentieth floor, two doors from the publisher's carpeted acre, and there's a rumor around the *Gazette* building that the old man doesn't sneeze before first checking with Lon.

Whatever the truth, Lon probably knows more about what's going on, both aboveboard and below, in the far-flung boroughs of New York on any given day than the mayor, the police chief, and the doorman at the Waldorf-Astoria combined. And he's also one hell of a poker player, as I sadly learned again last Thursday in our weekly game at Saul Panzer's, when I let him bluff me—I think—out of the biggest pot of the night.

Through the years, Wolfe and I have developed a mutual-aid society of sorts with Lon. He passes along information on cases we're working on, and, assuming Wolfe cracks said cases, the *Gazette* is rewarded with an exclusive. And Lon gets the bonus of dinner in the brownstone every few months, topped off with multiple servings of the Remisier brandy he loves so much.

It's almost two miles, north and a little east, from

the brownstone to the *Gazette* offices, but the wind had died down and the skies had cleared, so I chose to hoof it, leaving Wolfe to his book and his beer. It was almost three when my knuckles collided with Lon's oak door and I swung it open.

"Don't you ever wait for somebody to say 'Come in,' for God's sake?" he barked, cupping the receiver of one of three telephones on a desk strewn with newspapers, coffee cups, crumpled memos, and more felt-tipped pens and yellow pencils than you'd find in any stationery store in Midtown. Lon Cohen is dark—that description takes in his skin, his slicked-back hair, and his eyes, which are always moving. He muttered something to the person on the other end of the line and banged the receiver into its cradle, looking at me with a scowl that sent an unspoken but clear "I'm busy—what the hell do you want?" message.

"Sure, I'll sit down, thanks," I told him, easing into a chair in front of his desk, which also had a personal computer on it, the screen dark. "I just happened to be in the neighborhood and—"

Lon spat a word, then gave me a tight smile. "You never just *happen* to be anywhere, any more than I happen to suspect Nero Wolfe is hungry for information because of a case he's got his teeth into. Whatever you're here for, make it fast; we just got a tip that the police think they've finally nailed the guy who's done all those neighborhood bank jobs in Brooklyn and Queens."

"The one wearing the bulb-nosed mask?"

"That's the clown," Lon nodded, delivering the line deadpan. "Don't tell me this is a social call, because I'm not buying it."

"Okay, I won't. Charles Childress."

His thin face registered mild interest, and he leaned forward. "The mystery writer who lived in the Village and shot himself last week. What about him?"

"Interesting you should ask. What do you know about any enemies he might have had?"

"Aha. So a certain well-known and well-fed private cop suspects the suicide is not a suicide."

"Could be. But there's a question on the floor."

Lon leaned back and tugged on an already loosened tie knot. "Anything's possible, of course, but the best reporter we've got, J. D. Greifenkamp by name, dug around a little and found Childress was unstable, to say the least. He had fiddled with suicide at least once before, about four years back. Gas, that time. But somebody happened by and saved him, or so the story goes. Also, he'd had at least three shrinks, although in New York that's damn near par. We're told his mood swings would make a roller coaster seem like a horse-and-buggy ride by comparison."

"Had he been depressed lately?"

"Apparently. Something to do with a new contract for those Sergeant Barnstable books he was doing. You know about them?"

"Not much, except that he'd picked the character up from another author, right?"

Lon nodded and tugged on his tie some more. "Yeah, Darius Sawyer. I read two or three of Sawyer's books some years back. Pretty good stuff. This Barnstable is a middle-aged police detective, either a bachelor or a widower, in a small Pennsylvania city with a phony name. Someplace about the size of Scranton or Allentown. He's homespun, with more cracker-barrel philosophy than I care for. Sort of a slow-moving, 'aw-shucks' type, but his mind is in high gear all the time, and of course he always gets the killer in the last chapter. It sounds hokey, I know, but the writing was top-notch, and so were the plots, for that matter. Sawyer built quite a following over the years, and when he died, Childress was brought aboard by Monarch Press to keep the Barnstable series going. I hadn't seen any of his books, but I gather they were so-so or less."

"Who do you gather that from?"

Lon narrowed his eyes. "One of our book reviewers. Why?"

"Wilbur Hobbs?"

"That's right—oh, I see where you're heading. The feud between Hobbs and Childress over the panning Wilbur gave his books. If Wolfe is looking to blow that up into something, forget it. Wilbur Hobbs is one acerbic, arrogant specimen, but hardly the murderous type. If he's the best you've got, I'd tell your client to pack it in. By the way, who *is* your client?"

I smiled and shook my head. "Nice try, but uh-uh. I understand Childress really blasted your man in print recently."

Lon looked down at his cluttered desk top, then leaned on an elbow and rubbed his forehead. "Archie, I'm not one for washing dirty linen in public, although you're hardly public. What I'm about to say is for your ears only—which I realize means Wolfe's, too: If there were one person I could dump from the staff of this venerable journal, it would be Hobbs. Not just because he's arrogant and obnoxious, but because I don't trust him."

"How so?"

Before Lon could answer, one of his phones

bleated. He scooped up the receiver. "Yeah, yeah . . . Okay, I see . . . Yeah, all right, you can hold the edition for five minutes if you absolutely have to, but not one damn second more, got it?" He slammed the receiver down and turned back to me. "The police got the masked marvel, all right. The stupe dropped his plastic clown's face on the sidewalk half a block from his bungalow in Jamaica. Anyway, as I was saying, I don't trust Hobbs as far as I can throw him. There's scuttlebutt around, has been for several years, that he's not above taking a few shekels here and there in exchange for a glowing review. The piece Childress did for the *Manhattan Literary Times* was the first time he's been accused in print, though."

"Is there anything to it?"

Lon pressed his palms against his eyes. "Dammit, I don't know—maybe it's my nature, but I'm suspicious. And to be honest, I'm biased, too—against Hobbs. You know how much I love this business, Archie, but there are always a few rotten apples in a bushel, and my guess is this particular apple's got more worms than an Ozark bait shop. Every newspaper of any size has at least one or two reporters, feature writers, or critics who figure they hold their job by some kind of divine right and, cloaked in the armor of the holy and almighty First Amendment, have a license to write anything they please—fairness and the laws of libel and privacy be damned."

"That's quite a speech. You mentioned there's been talk about Hobbs."

"We've had a few random complaints through the years, including both a letter and a call a while back from Horace Vinson, the big kahuna at Monarch Press. He didn't back it up with any evidence, though."

"Horace Vinson—is he well-thought-of?"

"Are you kidding? The guy's like a god, particularly to the writers who eat their oats in the Monarch stable. They worship him. Hell, he's even been compared to Maxwell Perkins."

"Pardon my ignorance, but who's—"

"For a second, I forgot who I was talking to," Lon cut in, holding up a hand. "You may be street-smart, as we like to say in our columns, but your cultural literacy is deficient, to say the least. Perkins was a great editor, a legend back in the twenties and thirties and forties. He worked with Fitzgerald, Hemingway, and Wolfe—Thomas that is, not Nero."

"Thanks, I'll file that away in my memory bank. Back to Hobbs: Given the negative flak, is his job here at the *Gazette* in any jeopardy?"

" 'Fraid not. The man who signs all our checks is a big booster of his." Lon jabbed a thumb in the direction of the publisher's office. "He likes the controversy Hobbs generates with his reviews. Claims it draws readers into the book section. He may be right, but I'm still for giving the guy a one-way ticket to the unemployment line, and I've said so to the boss more than once."

"You're cold of heart in these tough times, old friend. While we're on the subject of Charles Childress, who came upon the body? Your story didn't say."

"I'm not sure who decided we're still on the subject, but because we are old friends, it was another writer, a woman named Patricia Royce. She found Childress in mid-afternoon on the floor of his office;

he'd apparently been dead about two hours, according to the medical examiner. Now, who's your client?"

"Is it fair to assume that Miss—or Ms., or Mrs.— Royce was close to the deceased?"

"For somebody who doesn't like to answer questions, you sure can ask a lot of them," Lon complained, swiveling to answer the bleat of his telephone again. He gave his caller two curt yesses and a nasty no before signing off and turning back to me. "I can think of a pair of reasons why I'm indulging you, Archie and you know damn well what both of them are. One, I like being asked to break bread at Wolfe's, and two, every so often you and your boss lob a scoop in this general direction. This may not be one of those times, but I can't take the chance."

I grinned. "You, sir, are a hard-headed, clear-eyed pragmatist."

"Flattery will get you nowhere. Patricia Royce— real surname, Reiser—is a novelist, historical stuff, heavy on the romance. Not my type of bedtime reading, but she's well-thought-of and has gotten good reviews across the board. She had known Childress for about ten years. To hear her tell it, their relationship was what people of my generation would have called 'platonic.' They apparently bolstered each other. When one was having trouble writing, the other would be encouraging, that sort of thing."

"Sounds like a good quid pro quo. How did she get into his apartment?"

"Had a key. She used his word processor from time to time—hers was always on the blink."

"Uh-huh. What do you know about Childress's agent and his fiancée?"

"Believe it or not, Archie, I don't have a shred of information about either one. And do you know why? Because I haven't inquired. And why haven't I inquired? Because nobody—except you, of course—has remotely suggested that this is anything but a suicide."

He leaned back and spread his arms, palms up. "And now, on the memory of my dear, departed mother, I swear solemnly that you have picked me dry. I know nothing more about Charles Childress or the means of his departure from this earthly life."

"That's good enough for me," I said, grinning and getting to my feet. "Will you also swear that if you get any more information on the late Mr. Childress, you'll pass it along to yours truly?"

Lon swore, all right, although not in a way that his dear, departed mother would have cared for. He then tossed a wadded-up piece of paper at me, but it missed. I picked it up and fired it into his wastebasket, which was ten feet away. "It's all in the wrist action," I told him as I bowed and quickly backed out the door.

FOUR

Walking home from the *Gazette,* I occupied myself with how to give Wolfe that gentle shove in the right direction that I had promised Horace Vinson I would deliver. Lon hadn't been much help, other than basically to confirm the low opinion Vinson held of the reviewer Wilbur Hobbs's ethics. It was five-twenty when I got back to the brownstone. I still had forty minutes to come up with a stratagem that would start Wolfe's motor, so I could hit him with it when he came down from the plant rooms. Little did I know that my work already had been done for me.

At six o'clock, the rumble of the elevator prefaced Wolfe's arrival in the office. I swiveled to face him, but before I could get a word out, he spoke. "Archie, we shall accept Mr. Vinson's commission, assuming we can agree upon a fee. Get him on the telephone. I will speak first. Then, if you do not already know how to reach Mr. Childress's fiancée, his agent, and his former editor, you will get that information from Mr. Vinson."

I worked to keep my mouth from dropping

open. "Don't you want to know how my talk with Lon went?"

"That can wait until after the conversation with Mr. Vinson," Wolfe snapped, ringing for beer.

I got the editor-in-chief's card from my center desk drawer and dialed his private number. He answered.

"Mr. Vinson, Nero Wolfe calling," I said as Wolfe picked up his instrument and I stayed on the line.

"Good evening, sir. I have chosen to investigate the manner of Mr. Childress's demise. My fee is one hundred thousand dollars, if I identify a murderer. If for any reason I am unsuccessful, the amount will be fifty thousand dollars. An advance of twenty-five thousand dollars, in the form of a cashier's check made out to me, will be due here tomorrow morning at ten o'clock."

I couldn't hear anything at the other end, not even deep breathing. I began to think Vinson had passed out when he finally cleared his throat and spoke. "That's . . . a lot of money."

"Just so," Wolfe conceded. "But you told me earlier today of your awareness that I do not come cheap."

"Hoist with my own petar," Vinson said, chuckling sourly. "And I also said you *shouldn't* come cheap, given your record. All right, Mr. Wolfe, I agree to your terms, and you'll have that check tomorrow at ten, delivered by messenger. I'm curious about one thing, though: What made you decide that Charles was murdered?"

"That can wait for another time, sir; we have other matters to discuss. Have the police sealed Mr. Childress's apartment?"

"No, not at all," Vinson responded. "No reason to, from their point of view. They're satisfied he was a suicide. In fact, I've been there myself. I was the one the police called first after Charles was found, because my name was on his billfold ID card on the line that says, 'In case of accident, notify . . .' And I also was the one who had to break the horrible news to his friends and family—they certainly didn't want to.

"First I telephoned his fiancée, Debra Mitchell—I told you about her when I was at your home—and then I called one of his aunts out in Indiana, a woman named Melva Meeker. After his mother died a couple of years ago, Charles had described Mrs. Meeker to me as his closest relative, and he'd made her the executor of his estate. When I broke the news to her, she sounded quite stoic, almost disconcertingly without emotion. At least that was the impression I got on the phone. I know this sounds terrible, but all I could think about was how relieved I was that she didn't break down when we talked. She also didn't want to come to New York—she was quite adamant about that. But she asked if I would sift through her nephew's personal effects and send back anything of either actual or sentimental value."

"And you did?" Wolfe asked.

"Yes. She sent a notarized letter, giving me permission to go through Charles's apartment. I got the keys from the police after they had verified with Mrs. Meeker that such was her wish, and I went to the apartment with my administrative assistant; her name is Laura Pyle. A sad experience, that was, like wandering through a cemetery. Anyway, Laura and I packed up two cartons of things and shipped them back to Indiana—his jewelry, which was mainly a wristwatch, a few rings, and some cufflinks—plus scrapbooks of his clippings and reviews, copies of some of his books, albums filled with family pictures, three bank passbooks, and a couple of stock certificates. His only safety deposit box, it turns out, is back in his hometown in Indiana."

"Did Mr. Childress have a life insurance policy?"

"He did not, not a penny's worth," Vinson said with disgust. "That came up once in a conversation we had a couple years back. I looked upon Charles—and several of our other young writers, as well—the way a parent might look upon his offspring. Not long after he had signed with Monarch, I talked to Charles and asked, in a general way, of course, if he was properly planning for the future. That question might seem rude, but I've known too many writers who have no financial sense whatever, and who ended up in pretty sad shape. He told me about a few investments he'd made, and when I mentioned life insurance, he laughed, said he didn't need it. He said he didn't have anybody to worry about but himself."

"Perhaps his attitude changed when he became engaged to Miss Mitchell," Wolfe suggested.

"I don't think so," Vinson said. "When he told me he was going to get married, I brought the subject up again, and he brushed it off. I remember what he said: 'Give it up, Horace, I'm not the insurance-buying type. The only thing I'd need a policy for is my funeral and burial costs, and the potter's field is good enough for me.' It sounded humorous at the time."

Wolfe drew in air and expelled it. "What is left in the apartment?"

"All his clothes and books, for one thing," Vinson said. "His aunt doesn't want them, so I've arranged for them to be taken away by the Salvation Army. And his personal computer—that will be sold, with the proceeds going to his estate. He had what he told me a few weeks ago was an almost-completed Barnstable novel on disks, and—I know this sounds unseemly—we plan to see whether we can get it in shape to publish. I haven't looked at it yet, but I'm going to in the next few days. His estate would of course share in any profits the book made."

"Can you facilitate a visit to the apartment by Mr. Goodwin?" Wolfe asked.

"Certainly, no problem at all. Do you have any idea what he, and you, expect to find?"

"I do not. The scavenger must ever be open to what awaits. I regret that I must now attend to other business. Mr. Goodwin is on the line, however, and he will require particulars regarding several individuals he will be visiting."

Wolfe cradled his receiver, and I took over our end of the conversation, getting addresses and in some cases, phone numbers. Vinson promised he would have the keys to Childress's apartment sent over by messenger. I thanked him and said that he'd be hearing soon from Wolfe or me.

"All right, what gives?" I asked after hanging up as I swiveled to face Wolfe. "Just what happened while I was away?"

He poured beer and watched the foam dissipate. "About ten minutes after you left, Mr. Cramer arrived, in his usual state of dudgeon. Because of your call to Sergeant Stebbins yesterday, the inspector assumed we were probing Mr. Childress's death, and he was affronted."

"As only Cramer can be affronted."

"Yes. I won't go into irrelevant detail, but he accused me of trying to generate business by manufacturing a murder where none exists."

"Déjà vu all over again."

Wolfe grimaced at my Yogi Berra-ism. "I saw no need to defend myself by pointing out that we did not originate the murder theory. Cramer continued to badger me, however, until *I* became affronted. That was his mistake."

"But our bank account's gain," I observed.

"The inspector hurled his cigar at the wastebasket, missing of course, and then he marched out. He was not smiling."

"Who picked up the stogie?" I asked, glancing at the wastebasket. "That's usually my job."

"I did." Wolfe's voice was icy. "I have washed my hands twice since."

"You *have* been through a lot, especially the way Cramer gnaws on those things. Well, what next?"

"Report."

I did, unloading an account of my visit with Lon. After I finished, Wolfe unloaded a laundry list of instructions. The first was to go to Childress's apartment and give the place a thorough combing, although, as he grumpily pointed out, "an army of others, including our well-intentioned client, have tromped through, likely obliterating any traces the murderer might have been thoughtful enough to leave." The next item was to visit Charles Childress's fiancée, Debra Mitchell, who, Vinson had informed us, worked as a vice president for public relations at the Global Broadcasting Company, one of the TV networks that presumes to shape our national culture.

At nine-forty the next morning, Thursday, a messenger wearing Spandex pants and an inane grin delivered a cashier's check for twenty-five thousand dollars and a small brown envelope from Vinson. The latter contained the keys to Childress's apartment and a note from Vinson giving the building's address and the name of the superintendent. After hoofing it to our neighborhood branch of the Metropolitan Trust Company and depositing the check, I flagged a southbound cab and gave him an address on what turned out to be a block-long, tree-lined street in the Village just west and a little south of Washington Square.

Childress's building was a five-story brick number that had been rehabbed, probably in the last few years, judging from its tuck-pointed and well-scrubbed facade. I entered the small and gloomy foyer, noted on the mailbox that C. CHILDRESS occupied 1-A, and used one of the keys from Vinson to open the inside door. I found myself in a hallway that led toward the back of the building. The first door on my right was 1-A, and this time I had to use two keys, one of which released the dead-bolt lock.

The place was stale and airless, hardly surprising given it had been closed up for a week. I started in the living room, which faced the street. The carpeting was beige and the furniture nondescript—a tired and slightly lopsided burgundy sofa, two easy chairs, the yellow one of which looked new, a TV set in a mahogany cabinet, a couple of unmatched mahogany end tables with unmatched lamps, and a cherry wood coffee table whose glass top was littered with recent copies of *The New York Times, The New Yorker,* and *The Economist.* The only picture on the yellow-and-brown striped papered walls was a print of a Renoir, the original of which, as she will be delighted to tell you, hangs in the sunroom of Lily Rowan's penthouse.

A copy of Childress's *Death in the North Meadow* lay on one of the end tables. I covered my hand with a handkerchief and flipped through it, finding no loose papers or notations. I was interested, however, in the author's head-and-shoulders photograph, which was on the back inside flap of the dust jacket along with his thumbnail biography. He looked younger than I had pictured, but no less surly. His face, topped by well-tended, sandy hair, was triangular—wide cheekbones tapering to a narrow, clefted chin. The dark eyes glowered, and a tight-lipped mouth turned down at one end. From this image, it was difficult to conceive of Charles Childress smiling or breaking into laughter.

I've searched scores—maybe hundreds—of rooms; I like to think I'm as good as anybody in the business, and that includes Saul Panzer. I scoured the Childress apartment from baseboards to light fixtures —living room, two bedrooms, one of which had been converted to an office, kitchen, and bathroom—in seventy-five minutes, including seat cushions, bookcases, and bureau and desk drawers. On the hardwood floor in the room used as an office were dark stains I assumed to be blood. But if there were any clues as to who plugged the apartment's tenant, they slipped by me. I was paging through the last of the volumes in the living room bookcase when a key turned in the front-door lock. A short, burly, sixtyish guy wearing brown coveralls stepped into the room. He was panting.

"I'm Carlucci, the super," he announced, tilting

his chin up defiantly and panting some more. "Heard somebody was in here. Can I help you?"

"Maybe," I answered in a pleasant voice. "Mr. Vinson, whom I believe you've met, gave me the keys." I held them and my notebook up. "I'm doing some checking on the contents of the dwelling."

"Oh, insurance stuff, eh?" The defiance seeped away. "Yeah, I s'pose you have to do that, huh?"

I nodded somberly, putting on my insurance adjuster's face. "A formality. As long as you're here, Mr. Carlucci, perhaps you can help." I fingered the knot on my tie. "The last few weeks, did Mr. Childress have any visitors who . . . well, who hadn't ever been here before, or whom you didn't recognize? It's just a routine part of our investigation, you understand."

Carlucci nodded grimly and pressed his lips together. "I really don't pay no attention to who comes and goes around here, you know? I'm just the super, that's all. I'm really sorry about what happened to Mr. Childress—he seemed like an okay guy, friendly, you know? But I never knew him all that well, except to say hi to once in a while and talk about the weather. I got so much to do that, hey, I barely got time to take a lunch break, you know?" He shrugged his burly shoulders.

"I know. Did you by chance notice if he had any visitors a week ago Tuesday—the day he died?"

"Uh-uh. After I found out what he done to himself, I wondered why I didn't hear the shot. Then I remembered I was away for a couple of hours, at the hardware store, you know, getting some paint, and then I stopped by to see my sister in Little Italy. She's just recovering from a stroke."

"Did you know he kept a gun in the apartment?"

He rolled his eyes. "Nah, but I'm not surprised. Who doesn't these days, you know? It's an awful world."

I agreed and said that I'd be leaving in just a few minutes, which seemed to relieve him. He backed out, pulling the door closed. I finished going through the books on the shelves, finding nothing, and I started for the front door. Don't ask why I reached up on my way out, because I can't supply an answer. Wolfe called it a fluke, I said it was instinct. Anyway, as I was leaving, I passed my hand along the top of the molding over the doorway to the foyer, expecting to get dust on my fingers. I did, but I also got a key. It was brass, for a door lock—I know that much after having studied locks and how to open them for the better part of my adult life.

This orphan was not a spare for any of the locks in the Childress apartment. I tried it on all of them, including the back door, which led to a gangway. And then, feeling stupid for having almost missed an obvious hiding place, I passed my hand along the moldings over all the other doors in the place. I got nothing but more dust—and a sliver in my right ring finger, which I couldn't get out until I used tweezers at home later. Cursing silently, I tucked the mystery key in my pocket and left, walking east to Sixth Avenue, where, after waving my arm for five minutes, I got a northbound cab.

At eleven fifty-five, I spun through revolving doors into the two-story-high, white marble lobby of the GBC Tower on Sixth, checking in with an overfed guard in a dark blue uniform who was manning a desk that looked like a flight deck from one of the *Star Wars* movies. I asked him to call Debra Mitchell.

"Got an appointment?" he drawled, eyeing me as if I were selling vacuum cleaners or encyclopedias.

"No, but she'll want to see me. The name is Archie Goodwin. You can tell her I'm here to talk to her about Charles Childress."

It was obvious that neither name meant anything to him. He opened what apparently was a company phone book, let his fingers do the walking, and located a number, which he punched out on his instrument. He spun in his chair, giving me his broad back as he murmured something into the mouthpiece. He paused, did some more murmuring, then hung up and spun to face me.

"Seventeenth floor," he said. "Here's a badge, number two-eleven. Wear it at all times in the building, return it on your way out, and sign your name right here." He thrust a loose-leaf notebook at me, and I scribbled my Hancock and the time on the lined paper.

The first thing I saw as the elevator doors opened at the seventeenth floor was a huge bronze eagle with outstretched wings—the logo of GBC—mounted on another white marble wall. Off to the left, at a white desk, was a pleasant-looking woman whose hair was—what else—white. "Can I help you?" she asked softly, peering over half-glasses.

I told her Debra Mitchell was expecting me, and she nodded. "Oh, yes, you are Mr. Goodwin, right? Ms. Mitchell said you were on your way up. Just go right through that door, then take a right. Her office is the third one on the left."

The door was white, the hall walls were white, the carpeting was white. I found Debra Mitchell's doorway just before snow blindness hit. I peeked in through the doorway and saw a mostly white office fully half the size of Wolfe's, with a desk in one corner and a sofa and chairs grouped around a coffee table in the other. A woman was seated behind the desk, talking on the phone. "Yes, correct. Yes, they've got the guests lined up for the next three weeks, except for next Tuesday. That damned, loopy inventor from South Dakota, or maybe it's North Dakota, the one who developed a car that runs on cornstarch or some-thing like that, pooped out on us, said he was too busy to make the trip. Can you beat that? *Too busy* to be interviewed live on network TV? No wonder he's never left whichever stupid Dakota he's in." She fi-nally looked up, saw me standing in the doorway, and nodded, telling the person on the other end that she had to go. Then she pressed another button and told someone else, presumably a secretary, to hold her calls.

"Please come in, Mr. Goodwin," she said with a cool smile, standing and coming around the desk. Debra Mitchell was worth a second look, as well as a third and a fourth. She was tall, at least five-ten in her heels, and whatever her weight, it was perfect for her height. Black, shoulder-length hair framed a face, high cheekbones and all, that would have looked just fine on the cover of any fashion magazine on any newsstand from here to Sri Lanka.

"I'm sorry I didn't notice you standing there." She gestured me to the sofa while she sat in one of the chairs at right angles to it, smoothing the hem of her emerald-green dress. "I recognized your name, of course. You work with Nero Wolfe. Horace Vinson told me he was going to try to hire Mr. Wolfe to find out what . . . what *really* happened to Charles." She looked down and then up at me, her golden-brown eyes shrewd. "Does your being here mean Mr. Wolfe will investigate his death?"

I nodded. "It does. Ms. Mitchell, I understand from Mr. Vinson that you agree with him that Charles Childress was murdered."

"Of course I do!" she snapped, slicing the air with a manicured hand. "He would never have killed himself. Never! It's too absurd to even discuss. Charles had everything to live for. His writing, our . . . our life together." Her face registered more anger than sadness.

"But he did have drastic mood swings, didn't he?"

"Of course he had mood swings. Charles was *artistic,* for God's sake. But if everyone here with mood swings killed themselves, this town would be smaller than Utica."

"Point taken. Had he been unusually depressed lately?"

"No, he had not," she said tightly. "Oh, he was ticked off about his new contract, and I don't blame him. Horace, whom I like very much, let Charles down badly and wouldn't agree to much more than what he had gotten for his first Barnstable books. Charles was upset about that, and about the review that weasel had done in the *Gazette.*"

"I understand he also was angry with his agent and his editor at Monarch."

"And with good reason in each case," Debra said, her voice still tight. "As you probably are aware, they became his ex-agent and his ex-editor."

"I am. Did Mr. Childress ever say anything to make you think that he was in danger?"

She shook her head vigorously and fingered the diamond pin on her floral print scarf. "No. In fact, Charles never seemed afraid of anything—or anyone. He was always ready to take on the world."

"I understand that he wasn't from New York."

"No, although he had lived here for, oh, I don't know, maybe twelve years. He comes—came—from some small town somewhere in Indiana. His parents are both dead. His closest relatives are a couple of aunts out there, both widowed, I think. I never met them, but I talked to one of them on the phone the other day, so did Horace; she made the arrangements to have Charles's body shipped back home for burial."

"Did you know he owned a gun?"

She nodded reluctantly. "Yes, he told me when he bought it—that was a couple of months ago. Some apartments on his block had been burglarized, even one in his own building, I think. Charles seemed almost proud of the fact that he'd picked it up. He grinned when he showed it to me, like a kid with a grotesque new toy. He laughed and said something macho like 'Anybody who tries to bust in here is going to get the surprise of his life—and if he gets cute, it'll be the *end* of his life, too.' "

"Did Mr. Childress carry any life insurance that you're aware of?"

She made a noise that I could only describe as unladylike. "Not a chance! Charles didn't have any use for it. He said insurance was the biggest waste of money since the building of the pyramids."

"Do you know who the beneficiary of his estate was?"

"His aunts back in Indiana would be my guess,"

she said defiantly. "It certainly wouldn't have been me—I'm pretty well set, thanks to an uncle who helped develop a computer chip. And Charles knew I was well set. I didn't need any of his money, if that's what you were suggesting."

"It wasn't. Ms. Mitchell, do you care to nominate a murderer?"

The question stopped her cold, as it was supposed to. She studied the glass top of the coffee table, tracing circles on it with an index finger, then looked up slowly, tilting her head to one side. "Have you met Patricia Royce?" she asked quietly.

"No, but I intend to. Why?"

"Do you know anything about her?"

"I know she is a writer herself, and that she discovered Mr. Childress's body the day of his death. I understand she was a close friend of his."

" 'Friend' has many meanings, Mr. Goodwin. It had different meanings to Charles and to Patricia."

"Go on."

She crossed her beautiful legs and tapped a shapely knee. "Let's just say that Patricia expected something more out of the relationship than Charles did." Her voice was chilly.

"Did he tell you this?"

"Huh! He didn't have to. Mr. Goodwin, it doesn't take someone with ESP to spot a woman on the make, and Patricia Royce was definitely on the make with Charles."

"How did he feel about her?"

Debra rolled her eyes. "He saw her as a fellow author, someone who he could bounce ideas off, someone he could compare notes with. At that, she leaned on him for moral support a lot more than he leaned on her."

"Did you and Childress ever discuss her feelings toward him?"

She nodded grimly. "We did. I told him I thought Patricia was in love with him, and he laughed at me. He just *laughed* at me! He said it was preposterous, that's the word he used."

"Ms. Mitchell, you're not going to like this next question, but I wouldn't be doing my job if I didn't ask it," I told her, raising one eyebrow and giving her what Lily Rowan calls my "almost-smile."

I got an almost-smile back. "Fire away," she said bravely. "You'll get a straight answer."

"Okay. Were Charles Childress and Patricia Royce having an affair?"

She handled herself well, but then, she probably saw the pitch coming. "Mr. Goodwin, if I got outraged and said 'no way!' you probably would chalk it up as the natural reaction of a woman who was being cheated on, wouldn't you?"

"I like to think I'm more enlightened than that," I responded with a full smile.

"All right, then the answer is 'no way!' " she said, not returning the smile. "Maybe it's arrogance, but I believe I was close enough to Charles to know what he wanted in a long-term relationship, and Patricia didn't have it. Now if you are going to ask me what 'it' is, we'll have a problem, because I don't think I can give you a definition."

"How did Patricia Royce feel about you?"

Now she was toying with the little bronze eagle that perched on the coffee table. "Oh, she was always very polite when we ran into each other—too polite. I got the feeling that she wanted me to think she was this humble little writer from—where's she from?—Virginia, I think it is. As you may know, she writes historical novels, mostly about the South. Charles always said they were very good, but I wouldn't know. You couldn't drag me kicking and screaming into a historical novel. Anyway, Patricia Royce was so damn self-effacing the few times we met that it gave me a pain. I know she never liked me. She and Charles had been friends long before I came along, and it was obvious that she deeply resented me, despite all that phony humility of hers."

"And I gather you think she could have killed Childress?"

"You are not going to get me to respond to that," Debra Mitchell said brusquely, giving the eagle another shove before she left it alone. "I know a little about the laws of libel and slander. Let's just say I hope you spend some time talking to Patricia."

I repeated that I planned to. "When did you last see Mr. Childress?"

"The night before he died. Last Monday night. We went out for dinner at a little Italian place we like on Second Avenue."

"Did he seem particularly depressed?"

"Oh, he was kind of sour, but no more than he had been lately. Actually, dinner was my idea; I thought it might take his mind off his problems and cheer him. He'd always liked that restaurant, and we hadn't been there for a while."

"Where were you on Tuesday, say from mid-morning on?"

"Well, I—" She recoiled as if she'd been slapped. "Why are you asking?"

"Just my native curiosity."

Her face went pale with anger, one of the better performances of outrage I've witnessed. "Listen, Mr. Goodwin, I'd hardly be encouraging your investigation if I were the killer, now, would I?"

"Probably not. But in my line of work, Ms. Mitchell, I've gotten in the habit of asking nosy questions. Do you have a problem with that one?"

Her face softened, but only slightly. "You'll have to excuse me. I'm still somewhat off-balance over this whole thing. Actually, I worked at home on Tuesday, editing press releases my staff had done for shows that we'll be running during the summer. I do that sometimes—work at home, I mean. I can get so much more done away from the phones. I live in a co-op on Park near Sixty-eighth."

"Did anyone see you during that time?"

"You really *do* ask nosy questions, don't you? Well, I guess you have to. No, nobody saw me. Wait— I'm wrong. I went out just before noon. I needed some air, so I took a long walk and ended up doing some grocery shopping at a deli in the neighborhood. Our doorman, Jake, saw me go, and he saw me come back."

"When was that?"

"I think it must have been close to two o'clock. I remember that I'd been home for about an hour and a half and I was thinking Charles would be phoning me soon. He had planned to spend some time at the library in the afternoon doing research on Pennsylvania for his next book. He had said he would call and tell me when he was picking me up—we were supposed to go to a cocktail party that the head of our news division was having in his place on Park. Well, I got a call, all right, but it wasn't from Charles. It was from my office, telling me *about* Charles." She fingered an ashtray on the coffee table, then looked up. "And that's it," she said, spreading her hands.

"But nobody can vouch for you between noon and two?"

She shrugged. "Maybe the clerk in the deli, but I didn't get there until after my walk, maybe about one-forty-five. Does that make me a suspect?" she demanded with a toss of the head.

"It might," I answered in a light tone. We were nothing if not civilized. "One more thing. Would you mind showing me the key to your apartment?"

Debra Mitchell started to frown but quickly erased it, smiling without warmth and tossing her head again. She knew that made her hair fall across her cheek. If I hadn't been so intent on getting something accomplished, the gesture might have impressed me no end. "If this is some sort of come-on that I'm not familiar with, call me naive," she said, narrowing her eyes and wrinkling her nose.

"I am by no means above a come-on," I conceded, "but only after hours. I only want to see your key—I won't even touch it."

She shook her head as if indulging a child and went to her desk, reaching into a drawer and pulling out a patent leather purse. "All right, here it is," she said, holding one key between her thumb and forefinger as she thrust her key chain at me with a flourish. "What does it tell you?"

"All that I want to know," I said. Even from two feet away, I could see that her key was not even a distant cousin of the one I had pocketed earlier in the Village. I thanked her for seeing me and started to rise. "Before you go," she said sheepishly, "I wonder if I can change the subject?" I nodded and she went on.

"You might have heard me on the phone when you arrived. A program of ours, *Entre Nous,* is an interview show—maybe you've seen it. It's on weeknights at seven. Anyway, we lost our guest for next Tuesday, an inventor from the Dakotas, and I wondered if we could get Nero Wolfe in his place. I know he doesn't like to leave home, but he won't have to. Belle Corliss, she's our interviewer, would come to his house along with a crew, and do the conversation right there. It would take—"

"Forget it," I told her with a smile. "Mr. Wolfe guards his privacy like a Doberman. And he has a powerful aversion to television. Call the latter a character defect on his part, but that's the way he is, eccentric through and through." I didn't bother to tell her that Wolfe also has a powerful aversion to having women in the brownstone.

"One more thing," I said, stopping just short of the doorway and reaching into my pocket, pulling out the key I had found above Childress's door. "Does this look familiar to you?"

Debra Mitchell took it and held it up. "No . . . It's not one of mine," she said, looking puzzled. "Why?"

"Just wondered. Well, thanks for your time."

She pressed me again about Wolfe being on *Entre Nous* like a good TV executive, but I held fast, and she finally surrendered gracefully. I thanked her again for her time and patience, and she gave me a firm handshake. As I walked down the hall toward the elevator, I found myself musing on two things: Debra Mitchell's beauty and her hardness, the latter underscored by what seemed to be a total lack of grief over the death of the man she had been going to marry.

FIVE

Wolfe had not stipulated the order in which I was to conduct my interviews after I had seen Debra Mitchell, so, in light of La Mitchell's comments, I opted to call next on Patricia Royce, which meant a trip back downtown. First, though, I stopped for lunch at a little diner on Seventh Avenue near Forty-eighth that I've patronized off and on for years. It's had the same counterman, a gravel-voiced guy named Bennie who's almost as heavy as Wolfe, since the days when you could ride the Staten Island Ferry for a nickel. The Reuben sandwich was as good as ever, and so was the mince pie, which I chased with a glass of ice-cold milk.

Vinson had given me Patricia Royce's address, on one of the east-west streets in the East Village between Second and Third Avenues. My watch read twelve-forty-five when the cab dropped me in front of a four-story brick building, which suffered by comparison to recently rehabbed neighbors on either side.

I climbed the seven steps to the dingy foyer and pressed the buzzer next to ROYCE 2-B. After a few seconds, I got a muffled "Yes?"

"My name is Archie Goodwin," I said into the

speaker. "I am here to talk about Charles Childress." There was a pause, followed by something that might have been "I'll be down." The entrance buzzer didn't sound, so I had no option but to stand in the foyer. While I waited, I tried to slip the key I'd found in Childress's apartment into the lock, but it didn't fit. After what probably was two minutes but seemed like ten, a very pale woman with dark blue eyes, sandy hair parted in the center and wearing jeans and a Boston College sweatshirt appeared at the inner door. She could have been anywhere from twenty-five to forty. "What do you want?" she asked through the glass.

"Are you Patricia Royce?"

She nodded, but made no move to open the door.

"I'm investigating Charles Childress's death," I said, talking more loudly than I needed to. "May I come in?"

"Are you with the police? I've already had one of their Homicide people come to see me."

"No, I'm a private detective working for Nero Wolfe." I pulled my laminated P.I.'s license out of my billfold and held it up to the glass.

Patricia Royce shrugged. Then she pulled the door open with a sigh. "I've heard of Nero Wolfe, and I guess I might have heard of you, too," she said. "I don't know what there is to investigate, but all right. Come on up." Her tone was hardly enthusiastic, although I didn't give her a chance to change her mind.

I massaged a slightly bruised ego and followed her up one flight and into a tiny living room furnished in some kind of modern—maybe Danish. We sat, me in a stainless-steel-and-leather chair that didn't look comfortable and wasn't, and she on a sofa built for people whose bodies bent only at right angles.

"I appreciate your seeing me," I told her. "The last few days must have been hard on you."

"They have," Patricia Royce said softly, looking at the worn toes of her running shoes. "Do you and your Mr. Wolfe represent some insurance company?"

"No. Our client is an individual, someone who feels Mr. Childress may have been murdered."

"Really? Why in the world would one think that?" Her face lacked both makeup and animation, although its parts were nicely arranged. There were pale freckles sprinkled across an upturned nose. I've always been a sucker for freckles.

"I'm not entirely sure. I understand you found his body."

She leaned forward and kneaded slender, pale hands between her legs, then looked idly around the room, but never at me. "Am I keeping you from something?" I asked after fifteen seconds, trying to mask the irritation I felt.

"Hmm? Oh—no, no," she said, acting as though she'd just been awakened. "Yes, I found . . . Charles. As I told the man from Homicide, and also the one newspaper reporter who called, I had gone to Charles's apartment—it's only a few blocks from here —to use his word processor, his PC, you know. I did that fairly often if he was going to be out. I have one of my own, but it hasn't been working."

She shook her head several times and looked at the wall above my head. I thought I was losing her again, but she tuned back in. "Last . . . Tuesday, it was, I had called Charles that morning to find out if I might be able to use his PC; mine has been acting up a lot lately, as I said. He was always very generous about it, and he said he'd be away all afternoon, and all evening, too, until late. I went to his apartment about three, and, well . . . I, I found him.''

"Where?"

"Is this really necessary?" she pleaded in a broken voice. "Are you aware that I gave the police a long statement?"

"Ms. Royce, I realize this isn't pleasant, but I'd like to hear it from you."

She glanced around the room before nodding. "Um, all right. Would you like some coffee?"

I told her no thanks, and she leaned back and ran her fingers through her sandy hair. "Well, where was I? Oh yes, as I said, I got to Charles's apartment about three and let myself in—he'd given me a key years ago. I went back to—you're not taking any notes."

I smiled. "I've got a good memory."

She made a half-hearted attempt to return the smile, finally looking straight at me. "You are fortunate, do you know that? I used to work as a newspaper reporter, in Hartford, for a short time just after I got out of school, and I felt I had to take down every single word when I was interviewing someone. Finally I got the good sense to buy a tape recorder. Anyway, as I was saying, I went back to the rear bedroom, which Charles used as his office, and . . . he was on the floor beside his desk, with a pistol next to him. There wasn't much blood, just a little on the side of his . . . on the side of his head." She passed a hand over the dark blue eyes that seemed even darker against her pale complexion. "Well . . . that's it, that's all. All there is. He was dead. I called the police, and they got there fast, just a few minutes later."

"Did you recognize the pistol?"

"Yes, it was Charles's—at least it looked like the one he had bought back in January or February. He showed me where he kept it—in the nightstand next to his bed. He said he wanted me to know where it was in case anybody tried to break in while I was working there alone."

"I understand there had been some break-ins on the block, and even in his building."

She nodded, studying her hands. "Yes, and that's why he said he got the gun. But you know, I've been thinking more about that, and I really wonder if maybe he really was planning to kill himself all along, and that's the real reason . . ."

"So you're convinced it was suicide?"

Patricia Royce folded her arms and twitched her shoulders. Another ten minutes with her and I'd start twitching myself. "Of course I am. Who would want to kill Charles?" she cried defiantly.

"Why would he want to kill himself?"

"Like I said, I've thought a lot about that. I probably knew Charles as well as just about anyone, and he was very moody. And I do mean *very* moody. His lows were really low, even when things were going well for him. He tended toward depression, and he'd been depressed and distracted more than usual lately."

"Why?"

"I think for several reasons," she replied, furrowing her forehead. She rocked back and forth for another half-minute before going on. "For one thing, he wasn't getting a lot of good reviews for his Barnstable books, particularly the last one. Have you read any of them?''

I shook my head.

"Well, I feel they're awfully well done," she said. "I'm probably biased because of our friendship, but I think they are as good as the ones Darius Sawyer had written. The reviews bothered Charles, particularly what that idiot Hobbs wrote in the *Gazette.* But he was also down because he didn't think he was appreciated by Monarch, his publisher."

"Did you agree with Childress's assessment?"

"Mr. Goodwin, you may be asking the wrong person," she responded, avoiding my eyes. "As you might be aware, I'm a novelist, too. Oh, nowhere near as successful as Charles was, but I have written four books, novels set either in the South or in England in the eighteenth century. I think every author is to some degree paranoid. We all feel that we're undervalued or are taken for granted—or both—by our publishers, whether or not that's really true. And in Charles's case, the feeling was intensified because of his latest contract offer, which he thought was insulting. And then there was something else . . ."

"Go on."

She looked at the ceiling. "Did you know that he was engaged to be married?"

"I've heard something to that effect."

"It's true," she murmured, eyes still fastened on the ceiling. "The woman—her name is Mitchell—Debra Mitchell—is extremely attractive, and extremely successful, too; she is an executive with GBC-TV. Well, in the last few weeks, Charles had been having . . . misgivings about her."

"Do you know why?"

Patricia pressed her lips together, then nodded. "Charles didn't talk a lot to me about it, but I sensed that he'd grown increasingly conscious of how, well . . . how *overbearing* she could be. He seemed to feel Debra wanted to run every aspect of his life. And Charles was an extremely independent individual. Extremely."

"Was he thinking of breaking it off?"

Another deliberate nod, and more lip gymnastics. "I got that distinct impression. I never pried into his social life—that wasn't how our relationship was structured. But a few days before, well, before what happened, he said something that made me believe he had decided to end their engagement."

"Can you remember what it was?"

"More or less. I had come by the apartment to use his PC. He was just on the way out, and he made some comment about being doomed to 'eternal bachelorhood.' That's the phrase he used. I remember very distinctly, he said it twice."

"Do you know if he did end the engagement?"

"No," she said, rising partway up and tucking her legs under her. "I never asked."

"Ms. Royce, you spoke a minute ago about the structure of your relationship with Mr. Childress. How would you define that structure?"

"Mm. Yes. Please call me Patricia. The only person who gets formal with me is the loan officer at my bank, and I don't want to be reminded of him. I know it sounds like a newspaper gossip-column cliché, but Charles and I truly *were* good friends—nothing more. We first met years ago, lord, it's been almost ten now, at a writers' workshop up in Vermont. We hit it off immediately. We found we admired the same authors

—and disliked the same ones, too. Back here in New York, we ended up growing into sort of a two-person support group, encouraging each other, propping each other up when the rejection slips came in. And they did, for both of us, before we started getting published. And we've bounced ideas off each other, and passed manuscripts back and forth for help in improving them. We were always comfortable together."

"But there was no romantic aspect?"

She almost smiled. "Mr. Goodwin, have you ever been married?"

"First off, I feel the same way you do about nominatives of address. My handle of first choice is Archie, and I implore you to use it. Second, no, I have never taken that walk down the aisle. Why?"

"My guess is you have one or more close woman friends. Am I correct?"

I nodded. "You are, and I think I see where you're headed."

Now she really did smile, which was a welcome sight. "I'm sure you do, Archie. How often do you get asked, 'When are you going to marry so-and-so?' "

"It has happened more times than I have thumbs."

"Like you, I never have been married, although I was close on one occasion, and even now, more than eleven years later, I don't know whether or not I'm sorry I backed out of it. But I do know it is possible to have a close relationship with a man without sex being its lodestar. I realize Debra Mitchell saw me as a threat to her relationship with Charles, but she needn't have. Debra's greatest enemy was her own personality."

"Uh-huh. I gather you have a book of your own in the works right now?"

Her whole body sagged, and she shook her head. "I did—about half of a manuscript of a novel set in Scotland at the time of the last Stuart uprising, at Culloden. But, after . . . after . . . what happened, I couldn't stand to even look at the stupid thing anymore. Everything in it reminded me of him, because I'd done so much of the work at his apartment."

"So now it's on hold?"

"Now it's as dead as the House of Stuart," she murmured. "I destroyed the disk. It's gone—completely."

"How does your publisher feel about that?"

She turned her palms up. "I haven't told them about it, but of course I'll have to. They weren't expecting anything until the fall anyway, and my editor had never seen even a sample."

"Seems like a shame. Patricia, can you think of anyone who might have wanted to kill Childress? Or who would have profited in any way from his death?"

She shook her head vigorously. "No! And that's why I can't believe he *was* murdered. Mr.—Archie, Charles shot himself, it's that simple. I know that doesn't make it any less tragic than murder. But he had tried suicide one other time years ago after what he called his 'Great American Novel' got rejected by the seventh or eighth publisher. He turned on his gas stove and—well, a neighbor smelled the gas, and the building super came in just in time. Charles was in therapy for a long time after, but in all the years that I've known him since then, he never went more than a few months without slipping into some sort of very deep depression. He was a very creative, very troubled spirit.''

''I understand he had no close relatives.''

''Just an aunt or two and a cousin out in Indiana. He came from a place called Mercer. His mother died about two years back. I remember it because he was there with her for a long time, six months or more, while she lingered. He was different when he returned to New York.''

''In what way?''

She closed her eyes tightly and started rocking again, then blinked awake. ''Oh, *older,* I guess, or more world-weary. Maybe that's to be expected when the person closest to you dies. He was an only child, and his father had been dead for years, so he had to bear the whole strain while his mother slowly slipped away.'' She shuddered. ''Sorry, I didn't mean to go and get morbid on you. It's just that Charles never seemed the same after that; he quit laughing and smiling almost entirely.''

I'll bet you don't do a lot of either yourself, I thought as I looked at her, wondering how many times she'd been in therapy herself. ''You mentioned that Childress had given you a key to his apartment. Speaking of keys, does this one look familiar?'' I pulled out my newfound brass acquisition.

''No . . . no, I don't think so,'' she answered, taking it from my palm and peering at it. ''Should it?''

''Not necessarily. Well, thanks for the time you've given me. If you think of anything that would be helpful, here's my card. Oh, and one more thing,'' I said, trying to make it sound like an afterthought, as I rose from a chair that should be tossed on the nearest New York City dump.

"Yes?"

"For the record, where were you a week ago Tuesday before you went to Childress's apartment—say from about noon on?"

"I've been expecting you to ask me that." Patricia Royce, too, stood. Her sandy head came just up to my shoulders. "I was here all day, until I walked over to Charles's place. Your next question, of course, is, 'Did anyone see me during that time?' And the answer is no, other than passersby on the street during my three-block walk, none of whom I knew.

"If that makes me a suspect in your eyes, so be it. I'm afraid I haven't been very helpful, Mr. Archie Goodwin, and I guess I can't be, at least if your goal still is to show that Charles died by any hand but his own."

Okay, maybe she wasn't the life of the party, but the woman did have a way with words. I thanked her again and we shook hands, but her dark blue eyes never met mine. If we didn't part as friends, we weren't enemies, or at least I didn't feel we were. After she closed her door, I lingered in the hallway long enough to determine that the lock on her apartment door was not a match for the mystery key.

SIX

It was a little after two when I got back to the brownstone, which meant Wolfe was still in the dining room consuming flounder poached in white wine. I wasn't about to interrupt him in mid-meal, but I wasn't about to pass on Fritz's flounder, either, so I marched directly to the kitchen.

"Archie, I kept a plate warm for you," he said, popping up from the high stool where he was reading one of his German-language magazines.

"I was hoping you'd say that," I told him, getting milk from the refrigerator and filling a glass. "Any calls while I was gone?"

"Mr. Cohen, at ten-fifteen—he sounded irritated, but he didn't leave a message. And Mr. Horace Vinson, at ten-twenty-five. He wanted to know if we had received his check, and I told him we had." Although Fritz did not know the amount of the check that had been delivered to our door that morning, he now had that cheerful "there's-money-in-the-bank-again" lilt to his voice. He was dying to ask me how things were going, but he didn't, and I didn't volunteer anything. I was too busy concentrating on the plate of flounder that he had just set in front of me.

After polishing off two helpings plus a dish of papaya custard, I carried coffee into the office, where Wolfe had settled in with beer and a fresh book, *Dreadnought,* by Robert K. Massie.

"Have you eaten?" he asked peevishly.

"Yes, sir, and I gave it the usual number of stars —the maximum. Sorry you had to dine alone, but as you know, I had assignments. Would you like a report?"

Wolfe set down his book, closed his eyes, and nodded. With that fresh check in the bank, he was committed to working, or at least to listening, and he didn't much like it. I had not been idly boasting when I told Patricia Royce about my good memory. I've been known to give Wolfe verbatim accounts of conversations several hours long, so filling him in on my chats with the two women in Charles Childress's life was a snap.

As I talked, he leaned back and got comfortable. When I finished, he didn't move. Any stranger walking in would have sworn he was asleep, but I know better; Wolfe ingests reports like he does food—with deliberation. At last he opened his eyes. "You told me how they looked and what they said. Now, what is your impression of them?"

At some point long ago, Wolfe got it into his noggin that I have no peers when it comes to analyzing the opposite sex and getting them to spill their innermost thoughts to me. Through the years, I've done a number of things—intentional and otherwise—to dissuade him from this belief, but to no avail.

"Debra Mitchell is as hard as the diamonds in a scarf pin she was wearing," I said. "Not the kind of woman who'd be likely to mourn the death of a fiancé for long, if at all. She didn't seem the least bit broken up. Her mind was on other things, like getting a celebrity guest for the *Entre Nous* show. I had no business speaking for you. I can call and have her schedule you for next Tuesday and—"

"Archie! Stop prattling."

"Yes, sir. Anyway, as easy on the eyes as she is, Debra Mitchell doesn't do a thing for me, if you can believe that. I think Patricia Royce's analysis of the lady is accurate: She's overbearing and would try to control every area of a mate's life, including the color of his toothbrush. Could she have knocked off Childress? Maybe, if she thought he was cheating on her. But if she did, the motivation wouldn't be a bruised heart, it would be cold anger over losing what she considered to be a possession.

"As for the Royce person, that's a mare of a different color. She's more than a little squirrelly, but possibly that's what comes from sitting in front of a computer screen all day dreaming up stories about Scotland and England in the eighteenth century."

"You seem obsessed with animal imagery today. By squirrelly, may I assume you mean eccentric?"

"I guess that's what I mean. I got the feeling talking to her that part of her was someplace else. Maybe that's the way it is with fiction writers."

Wolfe drained his glass and dabbed his lips with a handkerchief. "Did you sense she had a romantic attachment to Mr. Childress?"

"It's close to fifty-fifty, with maybe a slight tilt toward the platonic side. But even if Patty Royce did have a thing for the guy, I can't picture her as a killer. She's the type who would get revenge some other way than through physical violence. Like maybe in her writing."

"Have you made arrangements to visit Messrs. Ott and Billings?"

"Nope, but it's on the agenda to set up this afternoon. I assume you want me to chat with the *Gazette*'s very own Wilbur Hobbs, too, right?"

He made a face and poured more beer. "Yes, as abhorrent a task as that may be."

"Well, he's got to be talked to, right? And it might as well be by yours truly. Lon called earlier. I'll set it up with him."

Wolfe went back to his book as I punched out a familiar combination of numbers on my telephone. He answered after the first ring with his usual no-frills "Cohen."

"Archie."

"I recognize the name. You took enough time getting back to me. What's happening?"

"Let's see . . . the Mets won their third straight last night in Philly; Newark Airport was shut down for more than two hours because of the pea-soup fog—or maybe it's smog; the mayor has announced that—"

"Very funny, very bloody funny. You come to me and get information, I come to you and what do I get? Your version of snappy patter. Jay Leno you're not. Let's start over: What have you dug up about Childress's death?"

"Interesting you should ask. Mr. Wolfe suggested I talk to Wilbur Hobbs. Can you set it up for me?"

"Who's Wolfe's client?"

"I'm pretty sure I've heard that question before."

"And I'm still waiting for an answer," Lon fired back sourly.

"Patience is a virtue. All I can say is, you'll get an answer to that, and a lot more, too, before anybody else in the media does. It's always worked out that way."

Lon snorted. "I can't make Hobbs talk to you, but I'll tell him you'd like to see him."

"Should I call him?"

"No, dammit. I think he's in today; I'll wander by his office and ask him to call you." The line went dead before I could either thank Lon or send another zinger his way.

Next I located Franklin Ott in the white pages under the listing of "Ott Literary Agency," on East Fifty-fourth. "I'm off to the wonderful world of books," I told Wolfe as I rose and pointed myself at the door. He didn't bother looking up from his own book.

Ott's office was on the fourth floor of a narrow, drab building between Park and Lexington that had a Hungarian restaurant at street level. When I stepped off the automatic elevator, which was not much bigger than Wolfe's and almost as noisy, I found myself facing a door, the top half of which had frosted glass with OTT LITERARY AGENCY LTD. painted on it in no-nonsense black capitals.

I opened the door into a small, yellow-walled reception room with three chairs and a low table that was strewn with magazines. "Yes, may I help you?" The voice came from the pleasant-looking, well-nourished face of somebody's favorite aunt, who was peering through an opening that had a sliding plastic panel.

"Is Mr. Ott in?"

"He is on the phone, sir," the aunt chirped. "May I ask your name?"

"Archie Goodwin. I work for Nero Wolfe."

"Oh, yes—the famous detective." She favored me with a benign smile. "Will Mr. Ott know why you are here?"

"Tell him it's about Charles Childress."

The smile dissolved, replaced by an expression of earnest concern. "Oh. Oh, yes, I see, yes. Just a moment, Mr. Goodwin. Please be seated." She left her post and disappeared. Opting to remain on my feet after my experience with Patricia Royce's chair, I pawed through dog-eared copies of *The New Yorker, Sports Illustrated,* and something called *The Writer.* I was about to thumb the most recent *SI,* which had a picture of a blond golfer from Australia on the cover, when Aunt Sincere pulled open a door that led to the inner sanctum.

"Mr. Ott will see you now, Mr. Goodwin. This way, please." Her smile had returned, which comforted me. I followed as she shuffled down a short corridor, past a doorway through which I saw an underfed young guy wearing green suspenders, black-rimmed glasses, and a frown, who was hunched over a battered desk staring bleakly at some sheets of paper spread on his blotter. The next doorway led to the corner office, which of course had to be Ott's.

It was a long way from luxurious, but I am willing to concede that all those years in the brownstone have spoiled me. Except for two windows with closed blinds, the room was all bookshelves, to the ceiling. I'm used to being surrounded by bookshelves, but these were something else. They held a small-town library's worth of volumes, but also sheaves of typing or computer paper, bound by rubber bands, which were jammed horizontally or vertically into every space not otherwise occupied. And the desk was groaning with more of the same.

"Goodwin, eh? Yeah, I know who you are. Have a seat," Franklin Ott said absently, waving a hand toward three unmatched guest chairs while he studied something in a manila folder. Ott was thin all over —chest, shoulders, face, even his straw-colored hair, what little remained of it. I sat while he finished reading from the folder and tapping on the desk top with the eraser end of a gnawed yellow pencil. He shook his head, slapped the folder shut, and leaned back, cupping his hands behind his head.

"Let's see how good I am," he cracked with a lopsided grin. A bobbing Adam's apple caused his polka-dotted bow tie to vibrate with every syllable. "Your boss, the famed Nero Wolfe, has been hired by somebody—I don't know who but I can make an educated guess—to poke around into the death of Charles Childress, a death this certain somebody figures is murder, not suicide. Being the shrewd and thorough fellow that he is, Nero Wolfe knows, of course, that Childress had been on less-than-friendly terms with several people in this town, a certain literary agent among them. To steal a line from an ebullient former mayor of this great metropolis, 'How am I doing?' "

"Not bad," I said, nodding. "Anything more you want to add?"

Ott hooked his thumbs under his belt and shrugged. "No, it's your turn to sound off. I've read a lot of mysteries, but I've never seen a live detective before. Do you come out of the hard-boiled school, or are you the urbane type?"

"Beats me, although I don't recall that anybody's ever called me urbane. Why don't you take notes and tell me what you think when we're finished? First off, how long were you Childress's agent?"

Ott studied some of the bundled manuscripts on the opposite wall before replying. "Just about four years. He'd had somebody else, but he dropped her because he didn't think she had enough good contacts in the publishing houses, which was true—I know the woman."

"Were you glad to get him as a client?"

"Yeah, at the time, which doesn't say a whole lot about my ability to read character. Charles had done a few so-so mysteries for a small publisher, although they didn't make him much money. Horace Vinson at Monarch noticed him, though, and felt he had a lot of potential. This was not long after Darius Sawyer had died, and the shrewd Mr. Vinson wanted very badly to find a way to keep the Barnstable royalties pouring in."

"I gather Sawyer's books were big money-makers."

Ott made a face and twitched his shoulders. "Yeah, they did all right, but at least part of Vinson's strategy was that new Barnstable books would stimulate sales of the backlist, too. Backlist is the old books," he explained. "Hell, there must be at least two dozen Barnstable books by Sawyer, maybe more, and Monarch has the rights to all of them. Makes good business sense."

"So Childress hired you to strike a deal with Vinson, right?"

"That's pretty much it. Charles said he'd heard good things about me, and he knew I had several authors at Monarch."

"Was he happy with what you worked out originally?"

"Mr. Goodwin, Charles Childress was never very happy with anything or anyone, as I was to find out all too soon. He was a colossal pain in the ass at every step of the way, and if I had any brains at all, I would have dropped him right after I negotiated that first damn Barnstable contract. Now you, as a highly skilled interviewer, will no doubt ask me why I didn't drop him. I'll save you the effort. The answer is greed —pure, simple, unadulterated greed."

"That hardly sets you apart from the rest of us."

"I suppose not. I kept thinking there might be a film deal in the Childress stuff."

"But there wasn't?"

Ott curled his narrow lower lip. "No, and I should have realized it, but hope springs eternal. Not much of Darius Sawyer's stuff ever got picked up by the movies or TV through the years, and I learned that wasn't about to change. There's not a whole lot of Hollywood interest in an eccentric Pennsylvania bachelor geezer who lives in a farmhouse and goes around spouting Ben Franklin proverbs and drinking iced tea on his way to solving murders. The homespun approach may have worked on *Murder, She Wrote*, but nobody—and I mean nobody—on the Left Coast had the slightest interest in turning the Barnstable stuff into a TV show or a mini-series or a movie. Lord knows, I've spent enough time trying to make something happen. And all I got for my efforts from

Charles was a lot of bitching that I just didn't know the right people out there."

I nodded in sympathy. "Sounds like he was a real sweetheart to deal with."

Ott snorted. "You don't know the half of it. Things between us just kept getting worse. Charles never thought his first contract was big enough—that was for just one book, because Vinson wanted to see how well Charles could handle a Barnstable story before committing to more. I got him a better overall deal on the second contract, which was for two books, but he still wasn't happy. And several months ago, when we began negotiations on another two-book Barnstable contract, Charles insisted that I ask for about eighty percent more than the previous deal. I damn near spilled a cup of coffee into my lap when he came up with that. It was an insane proposal, and I told him so. You know what he said to me? 'You're supposed to have so much goddamn clout with people like Vinson and Monarch. Well, prove it.'

"What could I do?" Ott complained. "I told Vinson our asking price over lunch one day, and he looked at me like I'd lost my reason. Of course he knew damn well Childress was pushing me, and he also liked Charles, although I'll never know why. Well, we—Vinson and I—must have hashed things over for close to two hours, and the most I could get out of him was a bump of about fifteen percent over the previous contract, which I felt was fair, although I didn't tell him that."

"How did Childress react to the offer?"

"Hah! How do you think? Charles started screaming at me, right here in this office. The son of a bitch said I was worthless, and that he'd find himself a new agent, somebody who knew what he was doing. I told him to go ahead—that I didn't need the grief, which was true. Hell, I've got plenty of writers, and losing Childress wasn't about to break me. What really teed me off was that Charles couldn't stand his editor, Keith Billings, and I was the one who put pressure on Vinson to sack the guy, or at least take him off Charles's books, which he did.''

''Is Billings a poor editor?''

''I'd say so, yeah. He's arrogant, although that hardly makes him an oddity in our business. But he's also arbitrary and heavy-handed. He does way too much rewriting—not very skillfully, I might add. And he thinks all authors are totally incapable of taking a detached look at their own work. Well, dammit, I got him off Charles's back, and some thanks I received for the effort.'' He gave a stack of manuscripts on his desk a vicious shove.

''Then came that article of Childress's in *Book Business*, right?''

''Yeah. It shouldn't have surprised me, knowing what kind of a jerk he could be, but I've got to admit it was a jolt. Have you read it?''

I said I hadn't, and he went on, his thin face reddening. ''He didn't mention me by name, but he didn't have to. Everybody between the Village and the north end of Central Park knew who he was talking about when he wrote that, quote, 'Too many of today's agents are basically lazy, uninspired, and reactive.' He went on to say some more, too, none of it much fun to read, at least for me.''

''Did you talk to Childress after the piece ran?''

''I did not,'' Ott snapped. ''But I did call Vinson, and I blew, I mean I really blew. I've always had a good relationship with Horace, but that day I took my anger out on him, in spades. Hell, I told him I was going to sue both him and Childress.''

"Were you serious?" I asked.

He gave me a semi-smile. "I guess I was at the time. I thought the piece was going to really kill my business. But you know, almost every reaction I got was sympathetic. In the next couple of days, I'll bet seven or eight people called me, including three of my writers, and they all said Charles was an ass, or words to that effect. And obviously I'm not angry anymore, especially after what's happened. But I *do* have to call Vinson and apologize for what I said to him.''

"Did you lose any writers because of the article?"

Ott stared at the pencil in his hand. He seemed to be wondering how it got there. "Can't say for sure," he replied unconvincingly. "Agents are always gaining and losing clients, and we don't always know the reason. Hell, I got two new ones just last week— one of them a young woman you're going to hear plenty about in the next few years, believe me. Sorry I can't tell you what she's working on, but she's a winner, and just three months out of college.''

"Uh-huh. How good a writer was Childress?''

"Not as good as he liked to think. Oh, he was what I would call workmanlike, and he did a decent job—not perfect, but decent—of adopting Sawyer's characters and style. His dialogue was actually quite good, very lively, but his plots occasionally were a problem, although I always felt Keith Billings made too big a deal out of that. He—Keith—is full of himself.''

"Childress blasted Billings in that article, too, didn't he?''

"Yeah, not by name, but like with me, everybody knew exactly who he was crucifying."

"Do *you* think Childress killed himself?"

Ott pitched forward abruptly and rested his elbows on the desk, cupping his chin in his hands. "It wouldn't surprise me. In the few years I'd known him, he must have had at least three or four really bad depressions that I was aware of. He broke down and bawled once right here in this office—for no apparent reason. It would have broken your heart to see it. He was telling me about an idea he had for a new detective, a character he wanted to develop, and in the middle of a sentence, he just covered his face with his hands and started sobbing."

"Did he ever do anything with that new detective?"

"Not that I know of, but that was only a few months ago."

"Had he been in one of his depressions lately?"

Ott threw up his hands and shook his head. "I hadn't seen him since we had our set-to and he fired me or I quit, however you want to term it. That was over a month ago. But as I said earlier, he was really upset about the money he'd been offered for the two new Barnstable books, the one giving him the fifteen-percent increase. I understand that he accepted it, though, *sans* agent.

"Also, he was terribly thin-skinned about criticism. All in all, he'd gotten some fairly decent reviews on all three of his Barnstable mysteries, although as you probably know, the stuff Wilbur Hobbs had written in the *Gazette* bedeviled him. Then there were the Barnstable faithful—the people who'd been religiously reading the books since Sawyer started the series more than forty years ago. A lot of them are ferocious about detail. In fact, there are clubs of Barnstable fans in cities all over the country. They call themselves PROBE, but I forget exactly what the acronym stands for. Something with 'Barnstable Enthusiasts' in the title, I think. By and large, they applauded him and were glad that Barnstable was back. But they also caught him in all sorts of minor errors, things like the color of the pickup truck Barnstable drove or the kind of rug he had in his living room. Charles got a number of those letters, and this irked him when it should have pleased him that these folks, all of whom were polite, took the time to write.''

"Hardly worth shooting yourself over," I observed.

"Agreed. But Charles was wound tight. I warned him before his first Barnstable book came out that every word he wrote would be scrutinized with a magnifying glass. I also said I thought it was a small price to pay for getting to continue a character so many people loved. But you know, I don't think he ever fully appreciated the opportunity he was getting. To Charles, it was basically a way to raise his visibility fast —and to make money. I don't think he ever looked beyond the next hill.''

"Did he have many close friends?''

"Not that I knew of," Ott replied. "I'm sure you're aware he was engaged—to a young woman at one of the TV networks. In public relations, I think. I never met her. Then there was a writer he was friendly with, named Patricia Royce.''

"I've heard of her," I said. "What was their relationship?''

"I have no idea. Mr. Goodwin, I rarely if ever

socialize with my writers. No particular reason, except that my wife and I aren't big for the cocktail-party circuit or the Hamptons. Oh, I do go to some literary functions, but only because it's *de rigueur* in this business. And in fact, I did meet Patricia Royce once, at some book party, I forget where. She recognized my name, said she knew I was Charles's agent."

"But you've never worked for her?"

He shook his head. "She didn't ask me to when we met. And I've never taken on anyone in that genre —the romantic historical novel—although I did read one of her books sometime back, and I was impressed; her characters are nicely drawn and her plots are particularly solid and well-constructed. But I don't even know who represents her."

"Can you suggest anyone who might want to kill Childress?"

"With that personality of his, anybody who ever came within half a mile of him. No—scratch that last comment," Ott said sharply, twisting in his chair. "It was gratuitous, and I had no business coming out with it. Mr. Goodwin, let's just say Charles was an egotistical, moderately talented, immoderately unpleasant young man. I'd be a hypocrite if I told you his death deeply saddened me. But I didn't rejoice when I heard about it, either. Do I think he was murdered? Oh . . . probably not. Based on what I had seen of him over the last four years or so—and I hope that this doesn't sound callous—suicide seems consistent with his overall behavior. The man was a nut case. Sorry, but there it is."

"Did you know that he kept a gun in his apartment?"

"No, but I can't say I'm surprised. I was only in

his place once, several months back, while I was still his agent and we were on relatively good terms. I belong to a small club down on Gramercy Park, and I'd been having lunch there with a friend. Because I was nearby, I stopped by to see Charles after lunch and dropped off copies of the German edition of one of his Barnstable books which had just come in. He was all wrought up about one of the apartments in his building having been burgled or vandalized, or both, and he told me he was going to buy a 'piece'—that's the word he used, 'piece.' Ever the crime writer.''

"Do you know if he had drawn up a will?"

Ott spread his arms. "I have no idea, but I really doubt it. Charles was weird about money. On the one hand, he seemed obsessed with making it as fast as he could. On the other, he didn't seem to care about what happened to it once he got it. Possessions didn't seem to be a high priority with him. And his apartment—well, as I said, I was only there once, but the furnishings looked like they came from a resale shop.''

I nodded, then paused a beat. "Mr. Ott, where were you a week ago Tuesday from, say, late morning to late afternoon?"

"That was really quite well done." He nodded and smiled. "I wondered how long you'd wait to spring it. You did a damn nice job of pulling information out of me before you got to the part that figured to make the atmosphere tense, and which might cause me to ask you to leave. Except that I won't do that. Your question is legitimate.''

He opened a drawer and pulled out his date book. "Let's see, on Tuesday, I was at my barber's at ten-thirty, meaning I probably left him at eleven or a little past. You can check with him. Wallace Berkeley on Forty-sixth Street. Then let's see, I took a cab down to Gramercy Park, where I was having lunch with one of my writers at that club I mentioned. I got there early and walked around the park, which always makes me think of London. It relaxes me."

"How long did you walk?"

"Probably half an hour or more. Not much of an alibi, is it?"

"Certainly not if nobody can vouch for you. As you said yourself, Gramercy Park isn't all that far from Childress's place."

"You're nothing if not direct, Mr. Goodwin." Ott wasn't smiling, but he wasn't frowning, either.

"Direct is my middle name. One more question," I said, reaching into my pocket. "Any idea what this key opens?"

Ott took it between his thumb and forefinger and frowned. "You know, it looks like it might be to my apartment." He pulled out his key ring and took one off, holding it up next to the key I had produced. "Nope, not the same, see?" he said, giving me an up-close look at both of them.

I nodded as he handed me the key. "I've taken a lot of your time," I told him, getting up.

"Wait," he said, looking stern and holding up a hand like a traffic cop. "Do you keep a bottle of rye in your lower right-hand desk drawer?"

That stopped me. "No. But I always know where to find some."

"Not the same thing. No rye in your desk, no hard-boiled tag. Sorry to be the one to break it to you, Mr. Goodwin, but you are terminally urbane."

"A bitter pill," I admitted, donning my most

somber expression. "I suppose I can't change your mind with my Bogart impression and my British trench coat?"

Ott actually cracked a smile. "It's far too late for that. You are what you are."

I tried to think of something hard-boiled to say, other than "Same to you, fella." Nothing came to mind, so I gave him my most urbane smile and sauntered out.

SEVEN

When I got back to the brownstone, it was eight minutes after six, which meant Wolfe was down from the plant rooms. I was not surprised to find him seated behind his desk with beer and book.

"Home is the hunter, home from the sea," I said as I dropped into my desk chair.

He set the book down and sighed—not softly. "Archie, if you must quote Stevenson, make at least a minimal effort to get it correct: It is 'Home is the sailor, home from the sea, and the hunter, home from the hill.' "

"I'll work on it, thanks. Ready for a report on my meeting with Mr. Ott?"

"I sense that I am not going to be offered an alternative." Wolfe leaned back with his eyes closed as I gave him the conversation verbatim, ending with Ott's comment about me being urbane. "Indeed?" he said, raising his eyebrows and coming forward in his chair. "My dictionary defines urbane as, among other things, 'evincing the suavity and polish characteristic of social life in large cities.' That same defini-

tion also includes the words 'courteous' and 'polite.'
Mr. Ott must have been distracted during your visit.''

"I guess that's sarcasm, huh? Well, you know Lily
Rowan, and you've even admitted that you approve of
her, which makes her a rarity among human females.
Ask her about my suavity and polish and see what she
says. Any other reflections?''

He sniffed. "We are having roast quail for dinner." Then he picked up his book. He wasn't just
changing the subject to get me off his back, although
that was part of it. He also was aware that, since it was
Thursday, which means the weekly poker game at
Saul Panzer's, I wouldn't be eating dinner in the
brownstone. And he was rubbing it in because he
knows very well that roast quail ranks near the top on
my list of entrées.

I did not by any means spend the evening mop-
ing, however—far from it. First, Saul dished up a mul-
ligan stew Fritz would have been proud to serve. And
second, through a combination of reasonably good
play and incredibly good luck, I lightened the wallets
of all five of my comrades-in-cards.

The next morning, I settled in at my desk in the
office after breakfast and put in a call to Charles Childress's former editor, Keith Billings, at his current
publishing house. I got his "voice mail," which ranks
with wristwatch buzzers and beepers as elements guaranteed to bring the ultimate collapse of western civili-
zation as we know it. I left a message and was at the
personal computer entering Wolfe's dictation from
the previous day when the doorbell chirped at ten-
seventeen. Fritz was out gathering provisions, so I did
the honors.

As seen through the one-way glass, he was a specimen worth marveling at—for a moment, at least. His vested suit was pearl gray, with pinstripes, and it fit like it had been woven on him as he stood. His tie was a darker shade of gray, with thin yellow stripes spaced discreetly. He looked to be somewhere between forty-five and fifty-five; an angular face tapered from wide cheekbones to a pointed chin. Above his mouth was a well-tended little mustache that a British colonel would be proud to have nurtured. And atop his noggin, cocked at precisely the right angle, sat a bowler, which—you guessed it—also was gray. And damned if he didn't carry a walking stick. The only thing missing was spats.

As I swung the door open, I half-expected an English accent. I got New England instead. "Is Mr. Wolfe in?" our dapper visitor demanded in a clipped tone.

"Affirmative, although he's not available at the moment. Is he expecting you?" I asked, knowing that Wolfe wasn't expecting anyone.

"No, but I believe he wishes to see me. My name is Wilbur Hobbs." His pronunciation left no doubt that I was expected to kneel and kiss the green jade ring on his left pinkie. "And you, I presume, are Mr. Goodwin."

"Correct. Nero Wolfe is occupied until eleven. Would you care to come in and wait?"

"I would indeed," Hobbs answered, unsmiling. He stepped into the hall, placed his bowler on one of the wooden pegs after checking with an index finger to see if it was dusty, and carefully leaned his stick against the wall.

"You can wait in the front room—there are magazines—or you can come to the office, although I'm afraid I won't be terribly good company," I told him. "I'm in the middle of a project that may take the next hour or more."

"I prefer the office," Hobbs said haughtily. "Your friend and my colleague, Mr. Cohen, has led me to believe that Mr. Wolfe has a superb library, one of the finest private collections in New York City. I should like very much to browse it. With your permission, needless to say."

"Of course. Please come this way." I led Hobbs to the office and pointed him at the red leather chair while I went back to the letter I had almost finished. Within thirty seconds, he was up and over at the bookcases, making clucking sounds. My plan when I let Hobbs in had been to spring him on Wolfe when His Hugeness came down from the plant rooms, but as I typed, I revised the program. I have seen Wolfe march out of the office a few times when I've surprised him, and I didn't want to mess things up.

"If you'll excuse me, I'll be back in a few minutes," I told the critic. "Would you like something to drink?"

"Nothing, thank you." He didn't bother to turn from the bookshelves where his aristocratic nose was deep in a volume.

When I went to the kitchen, I came upon Fritz frowning and shaking his head over a pot on the stove. "I know that whatever you have in there will turn out all right," I assured him. "It always does. I have to run up and talk to Mr. Wolfe. There is a man in the office, waiting to see him. He's probably harmless, but I don't want him dashing out the front door with a first edition tucked under his well-tailored arm.

Keep an eye on him through the peephole. If he starts to leave, buzz the plant rooms."

Fritz, who knows how to throw a punch when he has to, nodded solemnly, marching to an alcove in the hall and silently sliding back a panel that reveals a seven-by-twelve-inch hole. On the office side of the one-way opening is a picture of a waterfall, custom-designed to allow a viewer in the alcove both to see and hear what's going on in the office.

I left Fritz to his surveillance and took the stairs by twos. As often as I've been up in the glassed-in rooms that occupy the fourth floor of the brownstone, I'm still awed each time I get hit by the colors of those ten thousand orchids that Wolfe unblushingly refers to as his concubines. I walked down the aisles through the cool, medium, and warm rooms, and stepped into the potting room, where both Theodore and Wolfe greeted me with cold stares. Wolfe, a sight to behold in his yellow smock, was sitting on a stool and contemplating a plant on the bench. "Yes?" he said sharply. He doesn't like to be disturbed during his playtime.

"We have a guest, name of Wilbur Hobbs. He came to the door a few minutes ago, and I put him in the office. Fritz is keeping watch."

He scowled, said something like "Grrr," and pressed his lips together. "Very well. At eleven." He turned back to the orchid.

There were two reasons Wolfe wanted me out of the plant rooms. First, as I mentioned above, he hates interruptions. Second, the longer Fritz stood in the hallway peering through the waterfall picture into the office, the more the preparations for lunch might be delayed.

When I got back to the first floor, Fritz nodded and silently slid the panel shut. "He has been looking at books the whole time, Archie," he whispered, although with the thickness of the office door, whispering wasn't necessary. I thanked him and marched in.

"Hi, sorry to desert you," I said to Hobbs. He was standing at the shelves with a book lying open in his hand, the one without the jade pinkie ring. "Are you keeping occupied?"

"Indeed. An intriguing collection."

"So I've remarked many times. To repeat my earlier offer, can I get you something to drink? Coffee? Tea? Beer? Bottled water?"

He swiveled from the waist up, compressing his lips, which apparently was his idea of a benign smile. "Again, thank you, no," he told me, returning to the book. I fiddled with the bank balance and performed a few other bookkeeping chores until I heard the whine of the elevator precisely at eleven. I felt like a boxing fan who'd just sat through the undercard at the old St. Nicholas Arena and was about to view the main event.

Wolfe stepped into the room, halted when he saw Hobbs at his bookshelves, and dipped his chin the requisite eighth of an inch. He slipped the orchid-of-the-day into the vase on his blotter before settling into his chair. Our guest got the hint and circled until he was in front of the desk, facing Wolfe. "I am Wilbur Hobbs; Lon Cohen said you wanted to see me—about the suicide of that *writer*, Childress." He made the noun sound like a malignancy.

"That is correct," Wolfe replied, looking straight ahead. "Please sit down, sir. I find it more comfortable to converse without craning my neck."

Hobbs nodded curtly and folded himself and his pearl-gray suit into the red leather chair. "Your library is most impressive," he pronounced, folding his arms and cocking his head.

Wolfe considered him without enthusiasm. "It is not my intent to impress, but rather to surround myself with works that merit periodic revisiting."

"I did not mean to suggest otherwise," Hobbs fired back tartly. "I was particularly interested to find William Smith's *History of the Province of New York*. And the 1895 *Almayer's Folly*, inscribed by Conrad himself, and using his Polish name, Korzeniowski. If I'm not mistaken, that's the edition with the missing 'e'."

"On page one-hundred-ten," Wolfe replied. "*Generosity* is misspelled. Would you care for something to drink? I am having beer."

"No, thank you. After Mr. Cohen told me of your interest in meeting with me, I decided to come unannounced on the chance you were available, although I realize that is a significant breach of etiquette, for which I apologize. Although he—Mr. Cohen—did not specify why you desired to see me, I assume it is related to the death of Charles Childress. And knowing something of your line of work, I further assume that you think he may not have died by his own hand."

"Both logical assumptions," Wolfe responded.

"I'm afraid I have little—presumably nothing—that will be of help to you in the pursuit of this line of investigation," Hobbs said, forming a chapel with his fingers. "But I came anyway, partially, I confess, because I was extremely interested in meeting you—and in seeing your library. I am leaving this afternoon for an extended weekend on Long Island and won't return to the city until Tuesday."

"I will not delay your departure," Wolfe said as Fritz entered with his libation. "Were you personally acquainted with Mr. Childress?"

Hobbs smoothed his mustache with an index finger. "I never met the man. I make it a point to avoid functions where authors are likely to congregate. I prefer to know them only through their writing."

"You had a low opinion of his work?"

"I have what you would term low opinions of many authors," Hobbs replied belligerently, "and I would be less than forthright with readers of the *Gazette* if I did not express my opinions both clearly and forcefully. Writers—the majority of writers, that is— understand and accept this as part of the price of plying their craft—or art, depending on the writer. Charles Childress did not. As you undoubtedly are aware, his bruised and fragile ego drove him to excoriate me in the *Manhattan Literary Times*. It was an unconscionable diatribe."

Wolfe sampled the beer and moved his shoulders. "Those who hurl javelins must be prepared to dodge them as well."

"Hah! But there is a difference," Hobbs snapped, punching the air with a fist. "I was reviewing his *work*, while his attack was *personal*—a vicious assault upon my integrity."

If that little speech was intended to impress Wolfe, it failed. "You reviewed all three of Mr. Childress's books about the Pennsylvania detective, Barnstable?"

Hobbs drew in air and expelled it, settling back into the chair, which dwarfed him. "I did."

"And you disliked each of them?"

"In varying degrees. I thought I was relatively kind to the first one that he penned. Bear in mind, I was never a great fan of Darius Sawyer's Barnstable books. Oh, Sawyer was a serviceable writer, I'll give him that much. *Better* than serviceable. He had two or maybe three interesting characters, and some of his dialogue was actually quite amusing. As you know, he developed an impressive following—some might call it a cult—in his later years. Then he died and along comes this continuator, a man of whom I had no previous knowledge.

"Now I must tell you, Mr. Wolfe, that on principle I do not abide life-after-death in the world of literature. But I read the new book with an open mind—as I of course always do. Charles Childress did a marginally adequate job of re-creating this Orville Barnstable character and other members of Sawyer's original ensemble company. His dialogue was acceptable in places, although uneven. But his structure . . ." Hobbs shook his head and compressed his lips. "His narrative structure was clumsy, ill-constructed, and—"

"And not challenging enough to befuddle a sixth-grader," Wolfe put in.

"Ah, you went back and found my review of Childress's first Barnstable book." Hobbs's well-tended face glowed with a satisfied smile. "That was three years ago."

"No, sir, I 'found' nothing. It was on a right-hand page, either five or seven, across the top, with a thirty-six point, one-line headline, photographs both of Mr. Sawyer and Mr. Childress, and a reproduction of the new book's dust jacket. I recall the review."

"I am flattered."

"Do not be; I retain what I read. Did Mr. Childress react publicly to your critiques of his earlier Barnstable books?"

"Not to the first. But to the second, I received a rude, boorish, handwritten note from him soon after my review of *A Harvest of Horror* appeared in the *Gazette*. Childress claimed I had it in for him because he was a continuator. He also claimed that I had not reviewed his book on its own merits, but rather had attacked it solely because it *was* a continuation. That charge was patently absurd."

"Did you reply?"

"I did not," Hobbs said primly, sounding offended and caressing his mustache again. "I answer civil letters, but Mr. Childress's was hardly civil. He resorted to puerile name-calling, which shouldn't have surprised me, given the paucity of his vocabulary."

Wolfe raised his eyebrows. "Indeed. What did he call you?"

"Huh! It does not bear repeating," the reviewer sniffed. "It is sufficient that he cast aspersions upon my parentage. Needless to say, I destroyed the missive immediately. I felt demeaned merely handling it."

"No doubt, then, you expected some form of response from him when you reviewed book number three?"

"In all candor, Mr. Wolfe, the possibility that he might respond did not enter my mind at any time," Hobbs answered crisply. "I review dozens of books each year. I never allow myself to be concerned about how their authors might react to what I write."

Wolfe readjusted his bulk. "How, sir, did *you* react upon reading Mr. Childress's essay in the *Manhattan Literary Times*?"

Hobbs jerked forward in the chair. "Essay! I wouldn't dignify it with that term. As I said before, it was a diatribe—vindictive rantings. I suppose if the man had confined himself to attacking my taste and my standards as a reviewer, I would have shrugged it off and let the whole business pass. But he also impugned my motives and suggested—none too subtly, I might add—that I accepted money or other largess in return for favorable reviews. I considered that actionable, and I said so, both to the editor of the *MLT* and to Horace Vinson at Monarch."

"Was it your intent to bring legal action?"

"I can't remember when I have been so angry," Hobbs said, accenting each word and folding his arms across his chest. "And yes, I did contemplate a suit—against Childress and the publication. But, well . . . on reflection, I abandoned the idea."

"Indeed. Why?"

"Mr. Wolfe, at the risk of sounding melodramatic, I state unequivocally that my work is my life. I have no family, and no hobbies, unless you include foreign travel—I own a modest villa in Tuscany that I visit at least once each year. I am a book reviewer, one fortunate enough to be on the staff of a major metropolitan newspaper, and as such I enjoy a certain anonymity. Oh, my *name* is well-known, but my face is not, at least outside a limited circle. I relish that anonymity. Some people in this city enjoy being recognized and approached in restaurants and other public places; I do not." Hobbs stopped for breath and contemplated his manicured fingernails. "After my anger over the Childress polemic dissipated, I realized—and my attorney concurred—that were I to bring a suit, the media, including the *Gazette*, would turn it into a circus, and I would be faceless no longer. For me, that was far too great a price to pay."

Wolfe scowled. "And you never spoke to Charles Childress after the article appeared?"

Hobbs shook his head vigorously. "I would not deign to communicate with him. I felt I adequately expressed my displeasure through his publisher, Mr. Vinson. Have you discussed the matter with him?"

Wolfe ignored the question. "Mr. Hobbs, you said Charles Childress charged that you accepted 'money or other largess' in return for favorable reviews. Was he correct?"

I would have given three-to-two that Wilbur Hobbs was going to take a walk. And the little man did get halfway out of the red leather chair before dropping back into it and—I swear—smiling.

"I am not going to dignify that question with a response, sir. Neither will I storm out in a snit," Hobbs replied evenly. If he was angry, he was doing a decent job of keeping the lid on. "I will reply only by saying that I see no need to respond to charges from a man who, tragically, I concede, subsequently chose to end his life violently. Mr. Childress had a host of demons—he hardly needed another in me."

Wolfe narrowed his eyes. "I have other questions, sir, and then you may depart for your Long Island weekend: First, can you account for your time a week ago Tuesday, from, let us say, ten in the morning till four in the afternoon?"

Hobbs snorted. "That was nine days ago—an eternity." He slipped a hand inside his suitcoat and drew out a kidskin pocket secretary. He opened it and flipped pages, murmuring to himself as he studied them. "Ah, of course, I was home all day, reading, which for me is the norm—I go to the *Gazette* offices once a week at most. I usually send my reviews in by modem from my PC. Yes—I remember now; it was that frightful biography of an obscure English playwright—justifiably obscure. I bled from every pore as I reeled through it. Abysmal."

Wolfe closed his eyes. "Did you see anyone that day?" he asked.

"Which is to say, can anyone vouch for me? Alas, I must answer in the negative," Hobbs replied, shrugging theatrically. "My building on East Seventy-ninth has both a doorman and a hallman, but it also has a service entrance, which I frequently use—that way, I can dispose of garbage in the bin when I leave. My comings and goings are rarely monitored. That day, as I remember, I didn't leave home at all, until I joined friends for dinner around seven at a wonderful little Szechwan restaurant on Third Avenue."

Wolfe, to whom the words *wonderful* and *restaurant* used together constitute an oxymoron, started to shudder, but recovered nicely. "What was your first thought when you learned of Mr. Childress's death?"

Hobbs blinked. "An interesting query, not that I would have expected less from you. But then, I am sure you are skilled at keeping unsuspecting people like me off balance. Let me see . . . I suppose I learned about the suicide—the death—in the *Gazette*. Yes, yes, I did. I remember now. I was actually in the office that morning. The first edition got dropped on my desk, and as I was thumbing through it, I saw the obituary. I was interested, of course, and no sooner had I finished reading it than the phone rang. It was the cultural affairs editor, inquiring if I knew Mr. Childress well enough to write a personal reminiscence, as a second-day story. I told him—truthfully—that I did not know the man at all, and that was the end of it."

"Had you ever been in his apartment?"

Hobbs jerked upright. "I . . . had . . . not," he said in an offended tone. "I am surprised you would ask such a question. I make it a point not to socialize with writers, and even if I did, Mr. Childress patently would not have been among them."

"Did you know that Mr. Childress owned a gun?" Wolfe went on, unfazed.

"Not until I read that it was the weapon that killed him." Hobbs sniffed. "But I was not surprised. I own a firearm myself. Although my building's security system appears to be adequate, in this city one can never be too cautious."

"Do you have any theories about Mr. Childress's death?"

"I assumed—and still do—that he took his own life. What's so unusual about that?" Hobbs shot back contentiously. "A lot of creative people, and far more talented ones than Childress, I hasten to add, have killed themselves, for whatever reasons: despair, depression, inability to live up to their earlier works or their reviews or their pathetically inflated self-images. Now I really must go," he said, looking at his watch with a flourish. "I do not know who your client is, although I can guess. If you will take the advice of someone who has been following the literary cavalcade in this city, and across the country, for more than twenty years, stop jousting with windmills. Charles Childress put an end to his own life. Now, I

really must be going. Mr. Wolfe, Mr. Goodwin."
Hobbs stood and bowed to each of us. "Good day."

"One last thing," I asked. "Is this by any chance
yours?" I held out the key to Hobbs. He plucked it
from my palm, contemplated it at arm's length, and
shrugged, handing it back. "No—not at all. Why?"

"Just a stab," I said. "Any objection to showing
me your keys?"

Hobbs glared. "As a matter of fact, I do," the
little man said. "I see no earthly reason to indulge
the fantasies and fishing expeditions of private inves-
tigators, whether or not they are licensed by the state.
Various governments around the world license ped-
dlers and prostitutes, too, among others. Again, good
day to you both." With that, he bowed again, and it
was a fine bow, although the gesture was wearing thin
with me.

I followed Hobbs to the front hall, where he re-
trieved his precious bowler and walking stick, favored
me with a faint smile—or maybe it was a sneer—and
stepped out the door, presumably in search of a taxi.
Here's hoping all the cabbies in Manhattan were on
their coffee breaks.

EIGHT

"Interesting specimen," I said to Wolfe when I got back to the office. "Just the kind of guy you'd like to sit around with shooting the breeze."

He snorted. "Mr. Childress was correct; the man is a preening poseur."

"Sounds right to me. Say, here's an idea: I tell Lon Cohen that unless he finds a way to get Hobbs tossed off the *Gazette,* he won't ever get any more invitations to dinner here."

Wolfe picked up his book and snorted again. "Archie, the fabric of your humor is frayed. Have you made arrangements to see Mr. Childress's editor?"

I was about to respond when the phone rang. As if on cue, it was the individual in question, Keith Billings, returning my call. Billings sounded harried, so I didn't waste words. "I work for Nero Wolfe, who is investigating Charles Childress's death, and I would like to see you for a few minutes, preferably today."

"Why?" he snapped.

"We are talking to everyone who knew Childress, in the hope that we can learn—"

"That you can learn how to turn his death from a suicide into a murder, right? I know enough about your famous boss to be aware that murder is his métier—not to mention a very profitable livelihood.''

"Then you also should be aware that Mr. Wolfe has a respect for facts. He doesn't twist or alter them, and he certainly doesn't have to manufacture murders in order to get business. A client is convinced that Mr. Childress was killed, and Mr. Wolfe happens to agree.''

"Just who is this client?'' Billings fired back.

"Sorry, that's something I cannot divulge at this time.''

"Yeah, that's what I figured. You're on a fishing expedition.''

"Look, I realize you and Childress weren't exactly the best of friends, but—''

"Oh, now I get it. If I don't sit still for an interview with you, the implication is that I've got something to hide, is that it, Goodwin?''

"You interrupted me—for the second time.'' I kept my voice even and amiable. "What I was about to say was: but I'm certain you'd do anything you could to help identify the murderer—if there is one.''

I knew he was still on the line because I could hear angry breathing. After about fifteen seconds, he strung a series of expletives together, none of which can be used on vanity license plates in any state. The man belonged in publishing, all right: He had a fine grasp of the language and used a few words I made a mental note to look up later in Wolfe's *Oxford Dictionary of American Slang.*

"All right, dammit, I've got a nightmare of an afternoon, but I can spare a few minutes,'' Billings said after he'd finished spewing venom. "Come at three—I'm on the eighteenth floor. I assume you know the address."

I assured him I did, and at two-fifty-six, I sauntered into the Art Deco lobby of a mature skyscraper on Madison Avenue in the Forties. The Westman & Lane Publishing Company occupied four floors, sixteen through nineteen, and its roster of employees, which included Keith Billings, took up more than one-fourth of the building directory. When I got off the elevator at eighteen, I found myself facing a massive reception desk. Behind it rose a large backlit display of Westman & Lane's current publications, artfully arranged on several glass shelves. Also behind the desk sat a young man with oversized dark-rimmed glasses and curly black hair tied in a ponytail. He looked up from the book he had been reading and blinked his complete indifference in my direction.

"I'm here to see Keith Billings," I said. "The name is Goodwin."

He considered me with more indifference. "He expecting you?" When I said yes, the young dynamo tapped out a number on his phone and pronounced my name. He then nodded, cradled the receiver, and twitched his ponytail to the left. "Through that door," he droned. "About halfway down on the right. Can't miss it."

I would have said thanks, but I didn't want to distract him from his book, which he had dived back into. I pushed through into a long corridor. Where GBC-TV had been white all over, this place was gray, from the fabric walls to the carpeting. Office doors were spaced every few feet on both sides. An identical nameplate next to each one proclaimed its occupant in sans-serif capital letters. Many of the doors were open, revealing rooms barely big enough for one medium-sized desk, a couple of guest chairs, bookshelves filling one wall from floor to ceiling, and editors, all of whom seemed busy, presumably editing.

That is what Keith Billings was doing when I cast a shadow across his desk from the doorway. He looked up from a sheaf of papers, ran a hand through a forest of brown hair that already looked like it had been styled by an eggbeater, and tossed a frown in my direction. "Archie Goodwin, occupation—detective. Come in, sit down," he said without warmth, gesturing toward his pair of standard-issue tubular chairs. Both had piles of books on them, so I took the smallest stack, placing it on the floor, and sat.

"Oh—sorry about the mess," Billings muttered. "As you can see, housekeeping's not high on my priority list." He got up, all five-feet-seven of him, stalked to the door, shut it with a bang that unquestionably put a kink in the heavy editing going on up and down the hallway, and returned to his desk. "That's the only way to keep from getting interrupted around here, and even a closed door is no damn guarantee. Now, you wanted to talk about Childress—go ahead."

Billings planted elbows on the two clear spots on the desk top, resting his chin on clasped hands. I put him at no more than thirty-five, and maybe a year or two younger. His neck was thick and his face was square and ruddy, with wide cheekbones and eyes that I would have called black, although they probably were dark brown, complete with deep circles under them. He looked like a man who took life seriously and smiled only on alternate Wednesdays.

He and the late Mr. Childress must have made quite a pair.

"As I said on the telephone earlier today, Mr. Wolfe has been engaged by someone who believes Charles Childress was murdered. And he agrees with—"

"Where's the evidence?" Billings growled. "And what do the police think? The papers haven't printed a single word about murder. Nothing—not one damned word."

"Interruptions can come from both sides of a closed door," I responded calmly. "On the phone, you told me how busy you are, and I don't doubt that for a minute. But this will go much faster if you allow me to complete the sentences I start."

He twitched a hand irritably. "Okay, go on, go on."

"I don't have hard evidence that Charles Childress's demise was anything but a suicide, and neither does Mr. Wolfe—or our client, for that matter. But I learned a long time ago that when Nero Wolfe has a conviction about something, he's invariably right. And he is convinced that Childress was murdered." Okay, so I was laying it on thick, but I needed to seize the offensive.

"Now, you had known Childress for several years," I went on quickly. "Was he the type who might have killed himself?"

"Mr. Goodwin, it may surprise you to know that I am not an expert on suicidal behavior. Until now, I have never known anyone who destroyed himself—assuming of course that Charles did. As you must be aware, he was given to extreme mood swings—believe me, I saw more of them than I cared to. In the course of a few minutes, the man could go from high to low and back again. But regardless of where he was on that roller coaster of his, it was never a picnic working with the guy.''

''Was he a good writer?''

Billings twitched his head. ''All depends on whom you talk to. My former boss, Horace Vinson—I suppose you've already met him—gave Charles higher marks than I did. And several critics around town had lower opinions of him than mine. In fairness, he did a pretty decent job of re-creating Darius Sawyer's characters. The biggest problem I had was his plots. They were clumsy and awkward, but whenever I tried to strengthen some part of the structure, he'd throw a fit. I mean, he'd really go into a rage. I've dealt with some difficult writers in my ten-odd years as an editor, but Charles was the corker.'' He scowled at the memory.

''What was wrong with the plots?'' I asked.

''Sheesh! What *wasn't* wrong with them? I don't know if you're familiar with whodunits, but the trick is to give each suspect—there's usually five or six of them, maybe even seven—a solid motive for having committed the murder, or whatever the crime is. Then, you've also got to make sure that each of the suspects gets more or less equal play as the story unfolds. Of course it helps to strew some red herrings along the way, too. But the toughest thing is to make the puzzle hard to solve while at the same time playing fair with the reader.''

''Meaning?''

''Meaning the clues need to be there for the reader to find. They should be well-hidden—damn well-hidden—but they should be there. For one thing, Charles didn't handle his clues well; the ones he bothered to put in at all were usually so obvious a semi-literate eight-year-old could spot them. And he normally spent all his time concentrating on one or two of the suspects and all but ignoring the others, none of whom had a very believable motive."

"I gather you had a hard time getting him to change anything."

Billings shook his head. "Huh—a hard time? It was damn near impossible, even after the first Barnstable book came out. At first, the reviews were mixed to mildly favorable, although the majority of the critics clobbered him for exactly the things I'd pointed out and had tried to get him to change. But he was almost as hard to deal with when we worked on the second book, and finally, I went to Horace. He promised he'd speak to Charles, get him to be a little more flexible. Horace did talk to him all right, but it didn't do a hell of a lot of good. Charles remained convinced he was Tolstoy incarnate, or at least Balzac. He was still miserable to deal with, and his plots still had more holes than all the golf courses in Westchester combined. He went ballistic any time I suggested changes. So what happened? The second book got worse reviews than the first, with most of the criticism focused on the plot. Why was I not surprised?"

"And after all that, you still were willing to edit a third Childress book?" I asked.

"Mr. Goodwin, it wasn't a case of being *willing*," Billings said sharply. "I was Monarch's mystery editor —that was my job. Vinson liked Charles, and his first two books sold well enough, in spite of the mixed reviews. If I wanted to stay with Monarch, and I did, those two factors left me with no options, other than to do what I could to make the Barnstable books as good as possible under the circumstances.''

"Then came the third book.''

Billings swiped at a buzzing fly and missed. "God, don't remind me. There's probably not much I can say that you don't already know. Things really turned ugly between Charles and me. The less-than-rave reviews he'd gotten, combined with criticism from some of the purists who had grown up on the Sawyer books, made him paranoid and defensive. Bear in mind that Charles Childress was not a Gibraltar of stability to begin with. Are you aware that he had attempted suicide before?''

"You've got my attention.''

"Actually, he did talk about it once, maybe to get sympathy, although I know that sounds cynical—in fact, I don't like hearing myself say it. Anyway, some years back, before I'd met him, he apparently got depressed when a manuscript of his for a big novel was rejected, and he turned on the gas in his apartment.''

"He told you this?''

Billings leaned back and put his hands behind his head. "Yeah, he did. And I couldn't think of a damn thing to say. I remember that after he told me about it, we sat in my office—that was when I was still over at Monarch—looking at each other like two stupes. Hell, I don't think either of us said a word for five minutes. But you know, I never felt closer to the guy than I did that day.''

"That feeling obviously didn't last for long.''

"No. Charles was always furious with me about something. He didn't take criticism well, and he accused me more than once of, to use his words, 'trying to turn my book into your book.' It got so that I found that I was even arguing with *myself* over every change I made in his work. I spent far too much time trying to figure out how he'd react to every change I made, and I don't have to tell you that's not a great way to edit a manuscript.''

''Maybe he was doing it intentionally, to keep you from fiddling with his writing,'' I suggested.

He turned his palms up. ''I don't believe Charles was that calculating. He honestly felt everything he wrote was without fault, and that an editor's role was simply to catch minor stuff—typos, punctuation errors, that sort of thing. He was stunned when the reviews of his first Barnstable book weren't all paeans to his towering talent.'' He grimaced.

''And you mentioned criticism from some of the purists. What about that?''

''Do you know about the Barnstable clubs?'' The phone rang. Billings ignored it.

''Just that they exist. Something to do with the acronym PROBE, aren't they?''

''Yeah. Standing for, if you can believe it, 'Passionate Roster of Orville Barnstable Enthusiasts.' Apparently, readers took to Orville Barnstable almost from the start. After Darius Sawyer wrote his first three or four books, so I've been told, this cult following sprang up. All over the country, and in Canada, too, Barnstable clubs were formed. 'Posses' is what the local chapters call themselves, and a newsletter was started out in California that had—and still has—a national mailing list. These people are as fervent as the Sherlockians; they know every detail about the stories, every idiosyncrasy about Barnstable and the other characters in the series. I know—I've given some speeches to a local chapter here, and the one in Philadelphia, too.

"Anyway, the clubs themselves on the whole were pretty kind to Charles—they were mainly delighted to have new Barnstable stories. And Charles, too, spoke to the local chapters; he was like a hero to them, and of course he liked that—who wouldn't? But he also got a lot of mail from individuals, not necessarily PROBE members, and some of it was on the nasty side. You know, in preparation to edit Charles's books, I read most of the ones Sawyer wrote—they all were published before I joined Monarch. I immersed myself in them and took a bookful of notes. But as well as I thought I knew the series, these people pounced on all sorts of minuscule inconsistencies in Charles's books. And some of them berated him for no other reason than because he had the effrontery to add to what they saw as a sacred canon."

"Did all this bother him?" I asked.

"Hell yes, it did. He'd pop his cork and fire off angry replies until finally, I just quit forwarding correspondence to him unless it was favorable."

"Pretty thin-skinned. Did any of these letter-writers threaten Childress?"

"Not that I'm aware of. They were purists, but they weren't *that* hostile."

"As far as you know, did anyone else ever threaten him?"

Billings leaned back and smirked. "No, Mr. Goodwin. I'm afraid that you and Nero Wolfe are really going to have to pull a rabbit, or at least a hamster, out of a hat this time to construct a halfway-believable murder scenario."

I smiled benignly. "In the years that you knew

Childress, did anything unusual happen to him? A personal crisis, a trauma of any kind?"

"You really are reaching, aren't you? Frankly, if you were hooked up with anybody except Wolfe, I'd ask you to get the hell out of here, but even I make allowances for genius, which is what I understand your boss claims to be. As far as personal crises, Charles always seemed to be immersed in one of his own making. Hell, as I'm sure you know, just in the last few weeks he had feuded in print with me, with his agent, and with that popinjay who masquerades as a book reviewer for the *Gazette*."

Billings paused to run a palm across his cheek and yawn. "The only time I remember Charles being upset by something unrelated to his writing was when his mother died. That was, oh . . . probably around two years ago now. He spent months in his hometown out in one of those interchangeable 'I' states in the Midwest—maybe Illinois or Indiana, while she deteriorated. It was pretty rough on him. When he came back, he seemed, I don't know . . . *distracted* is probably the best description. And he stayed distracted for months. During that time he even quit squabbling with me over changes I made in his precious prose."

"I suppose it's understandable that he'd be shaken," I responded.

"I guess so, except that he never seemed particularly close to his mother while she was alive and healthy. If I recall correctly, he told me just before he went home during her illness that he hadn't been back there in seven or eight years. And it's not exactly halfway around the world from here."

"Except maybe in outlook. During the period when he was 'distracted,' did he keep on writing?"

"Yeah. In fact, he cranked out quite a bit while he was with his mother, too. He'd send me batches of chapters periodically; they were okay, about the same quality as what he did here."

"Did he ever say anything about his months in the Midwest?"

"Not much. I asked once how he occupied himself all day, but he brushed me off with some comment about there being nothing to do except to write and talk to his relatives and take long walks down back roads. He said once that he didn't fish, he didn't hunt, and he didn't know a Jersey from a Holstein. And didn't want to."

"The apple fell pretty far from the tree. You made a reference earlier to his feuding in print with you, Franklin Ott, and Wilbur Hobbs. Did those attacks in *Book Business* and the *Manhattan Literary Times* surprise you?"

Billings screwed up his face. "Not really. I had already left Monarch to come here, but it made me mad, damn mad. I wasn't surprised because I'd had enough experience with the guy to know that his modus operandi was to blame other people for whatever writing problems he had. Hell, look how he took Ott over the coals in those articles."

"Franklin Ott?"

He nodded. "Charles wasn't stupid enough to mention him by name, of course, but everybody knew who he was writing about. Have you talked to Ott yet?"

"Briefly."

"Did he tell you that he lost three of his clients, including a top-flight science-fiction writer, within days after that damn piece of Charles's ran?"

"He mentioned that he has had some turnover," I said.

Billings slapped his leg. "Some turnover—ha! For a few days there, it was more like an exodus. Oh, I know, he's picked up a couple of new names since, but that can't match what he lost, at least not in terms of dollars."

"Interesting. What were the circumstances of your departure from Monarch?"

That raised the flicker of a smile, which disappeared as quickly as it arose. "Somehow, I think you already know a good deal about that, Mr. Goodwin. But of course you'd like to hear it straight from this horse's mouth. All right; after Charles's third Barnstable book, *Death in the North Meadow,* went to press, he went to Horace Vinson and demanded a new editor. He told Horace that we had 'irreconcilable personality differences'—that's actually the phrase he used, the intransigent bastard. Now you'll never get me to badmouth Horace Vinson—he's a wonderful bookman, and a true gentleman of the old school. The man redefines the word 'courtly.' But it's commonly known inside the business, and maybe outside, too, that whenever there's a conflict, Horace will invariably side with the author against the editor. And he did here. He told me that he was giving Charles a new editor, and that he hoped I'd understand.

"I'd seen something like this coming for a long time," Billings continued glumly, "so I wasn't terribly surprised. For one thing, I knew damn well that Ott, snake that he is, was lobbying hard to get me pulled off Charles's books. I was very calm during our conversation, but I told Horace firmly that as long as I was Monarch's mystery editor, I expected to edit *all* of the house's mysteries. To me, that was simply non-negotiable. In that pleasant, engaging way he has, he held his ground, and the result was that we agreed to disagree. I resigned, which I know saddened him. Off the record, he gave me a very handsome severance, something he was not obligated to do. And that's all there is to it. End of story."

"Are you happy here?"

"Happier than I thought I'd be. Westman & Lane is a smaller house than Monarch, and I'm handling a wider range of fiction, although I still get to edit mysteries, which are my first love. And of course, Mr. Goodwin, there is one more thing that you want to ask me."

"There is?"

"Absolutely. You want to know if I can account for my movements on the day that Charles was found dead. I know the drill pretty well. After all, I *do* edit mysteries, as you're well aware."

"Okay, Mr. Billings, where were you on—"

"On the Tuesday before last," Billings cut in, smirking. "I looked on my calendar right after you phoned, knowing that you and Wolfe would consider me a suspect. And frankly, I'm still a suspect as far as you're concerned, because I have no alibi—none whatever. I'd been working at home on Tuesdays—I can get infinitely more done away from the telephone and other office interruptions. And that was the case on the day Charles was found dead. I was at home all day—I have an apartment on the Upper East Side. Do I live with someone? No, sorry. Does my building have a doorman? No, it's not in that league. Did anybody see me? No, at least not until I went to a bar in

108 · ROBERT GOLDSBOROUGH

my neighborhood for a sandwich—corned beef, it was, on rye, and a beer. Any other questions?"

I showed him the key I was carrying, which he told me looked like hundreds of others he'd seen, but not that had ever belonged to him. "Here are mine," he said casually, tossing a ringful on his desk blotter. None matched the one I had.

"Anything else?" he demanded.

"Ever been to Childress's apartment?" I asked.

"You don't give it up, do you? No, I have never been there."

"Did you know that he died from a bullet fired from his own gun?"

"Yeah. Listen, I *do* read the papers. I don't know why he had one, but I wasn't surprised. I've toyed with getting a small-caliber pistol myself, for self-protection. Lord knows you need one in this town. Now if you'll excuse me, I've got a pile of stuff to do."

I got up, playing ever so fleetingly with the idea of making an anonymous, handkerchief-over-the-mouthpiece telephone call to one Lieutenant George Rowcliff of the Homicide Squad and telling him that a fellow named Keith Billings was seen leaving Charles Childress's apartment building on the day the latter was found dead.

NINE

T he walk home from Keith Billings's office cooled me off, so by the time I mounted the steps to the brownstone, I conceded that turning Rowcliff loose on the sawed-off, smart-mouthed editor would be a form of cruel and unusual punishment, the kind that was frowned upon by the framers of the Federal Constitution. Maybe I'd make my anonymous call to Sergeant Purley Stebbins instead; unlike Rowcliff, Purley is neither mean nor stupid. But the man sure loves to use his handcuffs.

It was almost a quarter of six by the time I settled in at my desk. Wolfe had left two handwritten letters on my blotter, to orchid growers in Marietta, Georgia, and Madison, Wisconsin. I dutifully entered each into the PC and printed them out twice—one for his signature and the other for our files. After I'd finished, I glanced at my watch, which told me it was eight minutes past the hour. It's a terrific watch, a quartz job Lily Rowan got me for my birthday two-plus years ago, and it's never been off more than a second or so—until now. I accused it of galloping until I shot a peek at the wall clock, which also read 6:08. Just as I began contemplating the implications of all this, Fritz appeared at the door, alarm both on his face and in his voice.

"Where is he, Archie? He did not ring for beer, and he did not call down on the house telephone to say he would be delayed."

"I was wondering the very same thing myself. I'll go up."

I took the stairs two at a time to the fourth floor. When I got there, I found Wolfe standing in the little hallway that led to the plant rooms, glowering into the darkened interior of the one vehicle in the world he trusted. Theodore Horstmann stood behind him, his face longer than the men's-room lines at Shea in the seventh inning on a warm Sunday afternoon when the Mets are playing the Dodgers.

"It doesn't work," Wolfe muttered.

I stepped into the elevator and pressed each of the buttons. He was right.

"Oh, well, at least the trip is southbound," I told him, trying to make light of the situation. "Beer awaits at base camp."

Wolfe was not amused, as his expression indicated. But he made the best of it and began the descent behind me. I beat him to the first floor by at least a minute. Fritz was at the bottom of the stairs, kneading his hands in his apron and looking up at me with a question mark on his face.

"The elevator's on the fritz, pardon the expression. He's coming—on foot. Have beer on his desk when he arrives," I ordered. I swear Fritz saluted before doing a snappy about-face and darting into the kitchen—probably a vestige of his days with the Alpine Patrol.

When Wolfe arrived in the doorway, two bottles

of beer and a frosted glass awaited on his blotter, and I was back at my desk. He marched into the office and got settled in his chair.

"I'll call the elevator maintenance outfit," I told him. "There's a chance somebody can come tomorrow, although it probably will cost extra because it's a Saturday." He grunted what I took to be his approval, so I found the number in my telephone file and punched it out. A recorded female voice informed me the office was closed but that I could try an emergency number, which I did. The guy who answered sounded like he'd just been roused from a deep sleep. I told him the problem and he responded with a few sluggish "uh-huhs." He was equally unenthusiastic when he said they'd send a crew out first thing in the morning—no later than nine. "Hafta charge you the weekend rate," he warned, and I responded that we would live with it.

I hung up and told Wolfe help was on the way, but he didn't appear to be impressed, so I changed the subject. "I talked to Keith Billings," I said as he set down his glass of beer, licked his lips, and picked up his current book, *Byzantium: The Apogee,* by John Julius Norwich. "Do you want a report?"

He scowled and closed the book. "Proceed," he said icily. I forgave him silently, knowing it had been an unsettling day for him, and gave him the conversation verbatim while he sat with eyes closed and hands on his chair arms. When I finished, he opened his eyes, drained his glass, and poured more beer before uttering a single word. "Indiana."

"Yeah, two people now have told me Childress seemed different when he came back from there.

Like I told Billings, maybe that's understandable, though."

"I detected no appreciable change in your personality or demeanor when you returned from your mother's funeral several years ago," Wolfe observed.

"True, but no two people react to a personal loss in the same way."

"Manifestly. How would one get to this place?" To Wolfe, any travel, even a few blocks by car, is an act of outright recklessness. I went to the bookshelves and pulled down the big atlas, taking it back to my desk. "Mercer, Indiana, population, four thousand six hundred eleven. Here it is, southwest of Indianapolis a little over a hundred miles, say a two-hour drive."

Wolfe shuddered. "And to get to Indianapolis?"

"Something over an hour by air, ninety minutes at the outside. Do I go?"

Another shudder. "I believe you are visiting Miss Rowan's dacha this weekend?"

Wolfe calls it a dacha, and Lily herself refers to it as "my country cottage." It actually is a spacious, stone-and-timber, tile-roofed, four-bedroom villa with an Olympic-sized pool and stables set on forty rolling and wooded acres near Katonah. "We were supposed to drive up around noon tomorrow, but I can cancel," I told him.

"No, Monday is soon enough. Make the necessary arrangements," he said, returning to his book. You might think he was being considerate by letting me keep my weekend plans, but he had a couple of ulterior motives: One, he wanted to be sure I was around in the morning to deal with the elevator repair crew; and two, he knew that if I were away toiling

on Sunday, he would have to give me a day off somewhere along the way as compensation, and he doesn't
like it when I'm not around on weekdays to carry out
whatever duties he dreams up. Actually, there was a
third factor, too. Wolfe, despite his overall opinion of
women, approves of Lily Rowan—whenever she
comes to the brownstone, she asks to see his orchids,
a request that is sure to get a positive response from
him. She had a weekend planned, and he did not
want to cast himself in the role of bad guy by messing
it up.

The next morning, after devouring a breakfast of
sausage, eggs, and pancakes with wild-thyme honey at
my small table in the kitchen, I finished packing my
overnight bag for the trip to Katonah and went to the
office to tackle some housekeeping odds and ends. At
nine-twenty, the doorbell rang. It was two men from
the elevator outfit we've used through the years, one
of whom, the tall bald one, I recognized. I ushered
them in, and we hoofed it up to the fourth floor,
where the car stood open and dark. While they surveyed it, I went into the plant rooms to confirm that
Wolfe had walked up the two flights from his bedroom on the second floor. Sure enough, there he
was, on his usual stool at the bench doing something
with the stuff in a pot, while Theodore looked on,
frowning. His frown predictably deepened when he
saw me. "Just thought I'd let you know that the elevator grease monkeys are here. Things may get a little
noisy," I said. Wolfe glowered in my direction and
turned back to the pot.

I went down to the office, where I balanced the
checkbook and read those parts of the *Times* I hadn't

gotten to at breakfast. At ten-thirty-five, the tall bald repairman stuck his head in the door and delivered the bad news.

"Sorry, but you've got problems big-time." He shook his head like an auto mechanic telling me that my car was on life-support systems. "I remember workin' on this baby years ago, and it was ancient then. They quit making this model before I was born, and I'm sneaking up on retirement. Howie and me have just now been on the roof of the cab, in the shaft from top to bottom, checked the cables, the counterweights, the motor, the bearings, the bushings, the electrical system, the works. And I gotta tell you, the thing's just plain dangerous the shape she's in right now. I'm surprised the city inspectors didn't whistle you on it the last time they was here. But I see by the certificate in the cab that they gave it a pass. Come on up—I'll show you just how bad it is." He—his name was Carl—and I walked up the three flights, where his partner Howie was packing up his tool box.

"See here?" Carl said, stepping into the elevator, crouching and playing his flashlight along the floor. "It's rusted through in four or five places where the wall joins the floor. Thing's ready to come to pieces. And the door"—he grabbed it and shook it—"is hanging on by its imagination. I'm surprised none of you had noticed how bad it is."

"How long will it take and how much will it cost?" I asked.

"Depends. There's so much wrong that we strongly recommend a new unit—including a cab. If the platform—the base of the cab, that is—was in better shape, maybe we could salvage it, but"—Carl shrugged—"that's not the case, not by a long shot.

"I know it probably sounds drastic to you, but startin' over's actually cheaper than tryin' to patch this old bus together, especially because a lot of the parts aren't even made anymore. And the motor's totally shot, too—totally. You may want to get a second estimate, but I think anybody else'll find the same stuff wrong that we did. If you go the whole nine yards, and I really think you should, we can start, oh, probably next Monday, assuming everything is in stock. We can have the new setup operational in ten working days, twelve at most. And we won't have to tear out any walls; the new cab can be assembled right in the shaft—after we dismantle the old one, of course, which is a big job. If you call our emergency number today with the go-ahead, I'm pretty sure that a crew can be here early next week." He thrust a clipboard at me with a list of things needing fixing and the cost of each. The figure at the bottom made me glad that we currently had a client.

I told Carl that I would check with Wolfe and get a decision, probably later today. He gave a thumbs-up, and the three of us descended the stairs to the front hall, where we said good-bye and I let them out.

Wolfe can be a trouper when times are tough, I'll give him that. It was only 11:04 when he strode into the office, and he wasn't even breathing hard from the mind-boggling exertion of walking down three flights. He placed a raceme of *Phalaenopsis* in the vase on his blotter and dipped his head in my direction but did not say "Good morning," since we already had seen each other earlier. I got up from my chair and walked to his desk, laying the estimate in front of him. He picked it up, pressed his lips together, and set it down. "Pfui. Exorbitant."

"Pfui, indeed," I agreed. "You're the only one who ever uses the elevator. Didn't it seem to you that the thing was getting pretty rickety?"

Wolfe shrugged away the question, ringing for beer.

"The work will take two weeks, maybe a little more, beginning early next week, or so the guy who was here thinks," I went on. "Do you want me to get a second estimate?"

"Would it be appreciably different?"

"Probably not. This outfit has a top-flight reputation, the best in the city—or at least they did. The reason we called them originally, you may remember, was that I checked with a high roller Lon Cohen knows who's in real estate, and he recommended them. But that was several years back, although we've used them for minor repairs three or four times since without any problems. I can do some calling around to see if they're still well-thought-of."

"No," Wolfe responded, holding up a palm. "Proceed." I did, and when I called them to give the go-ahead, the still-sleepy voice at the other end promised that a crew would be on the job Monday morning, "no later than eight-thirty." I reminded Wolfe that I would be on my way to Indiana on Monday and asked if he'd like me to get either Saul Panzer or Fred Durkin to fill in for me at the desk, as has been the case sometimes when I've gone out of town. "How long will you be gone?" he asked.

"That is a question I should be tossing at you," I said with a smile. "It all depends on what you expect me to accomplish while I'm there."

"Your notebook," he grumbled. "Instructions."

TEN

The weekend in Katonah could not have been improved upon. The weather was better than any New Yorker had a right to expect in mid-April: Sunny, light breezes, temperatures flirting with seventy. Lily and I rode two of her spirited Morgans for an hour or so Saturday afternoon, followed by a dip in the pool, and we dined down the road from her place at a just-opened restaurant in a two-hundred-year-old Tudor mansion. I had salmon *en piperade* and a few bites of her rack of lamb. Fritz would have given his blessing to both dishes. Sunday after brunch in the same restaurant, we rode some more, swam some more, and were back in town by six.

The memory of the weekend lingered pleasantly as I drove through the rain of a Monday morning in south-central Indiana, but I'm getting ahead of myself. My instructions from Wolfe on Saturday had been brief: Visit Childress's aunts and anyone else in Mercer who could reveal anything about the man, both during his hometown years and after he went to New York. When I pressed for more direction, he gave me his "Use your intelligence guided by experience" line, which I have heard more times than I can begin to count.

After making plane and car-rental reservations, I had called Debra Mitchell to get the names of Childress's aunts, only one of whom—Melva Meeker—she had talked to on the telephone. "She wasn't very communicative, to say the least," Debra told me crisply. "My guess is that you're wasting your time trying to phone her. And I'm sorry, but I don't know the name of the other aunt." I said thanks, not bothering to add that I was planning a face-to-face visit.

Maybe it was the rain, or the hills and curves and crawling farm vehicles, but it took me nearly two hours to navigate the two-lane blacktop through newly green and wooded rural countryside from the Indianapolis airport to Mercer, which trumpeted itself with a red-and-blue billboard proclaiming THE COMMUNITY WHERE HOOSIER HOSPITALITY WAS BORN—AND STILL FLOURISHES! Below it was a smaller, newer sign, in the same colors, that read CONGRATULATIONS TO THE MERCER METEORS FOR THEIR FIRST EVER STATE HIGH SCHOOL REGIONAL BASKETBALL TITLE. A few hundred yards farther down the road, I came upon a motel. The Travelers' Haven was far from posh, but it looked decent enough—a long, white, one-story stucco building between the road and a field that appeared to this city boy to be freshly plowed. A half-dozen cars were parked nose-first on the blacktop in front of the rooms. I wheeled my rented sedan up to the office and went inside, triggering a bell when I opened the door.

"Afternoon." A deep voice stretched it to four or five syllables, rather than the conventional three. The voice belonged to a dusty-haired, long-faced guy in baggy, gray flannel slacks and a red wool shirt who ambled through a doorway from the back, grinning and pushing wire-rimmed glasses up on the beak that was his nose. He was at least three inches over six feet, but if he weighed one-fifty, it was only because he wore his boots when he hopped on the scale.

"Afternoon," I countered, making no attempt to elongate the word. I know my limitations. "Can I get a room for a couple of nights?"

He puckered his lips. "No reason to say no. But we do like the cash up front. We've never been much for credit cards here."

"Always a good policy," I responded, returning his sober nod. "I will pay for the first night now, and if I decide to stay a second one, you'll get the greenbacks for that later today. Fair enough?"

He nodded again, this time with a slight grin. "Fair enough." He quoted me a price; it was higher than I would have guessed, but I was not inclined to negotiate. I opened my billfold and peeled off the bills, which he counted twice aloud and slid into an ancient cash register before handing me a brass key. "Room one-twenty," he twanged. "Down the line six doors on your right. Everything should be there, but if you need extra towels or another bar of soap, stop back. We'll take care of you, count on it. A good place for breakfast is the Old Skillet downtown. Right across from the courthouse. They serve a passable dinner, too. Although the best spot for that is Bill's Steak House, right on this road just south of town on the left—barely more'n a mile from here."

I thanked him, stifling the urge to say "much obliged," and walked to my room, which was a pleasant surprise. There was a king-size bed with a firm mattress and a bathroom that looked like it had recently been fitted with new fixtures and light blue tile. The TV set had a good-sized screen, although that was wasted on me: If you strung together all of the television I watch in a given year, not counting the news, the tape would not run as long as it takes me to walk from the brownstone to Lily's apartment up on Sixty-third between Park and Madison.

I unpacked, washed up, and went back to the motel office, where Indiana Slim was taking a reservation over the phone. "Where do I find the local newspaper office?" I asked as he cradled the receiver.

"It's right on the courthouse square. Two doors from that restaurant I was telling you about, the Old Skillet." He pushed his glasses up on his nose again. " 'Fraid we don't have a daily paper here; I suppose we're just too doggone small. The *Mercury* only comes out twice a week, Tuesday and Friday. It's all right, though—I always read it straight through front to back." He nodded with pride. "Fellow who's the editor, name's Southworth, comes from somewhere back East. They say he's a real crackerjack."

"Much obliged," I responded, deciding not to fight the urge. With a basketball team called the Meteors and a newspaper named the *Mercury*, the fine folks in Mercer either liked alliteration or they were big into astronomy—or maybe some of both. I half-expected to find a movie theater named the Mars.

The burg did have a movie house, all right, but it was the Roxy, and the aging letters on the marquee announced that it was CLOSED FOR REMODELING. From the look of the facade, the place more likely was closed for eternity. I parked on one side of the square just as the bell in the courthouse tower tolled twice, in near agreement with my watch. The newspaper occupied the street level of a solid, two-story red-brick building that was in far better shape than the Roxy, although it probably was older. On the big window, silver Old English type spelled out *The Mercer Mercury,* and beneath that logo, smaller black letters proclaimed it as *Proudly Serving Gilmartin County Since 1887.*

Entering, I found myself in a reception area manned by a strawberry blonde with a well-shaped nose who was busy driving an electric typewriter. The nameplate on her desk announced she was Barbara Adamson. I had the nose, and the rest of what appeared to be a nicely designed face, in profile while her fingers skimmed over the keys. She got to the bottom of the sheet and whipped it crisply out of the machine, then turned toward me with a smile that would have warmed a penguin's tootsies. The face was every bit as pleasing head-on as it had been in profile.

"I'm sorry to keep you waiting, sir," Barbara Adamson said softly, making me believe every word. "Can I help you?"

I told her I wanted to see Southworth, handing her one of my cards, the eggshell-colored number with only my name, address and phone number on it.

She studied it, nodded, and smiled, both with her mouth and her Scandinavian blue eyes. "Do you have an appointment, Mr. Goodwin?"

"No, but I wish I did. Would that help?"

Another smile, this one accompanied by a slight blush. "Oh, I didn't mean to sound rude or anything like that. Actually, Mr. Southworth is very accessible. He tries to see everybody. Does he know you?"

"I'm afraid not," I answered.

"You're from New York City," she said, nodding thoughtfully. "At the risk of sounding like this is some sort of backwater, I'll confess to you that we don't get a lot of visitors from New York. May I tell him what business you're in?"

"You may, Ms., Miss, or Mrs. Adamson. I'm a private investigator."

"It's Mrs.," she responded, breaking my heart. "A private investigator? Excuse me and I'll see if he's available." She got up and went through a doorway, leaving me to look at framed front pages of the *Mercury* that decorated the walls of the reception room. I was reading one from September 1945 with the headline OUR BOYS COME HOME TO CHEERING when a husky voice broke in. "I'm Chet Southworth; what can I do for you?"

He was about my height, but had the edge on me both in weight and years. His thick hair, which fell across one side of his forehead, was more gray than brown, and although I wouldn't have termed him fat, wide blue suspenders were being given a test. I asked if I could steal a few minutes of his time.

He moved his shoulders up and then down. "Why not? Come on back to my office." I nodded my thanks to Barbara Adamson and followed him through the doorway and along one side of an undecorated, high-ceilinged room where a half-dozen people worked at computer terminals. "We've only had VDTs for our editorial staff for a few months now," Southworth said over his shoulder, "but they're a godsend. I tried for two years to get management to invest in a system, and they finally got tired of hearing me carp and whine."

His office was a windowless cubicle in a back corner of the newsroom. "Not much, but it's home," he said with a smile, gesturing me to a chair as he dropped into the upholstered one behind his paper-littered desk.

"So, you're an honest-to-God, card-carrying New York private dick, eh?" Southworth chuckled, considering me over the tops of half-glasses. "Never thought I'd live to see one."

"I enjoy bringing excitement into people's lives," I said. "Actually, I'm the legs for another detective, Nero Wolfe."

He raised both chin and eyebrows. "Ah, *him* I've heard of, yeah. I'm from New York—the state, not the city. I worked on the Syracuse paper for fourteen years. Copy boy first, then police reporter, and on to the copy desk. After that I was city editor on a couple of small dailies in upstate towns nobody ever heard of. When my marriage fell apart, I came out here and —oh, hell, you don't want to hear my life story any more than I feel like telling it. Now what interests you and Nero Wolfe in this out-of-the-way corner of the Midwest?"

"Charles Childress."

"That's kind of what I figured, although I don't know why. From the reports we got, there wasn't any question but that it was a suicide."

"Mr. Wolfe has a client who thinks otherwise. And he agrees with the client."

Southworth chewed absently on a pencil. "And you're here to find out if there's something in the guy's background that might suggest a motive for murder, right? I'm afraid I'm not going to be a hell of a lot of help, Mr. Goodwin. Normally, going to the local newspaper in a situation like this would make

damn good sense. But here it doesn't, for two reasons: First, I've only been in Mercer a little over three
years, so I don't know where the skeletons are buried
like somebody who's home-grown would. And most of
the staff is even newer to the paper than I am. Second, when I took over as editor, I changed the character of the *Mercury* a great deal. It used to
concentrate almost exclusively on the folksy stuff—
club news, farm news, nonmalicious gossip. We still
do some of that, only because we have to, being a
community paper. But I've swung more toward what I
hope is probing coverage of things like the county
government and the board meetings of the towns
where we circulate. And believe it or not, the paper
has dug up some corruption here and there. Not
headline news by big-city standards, but we did get a
member of the county board indicted for taking
money under the table.

"And you know what—the readers love it! A local
family, the Kirbys, owns the *Mercury,* and to describe
them as conservative is like saying western Kansas is
flat. When we started getting harder-edged in our re-
porting, I was worried that one Kirby or another
would pressure me to back off. Wrong. It turned out
that their country club friends—the bankers, the re-
tailers, the owners of the big cement plant over in
Mapes—were all hoping somebody would get on the
case of the local politicos."

Southworth took off his glasses and pressed his
palms against his eyes. "Anyhow, that's a long-winded
way of saying that I don't know much about Childress.
Oh, we ran a piece when he died, of course. Apparently he was one of the three most famous people to
ever come out of Mercer. The other two were a Medal

of Honor winner in World War I and a high school basketball star back in the fifties who ended up going to the pros. Anyway, our obit on Childress was on page one—about eight 'graphs, most of it on his writing career, along with a picture we had in our files— it's the one used on his books. I'll get you a copy of that issue."

"Thanks. As I understand it, he spent several months in Mercer about two years ago during his mother's final illness. A couple of people who knew him in New York felt that he was different when he came back East."

The editor looked interested. "Yeah?"

"They said he seemed older, grimmer, and more distracted than before. Other than his mother's death, did anything happen while he was here?"

Southworth wrinkled his forehead. "Not that I'm aware of, but it just occurred to me that we did a feature on him, a profile, during the time he lived here taking care of his mother; I'd forgotten all about it until you mentioned her. Not a bad piece—Gina Marks did it. I'll get her." He sprang from his chair and went to the doorway. "Gina, got a minute? Come on in," he said in a voice that was neither a command nor a plea.

A slender woman of about twenty-five with straight black hair and dark, wide eyes gingerly stepped into the office, looking first at Southworth and then at me.

"Have a seat," the editor boomed. "Gina, this is Archie Goodwin, a private investigator from New York. He's looking into Charles Childress's death, got an idea there may be a possibility he was murdered.

You interviewed Childress for that feature when he was staying here. How did he strike you at the time?"

Eyes wider, she looked from me to Southworth and back again. "God, I don't know," she said in a throaty voice, spreading long-fingered hands, palms up. "That's hard to say, it's been so long ago, now. He wasn't terribly friendly, I remember that much. Darlene—she's our feature editor—" this explanation was for my benefit, "gave me the assignment, and the first time I called Childress at his mother's house, he started out being just plain rude, said he was in Mercer only for personal reasons and didn't want to be bothered with the press. When I told him a lot of people all over the county read his books and would love to know more about his work, he softened a little and asked me to call him again in two weeks or so. I did, and that time, he ended up talking to me."

"Where was the interview? At his mother's house?" I asked.

Gina Marks shook her dark head vigorously. "Oh, no. I did offer to go out there—it's on the county road about halfway between here and Clark's Grove—but he said he'd rather meet me in town. I ended up interviewing him one morning in a booth at the Old Skillet. It was about ten, so we pretty much had the place to ourselves."

"Was he forthcoming?"

"Not very! I got enough for my piece, but just barely. He seemed, I don't know . . . sort of distant, and resentful, too, like I was intruding on his time."

"Well, he *did* have a lot on his mind then," Southworth put in.

"Did he talk much about his life in Mercer?"

Gina gave me a thumbs-down and a sour look.

"No, and obviously, that's what I had wanted. But all I got was that it was his mother who stimulated his interest in reading, and literature in general, starting when he was twelve or thirteen. Beyond that, he didn't want to talk about Mercer at all. I think he looked down on this area as some sort of cultural desert. And it was obvious that he resented having to spend time here, even to take care of his mother. Frankly, Mr. Goodwin, the man didn't impress me one bit. He was a snobbish, arrogant, shallow transplant to the big city who tries to ignore the place he came from and what it taught him."

"So he didn't mention anyone else from here— relatives, friends?"

"Oh, he tossed off some obligatory, predictable compliment to one of his high school English teachers, who died years ago," she said hotly. "But it was so damn rehearsed, he'd probably used it in a dozen other interviews."

"Did you talk to anybody else for your story?" I asked.

"No—he made me feel so guilty for invading his privacy that I was just happy to pull what I did out of him. And what I wrote ended up being almost entirely on his approach to writing, with very little about his years in Mercer. To be honest, I'm not proud of that piece. I'd do it differently today."

I nodded in sympathy. "How many relatives does he have here?"

"Two aunts, and I think some cousins. I've never met any of them."

"Is there any scuttlebutt around town about Childress that you've come across?"

I got a glare. "Nothing I've ever heard. It may

surprise you, Mr. Goodwin, coming as you do from the self-anointed cultural capital of the western world, to learn that not all small-town newspapers are gossip sheets. We didn't win all those awards we've gotten since Chet took over by chattering about personal lives and peccadilloes." She sucked in air and let it out with an indignant whoosh.

"Whoa!" I leaned back and held up a palm. "I'm not taking shots at you or the paper. And I'm not interested in idle gossip for its own sake. Remember, we're talking about the possibility that a murder has been committed."

"Okay, sorry." Gina smiled sheepishly and slapped herself lightly on the cheek. "I guess maybe I get a little defensive sometimes."

"Dammit, *get* defensive!" Southworth barked, punching the air with a beefy fist. "I love to hear you defend the *Mercury*. I know Goodwin meant no offense, though. If he didn't come up with questions like that, then *he* wouldn't be a good reporter. Do you need to talk anymore to Gina?"

When I said no, she stood up and came over to me, offering a hand to show there were no hard feelings. I took it and smiled.

After she walked out, the editor motioned toward the doorway. "She's damn good," he said, "best we've got, and I know I'll be losing her before long. There's only so much variety and challenge you can offer an enterprising reporter like her in a town this size and on a twice-weekly. But . . . that comes with the territory—you train 'em to lose 'em. Tell me, what makes your boss and his client—and you, too, I assume—so sure that Childress was murdered?"

"Nothing tangible, except that life had been going more or less well for him," I replied. "And he was supposed to be married in the fall."

He nodded. "So I heard. I suppose you're going to talk to his relatives?"

"The aunts, anyway. Can you point me toward them?"

"Barbara—that's the woman you met out front—can give you directions to where they live." Southworth got to his feet and stretched. "Normally a few whiffs of a thing like this would get my old police reporter's juices flowing, but from what little I know and what you've told me, I don't see any arrows that point to murder. If you do find something, though, I'd appreciate a call."

"I have a prior commitment to a paper in New York," I told him. "But if you don't mind being second in line . . ."

He laughed heartily. "Don't mind a bit. I understand that you've got to keep your primary sources happy. But I'd sure as hell like to scoop the argyle socks off those arrogant bastards who run the fat, self-satisfied daily over in the next county."

"Sounds like a healthy attitude to me," I told him as we shook hands. "If and when something happens, I'll be happy to supply you with some boulders for your catapult."

ELEVEN

The twisting, two-lane blacktop took me southeast out of Mercer past small farms; all their houses and barns cried out for fresh paint and a handyman. Any dude from the city who feels the American farmer whines too much about his lot would be advised to take the route I did on that rainy April afternoon.

Following Barbara Adamson's neatly drawn map, I turned right onto a stretch of gravel called Bailey's Road and, after leaving a wake of dust for a quarter-mile, found the house, which was as Barbara had described it: two stories, faded yellow clapboard, with an almost-dead oak in a front yard that was more dirt than grass and a sway-backed barn off to the left. The mailbox, which had MEEKER hand-painted on it in faded red letters, perched atop a spindly post that didn't figure to survive the next strong wind.

I steered my car into the ruts that passed for a driveway and pulled up behind a grimy pickup truck of indeterminate color with more dents than a Manhattan messenger's bicycle. I climbed the three sagging steps to the front porch, which actually was just a stoop covered by a small roof. Finding no bell, I knocked on the screen door, which rattled with each rap of my knuckles.

After thirty seconds, the front door was pulled open. A chalk-white face with jet-black eyes and black hair pulled back against the sides of her head peered warily at me from behind the screen. "Yes?" she said in barely more than a whisper. Her skin was unhealthily pale.

"Are you Melva Meeker?" I asked, giving her what I hoped was an earnest smile.

"Oh, no, that's my mother," she replied with reverence. "What do you want?"

"My name is Goodwin, and I am investigating the death of Charles Childress." I held up my P.I.'s license, realizing that I sounded like somebody reading a grade-B movie script. "I would like to talk to Mrs. Meeker."

The woman, whom I guessed to be in her early to middle thirties, frowned, did an about-face, and silently dissolved into the murky interior of the house.

"It's a man about Charles," I heard her say. Another voice responded, but the rest of the conversation was muffled. Then footsteps grew louder on the creaking floor, and a second face materialized behind the screen. "I'm Melva Meeker," the woman said tentatively. Her broad face, framed by white hair that was pulled tightly back like her daughter's, had all the animation of her offspring's. "Why are you here, sir?"

Give both of them points for being direct. "As I told your daughter, I am an investigator from New York. My name is Archie Goodwin." I held up the license again. "There is suspicion that your nephew may have been murdered, and I'd like to ask you a few questions about him.''

She twitched her shoulders and sniffed. ''You with some insurance company?''

''No, I work for the private detective Nero Wolfe, and he has been hired by a friend of your nephew.''

''Huh. That television woman he was supposed to marry?''

''No, but she—Debra Mitchell—also believes that Mr. Childress did not commit suicide.''

''Why?'' she snorted, hands on hips.

''Both Ms. Mitchell and our client say that Mr. Childress had no reason whatever to kill himself. Do *you* know of any reason he would want to end his life?''

''Mr.—what is it?—Goodwin, Charles had been living in New York for years and years,'' she said icily, rubbing her palms on the light blue apron she wore over a print dress that reminded me of ones my own aunt back in Chillicothe fancied. ''He wasn't one of us anymore. We almost never saw him, except when he came back to Mercer to be with his poor mother during her last days.'' She looked down and shook her head. ''I have no idea what his life was like in that place or who his friends were. I mean no disrespect, sir, but why someone would want to live there, I have no idea. You couldn't pay me enough to even make a visit.''

It was clear that I was not about to be invited into the Meeker domicile. ''Was there anybody here who had any reason to want him dead?'' I asked through the screen.

''That's a fool question, a fool question,'' she snapped, her face still expressionless. ''Of course not.

As I just got done telling you, if you were bothering to listen, Charles hadn't lived in these parts for years. If someone *did* kill him, and I can't imagine why anyone would want to, the answer must be in your New York, where people murder each other every day for no good reason and don't give a second thought about it. Now I've got work to do," she huffed, taking a step back. The door was shut firmly. So much for Mercer's vaunted Hoosier hospitality.

As I went to the car, I looked over my shoulder. The white face of the younger woman peered out behind lace curtains at a first-floor window. It disappeared when I smiled and nodded my good-bye. I drove back along the gravel road after consulting the map again. Charles Childress's other aunt, who, I had learned from Barbara, also was a widow, lived another mile farther out of town. Her name was Louise Wingfield, and like Melva Meeker, she was a sister of Childress's mother.

The Wingfield farm was in far better shape than the Meekers'. The two-story brick-and-white-frame house, which hunkered on a knoll several feet above the main road, boasted a front porch that ran the full width of the house. The yard was green and neat, with tulips and other flowers I couldn't identify lining the base of the porch and two shade trees flaunting their new leaves. And the barn, unlike most of its neighbors, wore paint that looked like it would last through several more Midwestern winters.

I climbed the steps and was eight feet from the front door when it swung open and a tall, elegant-looking, gray-haired woman in a white, open-collared man's shirt, blue jeans, and brown cowboy boots tilted her head at me. She was not smiling.

"Mr. Goodwin—stop right there." The voice made it clear that there was no room for discussion. Her index finger was aimed at my navel. "Melva just called. She told me you had been there—and the reason *why* you were there. Hear me now—I have nothing, nothing at all, to say to you. If you do not leave my property immediately, I will call the sheriff, who is a personal friend, and has been for more than twenty years."

"Mrs. Wingfield, I—"

"Enough! I told you to git, and I mean it." With that, another Indiana door was slammed on me. What would the Mercer Chamber of Commerce say about this treatment of a visitor?

I took the motel clerk's advice and was glad that I did. The fare at Bill's Old-Fashioned Steak House—or at least the prime rib I ordered for dinner—was more than tolerable, it was first-rate, and at prices that New Yorkers haven't seen for at least twenty years. While I feasted in a booth in one corner of the dimly lit, half-filled dining room, I read Gina Marks's two-year-old feature story on Charles Childress and also the *Mercury*'s obituary on him. Barbara Adamson had photocopied both for me before I left the newspaper offices. Neither piece told me anything important that I hadn't already known, although the Marks feature quoted Childress as saying that "I have never—not for one minute—lost sight of my roots in Mercer. The experiences I had growing up in this area affect and color every thought that I have, every word that I write. Gilmartin County imbued me with the values I continue to live by, even though my home today is as

far removed from these green hills and quiet roads as
one could conceive.''

I don't doubt that Gina Marks set down the
words just as Childress said them. Whether she did it
with a straight face is another matter.

I got back to The Travelers' Haven a few minutes
before nine and peeled off my suitcoat and necktie.
What had I accomplished today? I asked the face that
stared back at me in the bathroom mirror. Damn
near nothing, that's what. I'd flown across parts of
five states and driven close to a hundred miles
through the Indiana countryside for the privilege of
having two widows tell me to mind my own business
and slam doors in my face. The local newspaper editor, although cordial and engaging, obviously
thought I was on a fool's errand, and his star reporter
pegged me as a scandalmonger from Gomorrah on
the Hudson.

I sat on the side of the bed, rereading both the
feature story on Childress and the obituary, trying to
find something—anything—that would justify this
trip. But I didn't, and I threw down the photocopies
in disgust, wishing I had a scotch and soda.

What I got instead was a soft tapping at the door.
I was on my feet in an instant, turning off the nightstand lamp, the only light on in the room, then moving to the door in three noiseless strides. I had no
gun—the airlines frown on passengers who carry
pieces—so I braced the door with one foot as I eased
it open a few inches.

Her colorless face was essentially the same as it
had been when I saw it through the screen door in
the afternoon—wide-eyed and almost totally without

expression. However, I detected something that I hadn't seen or hadn't noticed before—fear.

"Mr. Goodwin?" she said in the same whisper I had heard a few hours earlier.

"Hello again. You have the advantage of me," I responded, grinning and drawing the door back a few inches. "You know my name, but I don't know yours, except that you are a Meeker, correct?"

She nodded, swallowing and making a pathetic attempt at smiling. "Yes—I'm Belinda, Belinda Meeker. Can I come in?" Her voice had a faint, almost undetectable stammer.

Standing in the shadowy glow of the overhead light outside my door and wearing a brown zippered jacket and corduroy slacks, Belinda Meeker appeared as guileless as the Holstein calf I had seen following its mother in a field along the road that afternoon. But I have a policy against letting calves or any other beings into the room where I happen to be residing at the moment unless I know them well—real well. "I'll come outside," I countered, closing the door behind me. "What brings you here, Belinda?"

She took a deep, shuddery breath. "Ma doesn't know I came; I told her I had to get some stuff at the drugstore, which is mainly true, see?" She held up a bag from Mason's All-Purpose Pharmacy. "There's only the two motels in Mercer, and I figured you'd be staying here. It's the best one by a long shot. Tall Tom —he's the one who works in the office, we went to high school together—told me which room you was in. Are you angry?"

"Depends," I told her, eyeing a redwood bench along the wall a few doors to my right. "Let's sit over there."

The evening was mild, with a clear sky and a breeze that smelled of blossoms I couldn't name. It was more like late May than April, at least by New York standards. But then, this was farther south, not many miles from the Ohio River. Belinda and I sat side by side a foot apart on the bench watching cars and an occasional truck whirr by on the old highway. I knew she was having trouble getting words out, so I waited. After five silent minutes, however, I revised my tactics. "Is there anything you want to tell me?" I asked.

"Uh-huh," she answered softly. She didn't take her eyes off the road. "Uh-huh, there is. You won't say anything to Ma about my coming to see you, will you? I already made Tall Tom promise not to say anything, and he won't, I know that for sure. He's okay." The stammer got a little worse when she became anxious.

"No, I won't utter a word to her."

Belinda slouched down on the bench, jammed her hands into the pockets of the brown jacket, and made a sucking noise with her lips. Then she was mute again for another two or three minutes. It was all I could do to keep from shaking her by the shoulders until her teeth rattled.

A loud sigh told me the silence was about to end. "I heard what you told Ma this afternoon, so I know why you've come." Her whisper had me straining to hear her. "I think I probably know who it was."

"Who *what* was?"

"The one who killed Charles."

TWELVE

It hadn't taken me more than an instant to figure out that Belinda Meeker's visit to my motel was hardly a casual social call, but even so, I was not prepared for her pronouncement. When it came, I kept my gaze straight ahead and nodded, as if her words were precisely what I had expected to hear.

"I see," I responded in a voice that I hoped was unemotional. The last thing I wanted to do was scare her off, and she looked like the type that scared easily. I was mentally composing my next sentence when she saved me the effort.

"I prayed before coming to see you," she intoned, looking at the scuffed toes of her beige cowboy boots. "I prayed for a long time—a real long time."

"Well, I'm glad you're here," I told her, still treading on verbal eggs and trying to avoid making an omelet. "The weather's nice tonight, warmer than New York."

"After you left our place, did you go over to see my Aunt Louise?" Belinda asked.

"As a matter of fact, I did."

"Mama said you would, if you hadn't already

stopped there before you came to our place. The second you drove off, she was on the phone to Aunt Louise, telling her you was probably headed out there.''

''Your Aunt Louise was expecting me, all right,'' I said with a smile.

She actually reacted with a tiny grin of her own, if only for an instant. ''Yeah, I just bet she was. She's a pistol, that one is.''

''Based on what little I saw of her, I'd have to agree.''

Belinda made a clicking sound with her tongue. ''She say anything to you about Clarice?''

''No. Should she have?''

''I'da been surprised if she did, to tell the truth.'' She fell silent.

Clearly, this was going to take a while. But then, time was something I had lots of. ''Who's Clarice?'' I persisted.

''My cousin—Aunt Louise's girl. She's younger'n me, by what, seven, almost eight years. And a heck of a lot better looking, I'll tell you.'' She smiled again, this time sheepishly.

''There's nothing wrong with the way you look,'' I said to her. ''Does Clarice live with her mother?''

''No.'' She studied her boots again, wiggling them. ''She did up till she got married, and then again after her divorce. But she doesn't now.''

In case you're wondering, it had occurred to me by this point that her cryptic answers might be Belinda's way of having sport at a city slicker's expense, but I quickly dismissed the thought. Neither humor nor guile appeared to be in this country girl's repertoire. ''Where *does* Clarice live?'' I asked.

"Don't know for sure, but we all think New York."

"Why?"

"Because that's where *Charles* was," she said, matter-of-factly.

"I see. How long has she been gone?"

"Well . . . over a year now, I guess it is. Didn't surprise me one bit when she left. Both Aunt Louise and Mama acted shocked, but I really don't think they were. They knew Clarice had to do *something*."

"Why did she have to do something?" I asked, advancing the conversation only as fast as Belinda's measured responses dictated.

She made that clicking noise again. "Quite a few unmarried girls and women around Mercer go and get themselves pregnant, but hardly any do it by their first cousin. Clarice didn't want to stay around town and have everybody watch her get bigger, especially because people would figure out who the father was. Besides, she wanted to marry Charles, real bad."

"How did he feel about her?"

She kept looking straight ahead at the highway. "Far as I could tell, Charles didn't give two hoots about her. She was the one who pushed it; she was after him almost from the minute he came back to town to look after my Aunt Marian—that was his Mama."

"You said Clarice was married before."

"Yeah, she was, all right," Belinda sneered. "For less than two years, to Wendell Avery. Thank the Lord they had no kids. He was a bum before they got married, he was a bum *when* they was married, and he's a bum now. Drove a truck, whenever he was sober, that is. Lives in Evansville, last I heard. He left town right after they split up, which is pushing three years ago now. Far as I know, he hasn't been back to Mercer, good riddance."

Things were looking up. She was getting more talkative. We might not be here all night. "So when Charles stayed here caring for his mother, he and Clarice saw a lot of each other?" I asked.

Belinda made an unpleasant sound that came out as a cross between a chuckle and a cough. "Uh-huh. Like I said, she started chasin' him the minute he got to town. Said she wanted to help look after her aunt, but before he came, she hadn't been out to see Aunt Marian more'n maybe three or four times, if that. My mama and me, we were there almost every day, and so was Aunt Louise."

"Did Clarice have a job?"

"Same as me, she clerked in the mini mart that's part of the big gas station out at the Six Corners just south of town—you went right past it on your way to our place. We each worked four days a week, on different shifts from each other. Clarice always acted like she was too good for that kind of stuff, though. Wanted to be an artist. She was forever painting pictures at home, of flowers and trees and even their barn and cows, if you can believe it. Can't tell you whether the stuff was any good or not."

"How did you find out she was pregnant?"

"Aunt Louise told Mama. She told Mama that Clarice wanted to marry Charles and go back to New York with him. Thing is, he never asked her, though."

I nodded. "How long after his mother died did Charles stay in Mercer?"

"Oh, maybe two weeks, maybe three. We all helped him clear out the house, and then he put it on the market. His Mama had sold the land around it to another farmer a few years back. It took at least six months before the house sold, and at that, Charles didn't get nowhere near his asking price. Nobody does around here these days, especially the farms." She fell silent, maybe pondering the price of local real estate, and I had just about decided we would never get to the point when she spoke again. "Anyway, when he left town, Clarice was really low. She was maybe two months along, so she didn't show yet. And then one day, it was probably about three weeks after he went back to New York, she packed a few suitcases and was gone—just like that." Belinda clapped once for emphasis, but her facial expression stayed eerily unchanged.

"And you've never heard from her?"

"That is God's truth," she whispered, finally turning to face me. She shook her head. "Can you believe it? If Aunt Louise had gotten some word, any word, I know she would've told Mama, and Mama would've told me. In fact, Aunt Louise telephoned Charles in New York three or four different times, and he always told her that he hadn't heard from Clarice. But she didn't believe him—she told Mama that each time, he was real short with her on the phone, and that wasn't like Charles. He's always been real polite to Aunt Louise—and to all of us."

"Do *you* believe what he told your aunt?" I asked.

"No sir, I do not," she said quietly but very firmly. "A few days before Clarice disappeared, or whatever you want to call it, she told me she was going to marry Charles. 'When and where is this going to happen?' I asked. And she said, 'Soon.' That's all she said. She wouldn't tell me nothing else, but she sure sounded positive about it."

"Did Clarice's mother make any attempt to find her, other than the calls to Charles Childress?"

"Aunt Louise phoned Information for all the area codes around New York City—there must be about six—and none of 'em had a number for Clarice Wingfield or Clarice Avery—she took back her maiden name after she and Wendell split up. And she's never gotten a letter or even a postcard—nothing."

"Was your Aunt Louise upset about Clarice's pregnancy?"

"Yeah, I'd have to say so. Aunt Louise is the most religious one in the family. She goes to church every single Sunday. Not like me and Mama—we hardly ever go, except at Easter and around Christmas. And she's even been both an elder and a deacon. When Clarice got divorced, Aunt Louise was real unhappy for a long time, even though she didn't care for Wendell herself. Mama said she told Clarice that she was terrible, terrible disappointed in her."

"Miss Meeker, I'd like to go back to what you said first when you came to see me: Who do you think killed Charles?"

I got a look that suggested I was not playing with a full deck. "I thought that was pretty obvious to you by now," Belinda stated, folding her arms across her chest with finality. "Clarice killed him. He wouldn't wed her—his obituary in the *Mercury* said he had a fiancée in New York—so she shot him. Clarice had a temper, that's for sure. I saw her take a shotgun one time years ago and fire away at a cat on their farm who'd knocked over a pitcher of lemonade on a table out in the yard. She missed the poor animal, but that shows what she could be like when she was angry. Besides, who was the only relative who didn't come to the service for Charles at the Presbyterian church in town? Clarice, that's who. Doesn't that tell you something?"

"Wherever she is, maybe she didn't know he'd been killed," I put in.

"She knew, Mr. Goodwin," Belinda Meeker said, getting to her feet as though it were an effort. "She knew only too well."

"Do you know if Mr. Childress had made a will?"

"Mama said he did, and that he'd left a little money to her—she didn't tell me how much—and a little to Aunt Louise. That's all I know."

"One last question," I said as I stood to face her under the dim yellow light. "Did you mention your suspicion about your cousin to anyone else?"

She tilted her head up at me and shook it vigorously, her face expressionless.

"Why not?"

"Ah, ah, that makes two questions," Belinda answered, one corner of her mouth twitching slightly. Okay, scratch what I said earlier about her having no sense of humor.

"When we got the word that Charles had died— killed himself according to your police in New York— I knew right away it had been Clarice who shot him in a bad rage. No way Charles woulda done that; he was the kind who liked himself too much. But I figured, hey, if she got away with it, that's life. And besides, she's got herself a baby to raise. At least, I *suppose* she's got a baby, and that she kept it.

"But then you came around today," she said,

and the stammer worsened, "and I knew that the suicide idea had gone out the window. That meant *somebody* was going to get charged with murder, and I said to myself, 'What if you people back in New York pick the wrong person, someone that's innocent?' That's when I started praying. I never liked Cousin Clarice all that much, and that's God's truth, Mr. Goodwin. But I wouldn't wish her ill, except that it would be even worse if somebody who didn't do it got blamed. That would be a sin, wouldn't it?" This time she looked directly up at me, her eyes dark and unreadable.

"I guess that's as good a word as any," I responded. "Before I forget it, do you have a picture of your cousin?"

"Yeah, I do, I got one here. I thought you'd ask for one." She reached into the rear pocket of her slacks and tugged out a billfold. "It's getting old now, three or four years at least, but she still looks pretty much like this—at least she did when she left to go off to New York."

Belinda handed me a frayed, wallet-sized photo of a fresh-faced young woman with bangs, light brown hair, wide blue eyes, and a turned-up nose. The face was easy to look at, but the smile appeared forced, as if she'd had to hold it too long, waiting for the photographer to push the button.

"What would you guess her height and weight to be?" I asked.

"I don't have to guess on the height—it's exactly the same as mine, five-three in her stocking feet," Belinda declared. "Weight—well, I'm one-twenty-five, and Clarice was always thinner than me, small-boned, you know? I put her at maybe one-ten or so, unless she kept weight on after the baby.''

I fingered the photograph. ''I'd like to keep this for a while, if you don't mind. I promise I'll return it.''

She sniffed. ''Don't care anymore if I never get it back.''

''Would I be pushing my luck if I asked you something else?''

She hunched up her shoulders and looked down at a crack in the concrete. ''Aw, heck, I was just kidding before about that second question. Go ahead.''

''Do your mother and your aunt also think Clarice killed Charles?''

''It's never been talked about, at least not around me,'' she said after drawing in air. ''If I was to guess, I'd say they both are probably darn suspicious. They wouldn't ever say anything if you asked them about it, though. You won't tell them I came here, will you?'' She sounded scared again.

''No, I won't tell them. But I do appreciate your coming.''

Belinda shook her head. ''It wasn't easy to do. Nobody likes to think one of their kin is a murderer, even if it's true. I never felt worse in my whole life than I do right now.''

She turned and walked swiftly toward the battered pickup truck. I wanted to say something to comfort her, but I couldn't find words that would even begin to help. Maybe there were none.

THIRTEEN

The rattling of Belinda Meeker's pickup truck had barely faded when I hit the pillow. I got my requisite 510 minutes' sleep before rising, *sans* wake-up call. Taking the motel clerk's advice, I drove into town and sampled the breakfast fare at the Old Skillet.

The narrow, vaulted, cream-colored room with ceiling fans was crowded, probably for several reasons: Coffee on a par with Fritz Brenner's; buttermilk wheatcakes, only a shade below what I get dished up each morning in the brownstone; fried eggs that were neither too soft nor too firm; and sausages cooked precisely the way I like them. As I read the Evansville paper on a stool at the counter, I considered sending my compliments to the chef but opted instead for slipping an extra dollar to my waitress, a grinning, rosy-cheeked, white-haired specimen named Lettie who bustled from tables to counter and back and called everybody in the place by name except me. But I knew that all I'd have to do was come in three days in a row to develop a "Hi, Archie, Baby!" relationship with her, complete with a squeeze on the arm and a motherly pat on the cheek.

That was almost worth staying around for. As I ate, I thought about making another stab at Louise Wingfield but vetoed the impulse without even bothering to call Wolfe. He would have said something like, "Is it probable that she will be more forthcoming than on your previous visit?" to which I would have replied in the negative.

I checked out of The Travelers' Haven a few minutes before ten, which disappointed the long, lean clerk. "Sorry you can't stay longer," Tom twanged, sounding like he meant it. "We got our Spring Festival coming up in town starting Wednesday. It's a lot of fun, even for city folk like you."

I told him I was sure I would have enjoyed it, but that duty called. I exceeded the speed limit by ten miles an hour and sometimes fifteen as I headed north, and I settled into a seat on my plane at the Indianapolis airport all of seven minutes before take-off. On the flight back to New York, I closed my eyes, sipped bad coffee, and reviewed the events of my short stay with the Hoosiers, straining to figure out whether it had been worth either the time or the expense.

Well before we touched down at LaGuardia, I decided the answer to both questions was a qualified yes, although I was by no means confident Nero Wolfe would agree. We now had a new suspect, one Clarice Wingfield—or did we? Maybe I was overly reacting to Belinda Meeker's earnestness. She seemed genuine, all right, but did her outspoken dislike of her cousin color everything she felt about the woman? As for Clarice, was she really in New York? If so, would we find her? And if she was located, how would we—presumably I—approach her?

When my cab pulled up to the brownstone at two-fifty-five, I put these questions out of my mind and climbed the steps. I unlocked the door with my key, but the inside bolt was on so I hit the bell. Fritz answered after my second ring.

"Archie, I am glad you are back." His tone suggested I had been gone for decades rather than thirty-two hours. "The elevator business—*quelle horreur!* The workers arrived yesterday morning, about an hour after you left, and they have been so noisy. This is probably necessary, and it doesn't bother me, but I know it is very difficult for *him*." He cocked his head in the direction of the office as I set my bag down and hung my raincoat in the front hall.

"He'll get used to it," I answered without sympathy as I heard the shrill whine of an electric saw or a drill or some other power tool coming from the elevator shaft. "Has he been going up to the plant rooms on schedule?"

Fritz nodded grimly. "Always at the usual times."

"I read someplace that a crisis often brings out the best in us," I told him. "I'll go in and supply moral support before I unpack."

In the office, Wolfe was doing what he does most often at his desk—reading and drinking beer. He didn't look to be suffering from the rigors of the last two days.

"Don't worry, I'm not about to quote Robert Louis Stevenson this time," I said as I slid into my chair. "Fritz informs me the workmen have made their presence felt. If the racket right now is indicative, I imagine the last two days haven't exactly been a picnic."

He scowled his answer, then set down the book. "Are you well? Have you eaten?"

"Yes and sort of. Breakfast today was fine, no complaints. As for lunch, I know you haven't been on a plane in years, but my guess is that you still remember what airline food was like. I passed on it."

He nodded and made a face. "Indeed. We are having breast of veal with sausage-and-Swiss-chard stuffing for dinner."

"I find nothing to object to in that. Are you ready for a debriefing?"

He drained half the beer in his glass, then leaned back and closed his eyes, which is one of his ways of telling me to proceed without having to exercise his vocal cords. I went on, and for the next half-hour, I filled him in on my activities in the heartland, including my meetings with Melva and Belinda Meeker, Chet Southworth, Gina Marks, and Louise Wingfield. He sat through my recitation, much of which was verbatim, without stirring; when I finished, he came forward in his chair, placing his hands palms down on his blotter.

"After you have unpacked, we will begin the quest to locate Miss Wingfield," he said, returning to his book.

"I can start in on that right now," I told him. "I'll just—"

"No." He held up a hand. "You have been under stress. Tend to your ablutions first."

I could have pointed out what Wolfe already knows: That I find travel both stimulating and energizing, but rarely stressful. The effort would have been wasted, however. As I said earlier, he views any venture beyond the sanctuary of the brownstone to be extremely perilous, and one involving aircraft borders on the unthinkable. So lest you think he was being solicitous, forget it. He simply didn't want me working in what he viewed to be a weakened condition.

After unpacking, changing, and indulging in ablutions to the extent of splashing cold water on my face, I went down to the office and set about trying to find Clarice Wingfield. In the cabinets beneath the bookshelves, we keep the most recent month's copies of the *Times* and the *Gazette,* and also the current telephone directories for the five boroughs of New York City, as well as Westchester, Nassau, and Suffolk counties and the nearby areas of New Jersey and Connecticut.

Even though Belinda Meeker had said her Aunt Louise made a bunch of calls to directory assistance in the New York area, I started from scratch. First, I hunted for any listings in the books for a Clarice (or C.) Wingfield—or Avery. I read someplace once that women who disappear frequently go back to using their maiden name, and Belinda Meeker affirmed this about her cousin. In Clarice's case, though, I thought it was possible that when she made the move East, she went in the opposite direction and returned to the married name she had shunned. No dice. Ditto when I punched up directory assistance for each of the local area codes. I didn't even get a "This is a nonpublished number, withheld at the request of the customer" response from any of those automaton-voiced men and women at the other end of the line.

"A trio of possibilities," I said to Wolfe, whose book was between me and his face. "One, Clarice Wingfield is not in the New York area; two, she has changed her name; or three, she is somehow managing to survive without a telephone, inconceivable as that seems."

Wolfe, who himself would rather do without Mr. Bell's invention most of the time, lowered his book and glared at me. "Get Saul," he rumbled.

"Your wish, et cetera," I said lightly, wheeling around in my chair and punching one of the dozen-odd numbers I know from memory.

"Panzer," the familiar hoarse voice responded. Wolfe picked up his instrument and I stayed on the line.

"Saul, this is Nero Wolfe. Can you join Archie and me for dinner? We're having breast of veal, with a stuffing that Fritz developed. It has been called incomparable by no less than the owner of the most-renowned restaurant in Lyon—and probably in all of France. He had the exceedingly good fortune to dine with us two years ago."

"I know the dish, and the stuffing, that you're talking about, because I enjoyed it at your place once, too. And it *is* incomparable," Saul said. "I had an engagement tonight, but I just this instant decided to cancel it. Shall I be there at seven?"

The time was agreed on, and we hung up. Invitations to meals in the brownstone get issued about as often as Mets pitchers toss back-to-back shutouts, so I was surprised about Saul's invite, but only for a few seconds, before I figured out what was up.

At dinner, Wolfe directed the conversation as he always does. Maybe as therapy for his current miseries, he chose to elaborate on the history of the elevator, starting back in the third century B.C.: "Tradition has it that the Greek mathematician Archimedes invented a rope-and-pulley device that was capable of lifting one person." When he got to the development of elevator safety devices by Elisha Otis in the nineteenth century, Saul jumped in.

"How's this for a weird elevator story? I was in a six-story, block-square warehouse over in Long Island City about ten, maybe twelve years back. It was actually unoccupied at the time—which was the problem. The owners had hired me to try to stop whoever was hauling away their building piece by bloody piece. The thieves were getting in at night and stripping the building of the fluorescent light fixtures, the plumbing, even the doorknobs. Anyway, I holed up in a damp, dark little room in the basement for close to twenty-four hours, with sandwiches and iced tea which wasn't iced by the time I was done.

"At first I didn't think they were going to show up, but finally, just after dawn, they came—turns out they were sneaking in through a three-block-long tunnel that the owners didn't even know existed. It had been built at the turn of the century to bring coal from the East River into the basement in little mine-type railroad cars and to haul trash out the same way, but it had been boarded up God knows how many years ago. Somehow, though, these thieves knew about it.

"There were three of them dismantling the place," Saul continued. "And by God, they were even taking the freight elevator apart, piece by piece, for whatever the parts were worth as scrap metal. Well, I snuck out of my hiding place and was just about to blow the whistle on them when one guy fell four floors, probably sixty feet, down the elevator shaft.

The idiot had unbolted a section of the floor from the walls—while he was *in* the thing!''

"Of course that finished him," I put in.

Saul shook his head. "Incredibly, not even a broken bone. Some poor homeless creature had found his way into the building weeks earlier and had hauled three old mattresses in with him. He'd piled them at the bottom of the shaft and had been sleeping on them until he apparently found himself a better place to bunk. He left the mattresses behind, though, and this other guy fell, screaming all the way, onto the pile. He bounced a couple of times and ended up with a bunch of bruises and a burglary charge. If there's a moral, it got by me."

Wolfe damn near chuckled, although not quite. He both likes Saul Panzer and esteems him. A comment here about Saul: You wouldn't grade him high on looks; he's not much bigger than a jockey, and his face is mostly nose, and what isn't nose is ears. He always needs a shave, regardless of the time of day. His clothes never seem to fit quite right, and the closest thing he makes to a fashion statement is a flat wool cap that he wears except when the mercury goes above seventy Fahrenheit. All that might make you take Saul lightly, which would be a big mistake.

He is a free-lance operative, the best in New York —possibly in the world—at a number of things, including tailing people who don't want to be tailed and finding people who don't want to be found. Saul charges top dollar and gets far more business than he can handle, although he almost never says no to Wolfe, who has been throwing work his way for years without complaints.

I knew why Wolfe wanted to sign Saul on this

time, of course. The three of us were in the office with coffee after dinner, and I had also poured generous snifters of Remisier brandy for Saul and me. Wolfe sipped from his Wedgwood cup and set it deliberately in its saucer. "We need to locate an individual," he told Saul. "A woman. She is said to be in the New York area, but as Archie discovered this afternoon, she has no telephone listing. This problem may be too mundane for you, especially given your crowded docket. If so, I understand completely."

Wolfe was laying it on. As I mentioned, he esteems Saul, but he is not above using flattery, which is okay, because Saul knows exactly what Wolfe is doing, and Wolfe knows that Saul knows it, and Saul knows that Wolfe—well, you get the idea. Anyway, we had all been through this dance before. Saul, who always does have plenty of business, took a sip of the brandy, licked his lips, and nodded appreciatively. "Lon Cohen has mentioned more than once that this is the finest cognac in the world. He and I don't agree on everything—especially on the value of bluffing in poker—but I can't quarrel with his assessment of this nectar. Tell me about the woman."

Wolfe rang for beer and adjusted his bulk. "Her name is Clarice Wingfield, although it is conceivable she may be using the surname of her ex-husband, which is Avery."

"Or she may be using a completely manufactured moniker," Saul observed. "What else you got?"

Wolfe turned toward me. "A snapshot, taken three or four years ago," I said, pulling it from my center desk drawer. "Also, according to her cousin back in the Midwest, Clarice is a frustrated artist." I gave Saul the rest of the Indiana scenario, including

Clarice Wingfield's interest in art, and then quickly filled him in on our commission from Horace Vinson.

With his eyes roving around the room, Saul looked like he was daydreaming while I talked, but I knew better; he heard every word, picked up every inflection. When I was done, he finished the last of his brandy. "I'll start in the morning," he said. "I assume that you've tried Missing Persons?"

"No, sir," Wolfe replied, "but the question begs response. Archie shall undertake that tomorrow, as well as showing Miss Wingfield's photograph to others who might have seen her with Mr. Childress."

It is always heartening to be among the first to learn what my role will be. I threw a snarl Wolfe's way, but either he didn't notice or he was too busy concentrating on the bubbles that rose like spiraling strands of pearls in his beer glass.

"Do you see the need to utilize Fred?" he asked Saul. Fred Durkin is another free-lance operative we frequently hire. Fred is not as bright as Saul, not by light-years, and he is not as effective. But put him down as brave, loyal, and hard working.

Saul looked at his cap, which was perched on his knee. "Maybe, but for now, I think it will work best if I give it a go alone," he responded. "If you like, I can get a couple of quick copies made of that snapshot and have the original back here first thing in the morning. I'd like to carry one with me, and keep another in reserve in case Fred gets brought in."

Wolfe allowed as to how that was a capital idea, so I handed Saul the photo of Clarice Wingfield, then refilled his snifter with some of that cognac Lon Cohen swears is the finest in the world. Saul smiled his thanks and we retired to the front room for some gin rummy. That smile was even wider when he left the brownstone ninety minutes later; he had seventeen dollars in his pocket that hadn't been there when he walked in.

FOURTEEN

When I came down to breakfast in the morning, Fritz was waiting for me with the first of what would be several hotcakes, hot coffee, and a sealed envelope. "Mr. Panzer was here more than an hour ago; he told me you would be expecting this," he said, thrusting the envelope at me.

Saul is a morning person. But he's also a night person. In fact, I've often wondered how little sleep the guy can get by on. I asked him about that once, and he responded that after five hours of shuteye, he's ready for anything except acid rock music, and even some of that he can tolerate, although apropos of nothing, I happen to know he prefers Chopin to any other maker of melody, past or present.

Inside the envelope was the photograph of Clarice Wingfield that Belinda Meeker had given me, along with one copy and a piece of lined notebook paper with a scribbled message asking when I was available for another gin rummy session. I threw the note in the wastebasket, slipped the two pictures into my billfold, and sat down to compare Fritz's breakfast to the Old Skillet's effort. Fritz won, of course, but it wasn't a runaway.

After putting away life-sustaining portions of apricot omelet and hotcakes with bacon and honey, I carried a cup of coffee into the office and, settling in at my desk, punched the buttons on the phone. Horace Vinson's secretary answered crisply and, hearing my name, she put me through immediately to the editor.

"Ah, I was hoping you'd call this morning. Got anything yet?" Vinson asked anxiously.

I gave my standard response to that standard client question. "Nothing concrete. Did Childress ever mention a cousin of his to you? Her name is Clarice Wingfield."

"No, I can't say that he did," Vinson responded after a slight pause. "But Charles rarely discussed his pre–New York years, at least with me. Why?"

"Just a long shot." I thanked him and said he'd be hearing from us as soon as something was worth hearing. He wanted to string out the conversation, but I insisted that I had pressing duties related to the case, which was more or less true.

It was a splendid morning, spring in Manhattan at its absolute blue-skies-and-soft-breezes best, and I would have liked nothing more than to take a long, leisurely stroll Downtown. But I reminded myself that the faster I could keep events moving, the more likely that Wolfe wouldn't lose interest in the proceedings and begin feeling sorry for himself by dwelling on such mundane matters as his nonfunctioning elevator. So I walked only as far as Ninth Avenue, where I flagged a southbound cab. "One Police Plaza," I told the driver, giving him the immodest address of the blocky, brick headquarters building, which sits behind the Municipal Building on Centre Street near the approach ramps to the Brooklyn Bridge.

I'm not complaining when I say that I don't have a lot of friends inside the New York Police Department. Oh, I've got a couple of dozen *acquaintances* on the force, which is impossible to avoid, given my line of work. There's Inspector Cramer, of course, and Sergeant Purley Stebbins, both of Homicide, and both of whom I respect for their honesty and their devotion to duty. But I can't call them friends any more than they would refer to me that way; there simply is too much adversarial baggage in our long-time relationship. Let's not forget the earlier-mentioned Lieutenant Rowcliff, also of Homicide, whom I neither like nor respect—and the feeling is mutual. And there are others Wolfe and I have crossed paths with through the years, men—and a couple of women —I know by name. But friends? No—with one exception.

He is LeMaster Gilliam, and I have known him for at least fifteen years, maybe a few more. Gilliam is as honest as Cramer, as dedicated as Stebbins, and infinitely more civil than Rowcliff. He battled his way up and out of one of the poorest and roughest ghettos in the Bronx and into college, CCNY, from which he got a degree. I first met him when he was an energetic young patrolman and I was working with Wolfe investigating the apparently accidental death of a dockworkers' union official.

Gilliam had found the guy's body floating just off a Hudson River pier and was the only member of the NYPD who thought he'd been murdered. Wolfe, who had been hired by the union, listened with interest to this rookie cop's theory as to why the accident explanation didn't wash, if you'll pardon the expression. Anyway, after weeks of digging, and with Gilliam's unofficial help, Wolfe nailed the murderer, making sure Cramer knew that one member of the force had been of invaluable help.

LeMaster Gilliam still swears that was the beginning of his rise through the ranks. Maybe, but with his smarts, he was going to rise regardless. Our paths have crossed periodically since then, and once he mentioned with pride that he had a high school daughter who played the violin "like an angel." I passed her name along to Lon Cohen. After some nosing around, Lon ordered up a feature story on Sharelle Gilliam, who was described in a Sunday *Gazette* piece as "a brilliant prodigy with a great future."

The article, so Gilliam says, was a major factor in Sharelle's getting a university scholarship, and she has gone on to play with a number of big-time symphony orchestras. Her father was so grateful that he told me if I ever needed a favor, I should but ask. Attempting to take advantage of that gratitude, I invited him to sit in on our Thursday poker games, where he joined Saul and Lon in helping to lighten my pockets until he got switched back to a night watch.

I didn't mean to go on so long, but the man needed an introduction, especially because it was him I was going to see at One Police Plaza; Lieutenant LeMaster Gilliam now is head of Missing Persons for the department. "Archie Goodwin!" he roared when he'd been told I was waiting in the anteroom. "How the hell are you?" He pumped my hand with a meaty paw and steered me into his spartan office, which at least had a view of the small park in front of the building where flowering trees were showing off their blossoms.

"No complaints," I told him. "What's Sharelle doing these days?"

The smile got almost as wide as his broad chest. "Living in Chicago, and for a musician, that's the best of the best," he boomed. "Their ball teams may not always be so hot, but they've got the world's finest damn orchestra, and she's in it. Joined just last year. They're coming to Carnegie for a concert next month, and guess whose proud parents are going to be fifth-row center? But I don't think you ventured all the way Downtown just to ask about the world's most-talented young violinist, did you?"

I allowed as to how I did have some business and pulled out the photo of Clarice, giving him what few particulars I had and conceding it wasn't much to go on. Gilliam studied the picture, making a clucking noise with his tongue. "You say she hasn't been reported as missing, huh? Well, the chances are that if she is in Manhattan and has disappeared, she doesn't want to be located—probably for one of two reasons."

"Drugs or prostitution, right?"

Gilliam nodded. "Or more likely, both. But let me run a check to see if there's another explanation."

"Such as, an unidentified corpse that you now can put a name to?"

"You said it, Archie, I didn't." He narrowed his eyes. "By any chance are we looking for this woman, too?"

I grinned. "No, and it's because you guys in authority don't think a crime has been committed. But Nero Wolfe does.''

He returned the smile. ''Why does that particular scenario sound familiar to me? And why does it take me back a whole bunch of years?''

''I can't imagine.''

''Yeah. Well, I've got to get back to work. We're in the middle of something big right now. Then I'll run a check on your Ms. Wingfield, or whatever she's calling herself. Mind if I get back to you later today?''

What could I say to that? How many cops apologize for not being able to help instantly when you've barged in on them unannounced? But that's LeMaster Gilliam for you.

I left one of the photos of Clarice with him and grabbed a northbound taxi on Centre Street. Eleven minutes later I was at Childress's building in the West Village. In the entrance hall, I pushed the buzzer above CARLUCCI—SUPER. and I got a muffled ''Yeah?''

''I'm here about Charles Childress,'' I said into the speaker, getting an answer that, assuming I heard it right, I'm not going to share with you. I waited for close to a minute and was about to lean on the buzzer again when a scowling Carlucci burst into the foyer.

''You know, I've got a lot of work to do,'' the super snarled. I don't think he'd changed his clothes since I'd last seen him. ''People all the time comin' around and—hey, you been here before, right? Insurance investigation, right?''

I gave him my facts-and-figures nod. ''Sorry to bother you again, but this won't take long. We're looking for some of Mr. Childress's relatives, one of whom may have visited him here. Do you recognize this woman?'' I pulled out a picture of Clarice and held it toward him.

He frowned, then squinted at the likeness. ''Like I told you before, I don't pay a lot of attention to comings and goings—I got plenty else to do. But she does look familiar, yeah. If I had to bet, I'd say she's been here before. In fact . . .''

''Yes?''

He ran a thick paw over the off-white stubble on his jaw and took another look at the snapshot. ''Now I can't say for sure, because it was dark, but a few weeks back—more'n a month now—I was out in front of the building here, tapping down some of the bricks. A couple years ago, the guy who owns this place put a lot of dough into fixing it up—new windows, tuck-pointing, new iron railings, fancy coach lights, and a bunch of other stuff. Well, he also got the bright idea that it would look fancier to brick over the little patch of grass, which was mostly weeds and dirt anyway. Well and good, except the bricks were laid without mortar, and in the winter, the ground freezes and heaves 'em up so they're uneven. So what happens? I end up trying to level 'em up again. And that's what I was doing one night in March when a woman—coulda been the one in that picture, although the hair's a little different now, shorter I think, she comes out the front door, and she's screaming over her shoulder to Mr. Childress, who's standing in the foyer.''

''Do you remember what she said?''

Carlucci looked sheepish. ''I was mainly embar-rassed to be in the middle of something, you know? She was carrying on and I just wanted to get out of there. I don't like scenes. But the woman didn't seem to notice me anyway. She was crying, that I know for sure, and she said something like 'Money is not why I'm here.' And then she really lit into the poor guy. She called him a bastard and a few other things that were even worse. She stood on the bottom step, right there"—Carlucci pointed a stubby finger out through the glass doors—"and yelled at him. Really yelled. You'd have heard her a block away, maybe even two."

"Then what?"

He hunched his shoulders. "Then she left. Stormed past me like I was invisible—which truth to tell was what I wanted to be. After she tore out of here, Mr. Childress just looked down at me from the front door and shook his head. Didn't say a word. But then, what *could* he say? I dunno who felt worse, him or me. I still get embarrassed just talking about it. It was a real scene. Hey, mind if I ask you a question?"

"Why not? I've just asked you a few."

He crossed beefy arms over his chest and coughed nervously. "You think that woman might have been the reason Mr. Childress bumped himself off?"

"It's certainly worth considering," I told him. "Did you see her on any other occasions?"

"Not that I remember for sure," Carlucci said, shaking his head slowly and looking like he was straining to probe the dimmest recesses of his mind. "Mr. Childress had, well . . . he seemed to know quite a few women. Don't get me wrong, I don't mean anything bad by that. There was one lady, he told me about her, who came sometimes to use his computer. I think he said she was a writer, like him. Named Rice I think, or something like that. Said he wanted me to know about her because he'd given her a key to his place. Then there was the beautiful one who came to see him sometimes. I think maybe they was engaged or something. She was a real looker, dark hair, face like a movie star. Do you happen to know if she's somebody famous?"

"Sorry, I don't. And you don't remember seeing any of them here the day Mr. Childress killed himself?" I asked, purposely repeating a question I had posed to him six days earlier.

"No. See, I was away part of that day, including when he shot himself. Went to the hardware store and then to visit my sister. She's been sick, had a stroke."

He passed the consistency test. "You remember seeing anybody visit him in the day or two before he died?"

A shrug. "Nah, like I said, I don't pay much attention to who comes and goes around here. None of my business, you know?"

I said I knew and thanked him for his time.

FIFTEEN

A cab piloted by a gabby, neatly bearded Bulgarian who claimed to speak six languages fluently dropped me back at the brownstone at ten-fifty. I had my key poised at the lock when Fritz pulled the front door open.

"Archie, it's good that you're back before he comes down from the plants," he said over the cacophony of hammering, drilling, and yelling that came from the elevator shaft. "A woman is in there." He jerked a thumb toward the front room door. "She arrived at ten-thirty-five and demands to see you or Mr. Wolfe. She is a peri—the best-looking woman who has come here in years—except for Miss Rowan, of course."

"Ever the diplomat," I responded, making a note to look up *peri* in the dictionary. "Does our guest happen to be named Debra Mitchell?"

Fritz beamed. His faith in me had been confirmed. "I should have known you had met her before. You attract beautiful women like the flame draws the moth. You need to learn to share."

"In all honesty, I don't really think you'd enjoy being with this one," I told him. "I concede her beauty, but from what I have observed of the lady so far, that beauty is, to use the old cliché, only skin-deep."

Fritz nodded soberly. "Perhaps. But sometimes that is enough."

"So you say, and you might be right. Actually, the two of you might just find happiness together at that. You could admire her creamy complexion and raven hair and she would doubtless admire your shad roe with creole sauce. She seems like the type who enjoys the finer things of life, and your cuisine certainly falls into that category. But all of that remains for the two of you to work out. Right now, though, I had better see her before the lord of the manor makes his perilous descent. How's his mood this morning?"

"About the same as yesterday," Fritz responded glumly. He shook his head. "I don't know what bothers him most, the lack of an elevator or the terrible noise involved in getting a new one. He is more irritable than usual."

"And having a woman in the house will hardly improve that condition. Well, I'm off to see the peri," I said, opening the door to the front room. Debra Mitchell, dressed in a pleated, eggshell-colored skirt and a red blazer, was seated on the sofa flipping pages of *The New Yorker*. She looked up, unsmiling.

"Sorry you had to wait," I said amiably, getting a whiff of her perfume, which smelled like something Lily likes to wear. "But then, I was not informed you were coming."

"I didn't know it myself," was the cool reply. "It was spur-of-the-moment. I suppose I could have called, but I prefer seeing the people I'm speaking to.

I want to know what progress you and Nero Wolfe are making in finding out who murdered Charles." The last sentence was spoken in the tone of one used to getting her way.

I gave the woman points for directness if not for tact. "Technically, neither Mr. Wolfe nor I have to answer that question, as you are not our client," I said, still amiable. "However, in this house we try not to get hung up on technicalities. If you'll excuse me, I will see if Mr. Wolfe is available," I told her.

"Are you going to just leave me here waiting, like that Frenchman who answered the door did?" she snapped.

"He is Swiss, and, not incidentally, he also happens to be the finest chef in the world, no contest," I snapped back. I know Wolfe has said more than once that a guest is a jewel resting on a cushion of hospitality; but this particular jewel, glittering as she was, had flaws to the degree where I didn't feel much like playing the role of the hospitality cushion—or doormat.

"I will be gone no more than two minutes; time me on that beautiful watch of yours," I told her, stepping into the hall and closing the door behind me. If Fritz ever learned that she had called him a Frenchman, it would be all over between them. I vowed to keep silent.

Instead of using the soundproofed connecting door, I walked the eight paces along the hall to the office, where Wolfe was getting settled behind his desk. "Good morning, Archie. Did you sleep well?" he asked as he arranged his seventh of a ton and rang for beer. It was nice to see that even in time of crisis, he held to certain social niceties.

"I slept the sleep of the innocent," I assured

him. "But enough about my somnolence. At this moment, a person who may be a key figure in our current investigation awaits in the front room. I feel it is important that you see this individual."

He bristled. "Who is she?"

"I don't recall using a gender-specific pronoun," I said, trying to look hurt.

"Archie, you are as transparent as the crystal in a Czechoslovakian chandelier. I repeat my question."

"As we speak, Debra Mitchell cools her very attractive heels next door. She is eager, very eager, to find out how we—make that you—are progressing in the search for the murderer of her fiancé."

Wolfe scowled. "She is not a client," he murmured. "Talk to her; tell her we owe her no information and no explanations."

"Sorry, but I decline. If I did that, we would be turning our backs on a potential resource. As somebody once said, 'Waste not, want not.' "

"That somebody was named Rowland Howard, and he also penned such memorable phrases as 'Practice what you preach,' and 'You never miss the water till the well runs dry,' " Wolfe said, his facial expression making it clear what he thought about the wisdom of Mr. Howard.

"Those phrases make sense to me. Shall I bring Miss Mitchell in?"

He made a growling noise but said nothing, a tacit admission of surrender. I went to that sound-proofed door connecting the office with the front room, opening it. "Miss Mitchell, Mr. Wolfe will see you now," I told her over the sudden banging of the elevator crew and a metallic screech overhead I preferred not to contemplate.

The additional minutes spent waiting hadn't brightened her disposition any. Debra Mitchell marched into the office with smoke coming out of her pretty ears. I motioned her to the red leather chair and made the introductions before sliding in behind my desk. This figured to be interesting.

She wasted no time on preliminaries. Leaning forward, hands cupping one knee, she said: "Mr. Wolfe, last Thursday—six days ago now—Mr. Goodwin came to see me. He told me that you were investigating Charles's death. I want to know if you've made any progress at all." She kept the tone even, but it was obvious that anger simmered just beneath the surface.

Wolfe considered her through lidded eyes. "You look more intelligent than that."

"Meaning?"

"Meaning that I am not to be dragooned," he said, flipping a palm. "I have a client, and when I have something to report, that individual will be the sole recipient of the information."

"I am aware of who your client is—Horace Vinson," Mitchell fired back. "Why do I know that? Because he told me he was coming to you. I know Horace, and I am just as interested as he is—probably more interested—in seeing Charles's murderer caught."

"Just so. But I owe you nothing."

"I had been told you were arrogant, and that it was to be expected because you're a genius. Well, if you're so damn brilliant, why, after all this time, do you still fail to see the obvious?"

"Which is?"

"That Patricia Royce murdered him," she pro-

nounced venomously. "It hardly takes a genius to figure that out. It is entirely possible that Horace is
throwing his money away."

Wolfe eyed her without enthusiasm. "You sing a
different tune from the one you warbled to Mr.
Goodwin when he visited you last week," he said after
he had drained the beer in his glass. "At that time,
you stopped short of accusing Miss Royce of murder.
Something to do with the laws of libel and slander, I
believe."

She leaned back and folded her arms, a sour
smile creasing her photogenic face. "That was last
week, and in that time apparently not the slightest
progress has been made, so I'll chance it now. Besides, what's the penalty for libeling somebody who's
a cold-blooded murderer? To hell with worrying
about it."

"I know you told Mr. Goodwin why you think
Patricia Royce killed your fiancé," Wolfe said. "But
indulge me, please, madam, by repeating that litany."

"Hah! I guess that's really what it is, a litany,"
Debra Mitchell responded without hostility. "I know
I'm probably wasting my time going over this again,
but you asked for it. Patricia really had it bad for
Charles—maybe it takes another woman to see that. It
was obvious, though, and I met her only a few times,
three or four. She'd known Charles for years, since
long before I entered his life, and she had what she
felt were proprietary rights to him. Then I came
along and ruined everything for her, albeit inadver-
tently. She resented me, to say the least. She probably
made one last attempt to talk him out of marrying
me, and when that didn't work, she went into a rage
and shot him with his own pistol. She must have been

aware he had it. I knew about it, and she was at his apartment a lot more often than I was, using his word processor to work on her damn book. Claimed that her own PC was always breaking down.''

"Indeed. Did Mr. Childress inform you that Miss Royce badgered him to break off his engagement to you?''

She tossed her head in what had to be a well-practiced motion. "No, but then he wouldn't have. Charles had an irascible side—the way he lashed out at reviewers and editors and others he came in contact with in the professional world. But when it came to interpersonal relationships, he was very tight-lipped. For instance, he never wanted to discuss any of his old flames with me, or any other aspects of his private life, including his family.''

Wolfe glared accusingly at his empty beer glass. "Did you ever question him about the nature of his relationship with Miss Royce?''

"Just once. As I said to Mr. Goodwin when he came to see me last week, I told Charles on one occasion a few months ago that I thought Patricia was in love with him. He just laughed at me. He said they were just friends, *professional* friends, and that the idea of Patricia being romantically interested in him was laughable. So I dropped the subject. After all, *I* was the one who was going to marry him, not our Little-Miss-Phony-Meek-and-Mild.'' Debra Mitchell's voice rose with each word until she was almost shouting at the end of the sentence. She suddenly looked surprised, probably at hearing her own voice, and she sunk back into the chair, exhaling loudly.

"Did you believe Mr. Childress when he said Miss Royce was not interested in him?'' Wolfe asked.

"I believe that *he* believed it. But it's remarkable how many men, even supposedly sensitive ones, are totally oblivious to the signals women send out." She seemed to speak from centuries of experience.

"Did Miss Royce ever threaten you?"

"No, but threats aren't her style. I see her as more the sneaky type."

"Madam," Wolfe said, "if Miss Royce were as distressed as you suggest, and as enamored of Mr. Childress as you suggest, does it not seem likely that she would do violence to you, the interloper, rather than to him, the beloved?"

"Huh! You're being logical, which I would expect, but people in love rarely are." She sneered triumphantly. "They act on impulse. I know, I've been there on occasion myself."

"While in the throes of romance, you, too, have been impulsive?"

Debra Mitchell started to smile but checked herself. "Yes—not to the point of murder, of course. I was tempted to do violence to a man once, years ago, but . . . well, that's another story," she said, brushing her hair away from her face with a hand. "Back to Patricia Royce; there is no question whatever in my mind that she aimed that gun at Charles and pulled the trigger."

"I will not dispute the depth of your conviction, but there appears little substance behind it," Wolfe pronounced evenly. "Mr. Childress never spoke to you—or apparently to anyone else—about Miss Royce having a romantic interest in him. And when you questioned him, he laughed it off. Miss Royce said nothing to you—or apparently to anyone else—about her feelings toward Mr. Childress. Can you suggest some other individual who might be able to supply details about the relationship between these two?"

She shook her head. "I can't," she responded in barely more than a whisper. "I told you earlier that Charles was extremely closemouthed about his personal relationships. He was extremely uncomfortable discussing his feelings. I don't think he had any true confidants. He probably was as close to Horace as to anybody else—other than me, of course. And he only mentioned Patricia to him once or twice, and then just in passing. I know—I asked Horace about it after Charles was killed."

Wolfe rubbed an index finger on the side of his nose. "So we have nothing, other than your supposition, to link Mr. Childress and Miss Royce romantically?"

"All right—so there's nothing!" Debra snarled through clenched, capped teeth. "But you're supposed to be the genius. Talk to her. Question her. You can get the truth out of her if anyone can."

"Madam, what devices would you suggest I utilize? Bullying? Harangue? Intimidation?"

Debra threw up her manicured hands. "You've been questioning people for years, for God's sake. Use whatever works. How much is Horace paying you?"

I hid a smile behind my hand as Wolfe's eyes grew large. "If you were to reflect upon that question, I believe you would see it as inappropriate," he parried. This female was clearly pushing her luck.

"I don't see it as inappropriate at all," she told him firmly, tilting her head back. "I have some money socked away, a fair amount, actually. As I told Mr. Goodwin when he came to my office, my late uncle was a pioneer in developing a computer chip, and he was generous to me in his will—*very* generous. Anyway, whatever Horace is paying you, I will top it by a substantial amount. You will find me easy to negotiate with.''

''Your proposal is nonsensical, as you undoubtedly realize,'' he declared. ''Were I to start changing clients in mid-case, word of such harlequinade would spread, and soon I would be a pariah among those seeking to enlist the aid of a private investigator. Further, what you obviously desire is a resolution in which Miss Royce is found guilty of Mr. Childress's murder. I do not accept commissions that are contingent upon a specific finding, or that coerce me, however subtly, to reach such a finding. Now, if you will excuse me, I have a prior engagement.'' Wolfe rose, dipped his chin in his guest's direction, and stomped out.

''My God, he's arrogant,'' Debra Mitchell said to me in the wake of Wolfe's departure.

''He tends toward brevity,'' I told her. ''Some interpret that as arrogance.''

''Put me down as one of them,'' she replied caustically. ''Tell me, you did interview Patricia, didn't you?''

''Yes, not long after I visited you.''

She crossed her arms over her chest. ''And what did you think of her?''

''She seemed straightforward. Said her relationship with Childress was not a romantic one.''

''Which of course is precisely what she *would* say. And I'll bet she also said she was positive he committed suicide, right?''

''Right.''

"Did you find her believable?"

"That's a tough question," I responded. "Through the years, I've been lied to by experts, and I must admit that a few of them got away with it. But overall, I like to think I've got a pretty good batting average when it comes to reading people. On balance, I think she was straight."

Debra tilted her head back and sent me what I would call a knowing smile. "So she fooled you, too, eh? What did she say about me?"

I gave her my own knowing smile. "I'm not sure you want to hear it."

"Of course I do, or I wouldn't have asked."

"All right. She said she thought Childress was planning to break off his engagement to you."

Her dark eyes flashed. "That damn, lying—well, I guess I really shouldn't be surprised." She was struggling to put a lid on her anger. "What she told you just isn't true. You can believe that or not."

I smiled again. "I'll reserve judgment for now. Anything else?"

"That sounds suspiciously like a dismissal," she said. "All right, I'll go quietly. But I appeal to you and your boss to take another look at Patricia Royce." With that, Debra Mitchell rose, pivoted fluidly, and marched out the door and into the hall. Rarely has anyone departed from the office so gracefully. I only regretted that Wolfe wasn't there to see it.

SIXTEEN

The visit from Debra Mitchell on Wednesday was the most exciting event in the brownstone over the next twenty-four hours, unless you count the guy from the elevator construction crew who fell and bruised his arm while getting out of the truck on Thursday morning. He couldn't have been hurt too badly, though, because after sitting in the kitchen drinking coffee and eating two of Fritz's freshly baked apple turnovers, he was back on the job.

But things picked up Thursday, in the form of two telephone calls. The first was from LeMaster Gilliam: "Archie, sorry I didn't get back to you yesterday, but I had to put out a couple of dandy brush fires here, and I didn't get home until so late that the Letterman show was over. Anyway, that woman you asked about, Clarice Wingfield or Clarice Avery, has not been reported as missing, nor has anyone—living or dead—turned up in the last several weeks who even vaguely resembles the photo you left with me."

"I guess that's good news," I said, thanking him and trying to figure out what to do next. Wolfe's morale had begun to flag. He didn't seem overly concerned about our case, and the business with the elevator had gotten his goat. After lunch, he went up to his room instead of heading for the office. Fritz went up twice with beer and reported back to me with some distress that the patient was propped up in bed reading and apparently was going to skip his afternoon session with the orchids. And then a distraught Theodore Horstmann stormed into the office, demanding that I speed up the work on the elevator.

"It's a pity that you are unhappy," I told him, "but you're yapping in the wrong direction; try those fellows working in the shaft. But if I were you, I'd steer clear of the one with the long scar on his left cheek. He looks like he quit smiling permanently the day he learned the truth about Santa Claus. And besides, he banged up his arm this morning when he tripped getting out of the truck." Theodore didn't enjoy my stab at humor, but then, I've never viewed it as a high priority to keep him amused. He went back up to the plant rooms muttering, and I went back to pondering a strategy.

As I pondered, the phone rang again, and I gave the standard spiel: "Nero Wolfe's office, Archie Goodwin speaking."

"Ah, yes, I was told you would be the one who answered." It was a raspy but precise male voice. "My name is Pemberton, Claude Pemberton, and I am a member of an organization called PROBE, which stands for—"

"Passionate Roster of Orville Barnstable Enthusiasts," I put in.

"Ah! I'm so glad that you have heard of us, but I suppose I shouldn't be surprised. After all, our national, dues-paying membership is well over a thou-

sand, and . . . well, we know from talking to Horace
Vinson that Mr. Wolfe is investigating the death of
Charles Childress, so doubtless, you and he—Mr.
Wolfe, that is—have heard of our existence.''

"That is correct, Mr. Pemberton. What can we
do for you?''

Claude Pemberton cleared his throat. "Well, it
actually may be the reverse, which is to say, what *we*
can do for you. Two other members of PROBE and I
would like to pay Mr. Wolfe a visit.''

"For what purpose?''

"I would prefer to discuss that with Mr. Wolfe in
person, if you and he have no objection, of course.''

"When could you be here?''

"The others are with me now—we all are New
Yorkers. We could be there whenever you say, sooner
rather than later—preferably this afternoon.''

I told Pemberton to hold on, and I called Wolfe
in his room. "Me,'' I said when he picked up his
instrument. "A guy from PROBE, the Barnstable fan
group, is holding on the other line. He and two colleagues from the group want to stop by, preferably
yesterday. He doesn't want to say why. Should I lean
on him for specifics?''

I could hear Wolfe exhaling. "No. Tell them to
come at four.''

"So you really are passing up your afternoon visit
with the plants?'' I asked. My answer was a line that
had gone dead. I reconnected with Pemberton, who
sounded pleased that Wolfe would see him and the
others—whom he identified as Wilma Race and Daniel McClellan—in less than ninety minutes.

No sooner had I cradled the receiver than the
phone jingled again. "Debra Mitchell tells me she

stopped in to see you and Wolfe yesterday," Horace
Vinson said with irritation in his deep voice. "First, I
want you to know she made the visit without my
knowledge. Second, I am concerned that you haven't
kept me apprised of your activities. And third, I am
disturbed that almost no progress has been made, at
least according to Debra."

"Your first point is duly noted," I told him. "As
for points two and three, you have presented the explanation yourself: We haven't kept you apprised simply because there hasn't been anything to apprise you
about."

"Any idea when there will be?" He still sounded
irked.

"Mr. Vinson, we are following several intriguing
leads right now," I half-lied. "I will tell Mr. Wolfe that
you called."

"Please do," he responded, saying a good-bye
that contained not a dollop of warmth or goodwill. So
now our client was riled up.

I reported the conversation with Vinson when a
grumpy Wolfe came down at three-forty-five, but he
waved it away, busying himself with signing the correspondence that I had completed and stacked neatly
on his blotter. Undeterred, I plowed onward.

"I know you are dying to know if Saul has
checked in with any information about the elusive
Clarice," I said. "Alas, the answer is negative, and I
can't very well question him tonight, being that business is every bit as *verboten* at our poker table as at
your dinner table. But then, you already know that."

"Which of course means it was unnecessary for
you to remark upon it," Wolfe replied offhandedly,
not bothering to look up. He was showing that I

hadn't gotten under his skin, but he was trying to get under mine.

The doorbell rang precisely at four. I went to the hallway and sized them up through the one-way glass: A motley crew of three, one long, thin man with a long, thin, sorrowful face; one medium-sized, auburn-haired woman of indeterminate years with a pleasant half-smile and the smooth, creamy complexion of an acne-free teenager; and one compact young man—I put him at twenty-eight—wearing a pink crew-neck sweater and a guileless expression. Lest you think I used a disparaging term by calling them motley, I quote from that word's definition in *Webster's Second,* the only traditional dictionary Nero Wolfe will allow on his shelves: "Composed of different or various parts . . . diverse; heterogeneous . . . discordantly composite."

I opened the door to this diverse, discordantly composite trio, and the tall one—he must have been more than six-and-a-half feet from wing tips to wispy, graying hair—almost smiled down at me. "Hello. Would you be Mr. Archie Goodwin?"

I answered that I would be and he, stooping slightly, held out a large hand. "I am Claude Pemberton, president of the New York posse—that's what we call our chapters—of PROBE. Meet Wilma Race and Dan McClellan, both of whom are officers in our posse. Thank you for allowing us to come, Mr. Goodwin, especially on such short notice."

"Thank you for coming," I said, steering the three down the hall to the office. I introduced them to Wolfe, who dipped his chin a fraction of an inch but remained otherwise impassive, which is standard. Because Pemberton appeared to be their spokesman,

I gave him the red leather chair and gestured Ms. Race and Mr. McClellan to the matching yellow ones.

"Will you have anything to drink?" Wolfe asked, adjusting his bulk and studying the visitors without pleasure. "I'm having beer."

They shook their heads or made other negative gestures. Claude Pemberton cleared his throat. "Mr. Wolfe," he said, leaning forward and kneading his large hands, "we have come on short notice, for which we thank you. As I told Mr. Goodwin, we are conscious of this sudden intrusion upon your privacy. We are officers in the New York posse—a fanciful name for chapter—of PROBE, which is a national organization made up of people who follow the exploits of Sergeant Orville Barnstable. Now I know you probably think we're a bunch of eccentric weirdos who dote on a fictional character, but—"

Wolfe held up a silencing hand. "I start with no preconceptions whatever either about you"—he took in the three with a sweeping glance—"or your organization. What one person perceives as eccentricity may appear as commonplace behavior to a second and tedious normality to a third."

Pemberton actually smiled. "That's nice, very nice—who said it?"

"I did," Wolfe replied, dabbing his lips with a handkerchief after drinking beer. "Continue."

"Well, as I was telling Mr. Goodwin on the phone earlier, PROBE is a nationwide organization, plus Canada and the U.K., and we have more than a thousand dues-paying members on our rolls. About half are concentrated in and around New York, but we also have posses in at least a dozen other cities, including Toronto, Chicago, London, and Los Angeles. We loved Darius Sawyer's books, and we were delighted when Charles Childress continued the stories after Mr. Sawyer's death."

"Was there a consensus within your ranks as to the quality of Mr. Childress's writing?" Wolfe asked.

"We *loved* it," Wilma Race interposed, her animated hands accenting her words. "Most of us felt it was remarkably similar in style to Mr. Sawyer's, wouldn't you say so?" She looked for affirmation from the men who flanked her.

"In some ways, I actually liked the Childress books better," replied Dan McClellan, with a somber nod. "For one thing, he was more contemporary, you know? His books had a lot more current references."

"Well, now, Dan, that's because his last book was written more than five years after Darius Sawyer died," Pemberton chided gently. "Of course he was more contemporary."

"I only meant that—"

"If I may move along," Wolfe rumbled, cutting McClellan off cleanly and boring in on Pemberton, "you told Mr. Goodwin on the telephone that you had something to discuss with me."

"Indeed we do," the tall man said, straightening up. "It has only been—what, Wilma, five days?—since we learned from Horace Vinson that you had been asked to investigate Mr. Childress's death." Wilma nodded vigorously. "I had called Mr. Vinson, who I met at a PROBE meeting some years back, and I asked if he knew anything about what happened beyond what we've learned from the newspapers. He told me that although he had no proof, he was convinced that Charles Childress was killed—and that he had hired you in the hopes you would find the murderer.

"Well," Pemberton went on after pausing for breath, "we got excited about that, and we conducted a national telephone canvass of our members, using volunteers both here and in a half-dozen other key cities. We divided the whole country, plus Canada, into regions. And in seventy-two hours, we got firm commitments for twelve thousand, three hundred dollars." He pronounced the figure precisely, and with unabashed pride.

"For what purpose?" Wolfe growled.

Pemberton hit the side of his head with a palm. "Oh—I'm sorry. I guess I'm not telling this in a very orderly way, am I?" he said apologetically. "This money is to help compensate you for the investigation. Here is a certified check, made out to your name, for the figure I mentioned." He leaned forward and slid an envelope across the desk toward Wolfe.

"I admire your resourcefulness, sir, but I must decline your offer," Wolfe replied, eyeing the envelope without interest. "I prefer to work with a single client, and as you know, I already have one."

Wilma Race took over. "As Claude mentioned, when our members learned that you were working to discover the cause of Charles's death, they, like we, were heartened, and all of us felt that PROBE should bear a portion of the cost." If I had seen a more earnest face than her pleasantly round one recently, I couldn't recall it.

"Incredible," Wolfe murmured, his eyes wide. "Did they all electronically transfer money to New York?"

"Oh no," McClellan put in. "We've gotten only a few checks and money orders so far, those by mail and mostly from the New York and Philadelphia and Boston posses, plus the one in Princeton, New Jersey. But we have the verbal commitments, which, considering our members, is the same as cash. And Claude here made up the difference out of his own pocket so that we could present you a check today."

"I know that the members are good for it," Pemberton said, nodding. "It will all come in, every last cent."

"Madam. Gentlemen," Wolfe said as his gaze moved over the trio, "I appreciate your confidence. However, I reiterate that I can serve but one master at a time. Your organization and Mr. Vinson have identical aims: To learn whether Mr. Childress was murdered, and if so, to have the perpetrator exposed. Assuming I find answers to both, you will have achieved those ends, and with no financial outlay on your part."

"True," Wilma Race conceded eagerly, "but we —PROBE, that is—desire to buy into the resolution of the case, indeed, to play an integral role. If Charles Childress was the victim of foul play, as we all believe he was, and if you identify his murderer, as we all believe you will, we want to feel that we have been a part of it. Call it pride, or hubris, or whatever you want to, but it is very important to those of us who have enjoyed the Barnstable stories that we be involved."

"There is something else," Daniel McClellan said. "Maybe I shouldn't say this, but hell, why not?" He shrugged his pink shoulders and pressed his lips together. "We've all read about how you gather all the suspects right here in this office when you are about to finger a killer, and we were hoping—"

"Dan! That's really out of line!" Pemberton admonished, sounding remarkably like my high school chemistry teacher, Orrin Fitzmorris, when he bawled out someone who was talking or, worse—sleeping—during one of his interminable lectures.

"What is it you were hoping, Mr. McClellan?" Wolfe demanded. He thinks nothing of cutting someone off in mid-sentence, but he does not tolerate it in others.

I felt sorry for the young guy, who hunched his shoulders in embarrassment and looked like he wanted to withdraw like a turtle into the shell that was his bulky sweater. He glanced at Pemberton, then at Wilma Race, and finally at Wolfe, swallowing. "We were hoping that as a co-client with Horace Vinson, we could have someone from PROBE be in the room—this room—when you . . . well, name the murderer. Assuming there is one, of course."

Wolfe scowled. "Sir, this is not a theater, nor does it magically transmogrify into one on those occasions to which you refer. Your suggestion is impractical at best, absurd at worst."

"Mr. Wolfe," a flustered Pemberton interjected, "if I may take the liberty of amending what Dan said, PROBE's primary interest is not in having someone attend one of your denouements, although I confess that we discussed the possibility with some relish. Rather, we want, as Wilma said, to buy into the investigation, thus showing the depth of our support for your efforts."

"I acknowledge that support," Wolfe said. "It is not necessary to affirm it with mammon. However, I have some questions, the answers to which might prove illuminating."

"Ask anything," Pemberton replied, spreading his long arms with a flourish.

Wolfe drained the beer in his glass and poured from the second bottle Fritz had brought in, watching the foam dissipate and the bubbles rise. "Do you know of anyone within your sodality, either in its New York chapter or elsewhere, who had reason—and desire—to dispatch Mr. Childress?"

Claude Pemberton looked at Wilma Race and then at McClellan, relaying Wolfe's query with his facial expression. Both responded with a shake of the head, as did Pemberton himself. "No, I can't imagine anyone from PROBE doing this, although of course most of the members we know are in the local posse," he answered. "But Mr. Childress was *very* popular with our members. He spoke about his writing twice at New York meetings and each time, he answered questions for almost an hour."

"And very graciously, too," Wilma added, her pretty hands dancing once more. "The first time we invited him, it was with some trepidation, because we had heard that he could be, well, *difficult*. But Mr. Wolfe, that was not the case at all. He was engaging and humorous."

Wolfe frowned. "On either appearance, did Mr. Childress mention receiving angry letters or calls from readers?"

"I don't recall," she answered. "Do you, Claude, or Dan?"

McClellan shook his head, and Pemberton leaned back in the red leather chair, wrinkling his brow, presumably in deep thought. "Oh, he did mention a couple of notes that he'd gotten from readers who had minor bones to pick over details in his books. I got the impression that kind of thing mildly irked him, but it was passed over quite briefly."

"You said Mr. Childress answered numerous questions posed by your members," Wolfe continued. "What was the nature of the queries?"

"Oh, they were pretty much what you'd expect," Pemberton replied promptly. "Things like 'Where do you get your plots?' and 'How hard has it been to recreate the Sawyer characters?' and 'When do you do your writing?' "

"Did you find any of his responses either surprising or unexpected?"

"I didn't think so," Pemberton said, and his PROBE colleagues nodded their agreement. I could tell that Wolfe was losing interest in the proceedings, and I wondered how he would terminate them. I didn't have long to wait.

He levered himself upright, dipping his head slightly to each of our guests. "I must excuse myself because of a previous engagement," he told them. "Mr. Goodwin will want to know how to reach you in the event that I have further questions. Good day." He moved around his desk and marched out of the office.

Following his directive, I wrote down the names and addresses of the threesome and also returned the check to Claude Pemberton, who was reluctant to accept it. "Take the thing," I urged. "If you don't, Mr. Wolfe will tear it up, and that will rile him, given his distaste for physical exertion of any kind. Besides, Horace Vinson can afford the exorbitant fees we charge."

"But our members already have pledged the money," he protested.

"So? Send it back, or set up a fund for a Christmas party, or a newsletter."

"We already have a national newsletter, financed by dues," Pemberton grumbled, but he gave up, sliding the envelope with the check into the breast pocket of his gray herringbone sportcoat. I saw the PROBE trio to the front door, thanking them for their time, which I thought was unusually gracious of me, given it was they who requested the parley.

After locking the door behind them, I went to the kitchen, where I found Wolfe watching Fritz prepare dinner from the wooden chair with arms near the window that had been constructed to his specifications. He threw a glower my way.

"Ah, the 'previous engagement' trick, eh?" I said. "Leaving good ol' Archie to shovel the intruders unceremoniously into the street. Well, I did, and you'll be pleased to know that the check is gone, too, although Pemberton was none too happy about it. Any observations on them?"

Wolfe drank beer and closed his eyes. "Well-meaning, although not particularly helpful," he pronounced.

"You were perhaps expecting them to supply the murderer's name, along with a signed and notarized confession?"

He kept his eyes closed, probably hoping I would disappear. I obliged.

SEVENTEEN

Although I had told Wolfe otherwise, business actually did get touched on at Saul's place that night, albeit briefly. We had finished playing and I had pocketed my modest winnings, thanks mainly to the last hand, where I held three tens to beat Fred Durkin's two pair. As I said my good-nights to the others and started to leave, Saul collared me. "I'm still on this Clarice Wingfield business," he said apologetically. "Nothing yet, but I've got an idea, or maybe it's just a hunch. Tell Mr. Wolfe that if I don't turn something up by the weekend, there's no charge, and that includes expenses." Vintage Saul Panzer; he takes his work seriously, and he hates to let Wolfe down—and Wolfe knows it. Which is why Saul will always get paid out of our coffers, whether he's successful or not. Come to think of it, I can't remember a time when he hasn't been successful.

The next morning, Friday if you're the type who likes to keep track, I was in the office balancing the checkbook and trying to ignore the pounding and drilling from the elevator shaft when the phone rang.

"Bingo!" It was Saul.

"I assume that means something positive," I replied, trying to sound sedate.

"Damn right. The lady in question is over in Hoboken, working in a small art gallery. She's there right now."

"You're positive?" I asked unnecessarily.

"As positive as I am that I'm standing at a pay phone in the old Hoboken railroad station. I saw her not fifteen minutes ago."

"Damn and double-damn. How'd you find her?"

"Long story, professional secret and all that. But I might just tell you some time during a gin rummy game. I didn't talk to her, of course—I leave that to the pros like you. I assume you want the particulars?"

I told him I did, and while he unloaded, I took notes. We hung up at ten-fifty-two, leaving eight minutes before Wolfe's descent from the plant rooms— assuming he had gone up there after having breakfast in his room. And during the current crisis, I wasn't about to assume a thing.

Sure enough, at 11:03, he walked into the office, not even breathing hard, slipped an *Oncidium truliferum* into the vase on the desk, and eased into his chair. "Good morning, Archie. Were you successful at poker last night?"

At least it was a change from his usual "Did you sleep well?" I replied that I was a few pesos richer and then filled him in on Saul's discovery.

He listened, dipping his head a fraction of an inch. "Hoboken. That is just across the river, I believe."

"You'll never get a medal for your knowledge of local geography, but this time you are on target. I can probably get there by train from Herald Square in twenty minutes or so.''

That brought a slight shudder, but he recovered nicely. "Very well. After lunch.''

In fact, the trip from Thirty-third Street on the PATH train—or the Hudson Tubes, as it's known to longtime New Yorkers who aren't big on acronyms—took only sixteen minutes, and that included several lurching stops in the dank old tunnels under the Hudson River. When I got off the train and emerged into bright sunshine on the Jersey side, I realized it was the second time I'd left the state on the same case. If that happened before, I couldn't recall it.

I did recall the last time I'd been in Hoboken, though. Several years back, the husband of a friend of Lily Rowan's started an Italian restaurant there, and we went to the grand opening. The food was well above average—Wolfe himself would have approved —and the atmosphere was pleasant, even festive. But the couple had a yearning to live in Italy, so they sold the place and, last I heard, the two of them were running a fancy eatery in Siena. Lily thinks we should visit them some time, and maybe we will.

Downtown Hoboken was about as I remembered it, although there were a few tall apartment buildings now, and many of the old brick office buildings and hotels in the business district had been spruced up and painted, some in pinks and light blues. All in all, the old burg on the river facing Lower Manhattan looked to be thriving.

I walked west from the depot along Hudson Place, passing the Italian restaurant we'd helped to christen that night years before. Judging by the facade, it was alive and well. When I got to Washington Street, the main drag, I turned right. The art gallery was in the second block, where Saul said it would be. I peered in through the plate glass and spotted her right away. She wore a navy blue dress with white trim and big white buttons the size of bar coasters, and she was standing next to a desk, talking on the telephone. Her hair was shorter than in the old picture, but otherwise she looked pretty much the same. And her cousin Belinda's estimate that she was five-three and one-hundred-ten pounds seemed about on target.

After looking in at Clarice for a few more seconds, I went north to the next cross street and headed west. Hoboken's business district quickly gave way to residential streets, and within three minutes, I found the one I wanted.

It was a tree-lined block with three- and four-story brick flats on both sides, many also painted in bright colors and every one of them well-kept despite their age, which in most cases was pushing the century mark. I found the address Saul had given me—a light green brick building with a maple tree poking up through uneven bricks in a small courtyard enclosed by a black iron fence with a gate. After glances to the right and left, I opened the squeaking gate and walked to the door of the garden apartment, which had a typewritten C. WINGFIELD in the plastic-covered holder above the bell. Pulling a key from my pocket, I took aim at the lock. It slipped in smoothly, and I could feel it slide the bolt, which was all I had come for. I eased the key back out, did a snappy about-face, and returned to the art gallery.

This time I went in. Clarice, now seated at the

ornate cherry wood desk shuffling some papers, rose fluidly as I entered and smiled. "Hello, may I help you?" she asked in a pleasant, cultured voice.

"Possibly. Are you Clarice Avery, née Wingfield, formerly of Mercer, Indiana?"

She recoiled as if she had been slapped. Her "What do you want?" came out in barely more than a whisper.

"Just to talk," I said, trying unsuccessfully to disarm her with a smile. "Is there anybody who can take over here so we can grab a cup of coffee?"

"Who *are* you?" Her voice was slightly stronger than before, but her face stayed frozen and white.

"I work for the private investigator Nero Wolfe in Manhattan," I responded, holding up my license. She stared at it, and then at me. As she began to hyperventilate, another young woman, this one Oriental, emerged through a doorway from the rear.

"Anything I can help with, Clare?" she asked, obviously puzzled.

"No—well, yes," Clarice said, recovering her composure. "Amy, this is someone I know, Mr. . . . Goodwin. And we need to talk for a few minutes. Over coffee. I won't be gone for long."

Amy nodded and said she would hold the fort. We were outside in the sunlight before Clarice turned to me again. "Really, what *is* it you want? I've never heard of you, or—who's that person you work for?"

"Nero Wolfe, and he happens to be a legend. Where's a good spot for coffee?"

She gestured toward a sign a few doors down the block at a corner. It was an Italian restaurant—there is no shortage of them in Hoboken. The pink neon-bordered clock on the wall above the bar read two-thirty, so whatever lunch crowd they attract had dispersed; the place was almost empty, and we slipped into a booth near the door.

After a tired, indifferent waitress took our coffee orders and shuffled off, Clarice leaned forward and fixed me with light blue eyes. Close up, she looked surprisingly young and fresh-faced. "All right, you got me to come here," she said, lapsing into a twang not unlike what I heard—and probably used myself—growing up in Ohio. "*Now* will you tell me what this is all about?"

"I've got to believe you have at least an inkling," I responded as thick mugs of very black coffee were plunked unceremoniously on the spotless Formica in front of us. "It has to do with Charles Childress."

I thought she might start her panting again, but she fooled me. "Yes, I did have that inkling," Clarice said, letting out air and leaning back against the brown leatherette seat. "How did you find me?"

"That's not important. Almost anyone can be located if the resources are available. I assume you are aware that people in Mercer are worried about you and wonder where—and how—you are?"

She forced a smile. "That's a gallant thing for you to say, Mr. Goodwin, but I happen to know that it isn't true. And I'm damned if I'll ever go back there. Did someone from Mercer—or Merciless, as I like to call it—send you to find me?"

"No, although I won't deny that I've been there. Returning to Charles Childress—he was your cousin."

"That's right," she said stiffly.

I drank the below-par coffee, cupping the mug with both hands. "Miss Wingfield, or Mrs. Avery, or whatever name you prefer, we could dance around each other for another half-hour or more, or we could get straight to the point. I prefer the second option. When did you last see Charles Childress?"

Now it was Clarice's turn to sip coffee; her pale, unmanicured hands trembled slightly as she lifted the mug to her mouth, then made a face. "Wingfield is my name. Forget Avery. I did, long ago. What did they tell you about me in Mercer?"

"I know about the pregnancy, if that's what you're asking."

She nodded. "Uh-huh, that's part of it. You must have seen my mother, right?"

"Briefly. *Very* briefly. She wasn't inclined to pass the time with me."

That brought a slight smile. "I'll just bet she wasn't. Did she threaten you?"

"With the wrath of the sheriff, which was enough to discourage me. I left."

"She uses his name more than once when it serves her purpose. So then you went and saw Aunt Melva and Cousin Belinda, right?"

"Your order is slightly off, but yes, I talked to them, too."

Clarice nodded and let her eyes roam idly around the nearly deserted room before coming back to me. "And they—Belinda in particular—were no doubt eager to fill you in on my wanton ways. Am I going too fast for you?"

"Good line," I replied. "Bogart used it on a court stenographer in *The Maltese Falcon*."

"Where do you think I got it? You may be surprised to learn that not everybody from small-town Indiana is culturally deprived."

"Tell me. I'm from small-town Ohio, myself. What made you come East?"

She set her mug down hard. "To use your own words, 'I've got to believe you have an inkling.' Don't play dumb with me, Mr. Goodwin. Stop shilly-shallying; it doesn't become you."

"All right. Childress returned home to Mercer to take care of his dying mother. While he was there, the two of you, cousins who had known each other since childhood, renewed an old acquaintance. Among the results was that you managed to get pregnant. After his mother's funeral, et cetera, Charles returned to New York. You followed him and covered your tracks so that the folks back home couldn't locate you."

Her expression didn't change. "Obviously I didn't cover my tracks well enough."

"As I said before, it's damn near impossible for people to lose themselves today. I'll concede it can be done, but not easily. Two questions: Did you have the baby? And did you keep in touch with Childress?"

Clarice desperately wanted to be anywhere except in that little Hoboken restaurant. I felt for her, but not enough to let her loose. We looked at each other for what seemed like minutes but was only a few ticks.

"Not that it's any business of yours, but I do have a child now," she murmured, breaking off to stare into her mug. "A little girl. There's somebody who takes care of her while I'm at the gallery. I live close by, just a short walk, and I paint when I'm at home."

"That answers the first question."

She glared at me. "You don't let up, do you? Yes, I saw Charles several times after I got here."

"And?"

"And *what?*" she shot back angrily.

"Miss Wingfield, you picked up and moved from Indiana to New York, or technically, to a place in the shadow of New York. You were pregnant, and the father of your child—or unborn child—was here. You sought him out, which is natural, for a number of reasons—emotional, psychological, financial."

"Well now, aren't we the psychiatrist?" she mocked. For the first time, color blazed in her cheeks. "I think it's simply wonderful when men analyze what women do, and why we do it. However would any of us be able to survive without any of you?"

"Okay, I stand corrected, chagrined, and whatever else you want to hang on me," I replied, turning both palms up. "Did you get together in New York? Or did he come to see you? Or both?"

"He did *not* come to see me, not ever, although I wanted him to. But I did go to his place over in the Village. And, as I said before, I went several times."

"What happened on those visits?"

She drummed her fingers on the Formica, then looked up. "Not much. The truth is, I wanted Charles to marry me. Since you're into analyzing my actions, does that seem outrageously forward?"

"No. Should it?"

"It would in Mercer, at least in my family. But then, I already had been ostracized, including by my own dear mother. She couldn't stand the idea of a pregnant, unmarried daughter around where everybody could see her and gossip about her and, worst of all, pity her. Reflected badly on a pillar of the community, you know?"

200 · ROBERT GOLDSBOROUGH

I nodded. "Apparently Childress wasn't interested in marriage?"

"At least not to me. He said he was engaged to a woman at one of the television networks, but then you probably already—" Clarice stopped herself in mid-sentence and jerked upright in the booth as though she just remembered something. "Wait a minute. Just what is your interest in all this, anyway? Here I am spouting personal things to a man I don't know from Adam. I haven't the vaguest idea what you're after. Explain, and explain fast, or I'm gone." She sounded like she meant it.

"All right," I answered. "Someone, it doesn't matter who, hired Nero Wolfe to investigate Charles Childress's death. That individual felt this was not a suicide, but murder—and Mr. Wolfe agrees. What do you think?"

She paused a beat too long before responding, and when she did, she was reading her lines. "I— That's terrible! I don't believe it. Who would want to kill Charles?"

"I was about to lob that very question in your direction," I told her. "You said you saw him a few times. Did he seem particularly concerned about anything—or anyone?"

Another pause. "Not that I could see. Oh, he was always worried about his writing, his work. He was the high-strung type, tense, you know? That was his nature. Always a little jumpy, always on edge."

"How many times did you go to his place in the Village?"

"Too many," Clarice said ruefully. "The first time, he was shocked to see me; I had gone without phoning. He didn't even know I'd moved East, and he didn't know I was pregnant, either. Believe me, he was not happy to learn either fact."

"Was he willing to help with the support of the baby?"

"Yes, absolutely," she answered without hesitation. "I didn't mean to make Charles out to be some sort of an ogre. When I told him about, well, about the baby, he said he'd pay for everything. That's what he said—everything. In fact, he set up a trust fund with one hundred thousand dollars. I can draw a certain amount from it each month for my baby, and the rest is drawing interest. I'm not quite sure of all the details. That's very comforting to have, but what I really wanted was him, more than his damn precious money," she said bitterly.

"But he wasn't interested?"

"Not at all." She underscored each word. "I was too stupid to accept his rebuff the first time I was there, so I kept coming back, begging, I mean really begging, for us to get together. It was pathetic. *I* was pathetic."

"You also were under a lot of strain, and understandably so."

She looked at me dismally, then shook her head. A shadow of a smile touched her lips. "I'm sorry for what I said before, about you trying to analyze me. That was a cheap shot."

"Don't worry about it, please. I've got the hide of an armadillo. Did you ever spend much time at Childress's apartment?"

That drew a hollow laugh. "Usually just long enough to get into a shouting match. One night I got really angry with him about—well, about how he had dumped me. I was frustrated, and I was still yelling when I walked out the front door. And who was out in front but the janitor—I guess you call them supers here, don't you? Anyway, this super, who's really nosy anyway, was puttering around. He must have heard every single word."

"But Childress never came over to your place in Hoboken?"

"Never, not once. I left him a key, and I even tried to get him to come and see . . . his daughter. But he never would. He sent money, all I needed and then some. And, as I said, he set up the trust fund."

"When's the last time you saw him?"

Clarice blinked twice. "That's the worst part."

"How so?"

A shudder shook her. "I went to see Charles the night before he died. It was sort of a last-ditch thing for me, one final chance to find out if maybe we could get back that feeling we had during the time we had in Mercer when he was taking care of his mother."

"But now he was engaged, wasn't he?" I asked.

"No-o-o, not any more he wasn't, or at least he was about to end it with the Mitchell woman, whom I never met, never laid eyes on. He had told me that a few days earlier, which is what really pushed me to try again."

"Why was he breaking off with Debra Mitchell?"

"He said something melodramatic about how they lived in different worlds. I got the impression she had a very public life, and thrived on it—you know, parties, dinner out with important people every night, that sort of thing. Charles was no recluse, but he really didn't care for the cocktail-party circuit or whatever they call it in New York. I think in many ways he was still sort of small-town, even after all these years in the big city. Although he would have hated to hear someone describe him that way."

"I'm curious. How did he happen to tell you he was ending the engagement?"

One corner of her mouth turned up. "You're curious about all sorts of things, aren't you? Well, the second-to-the-last time I went to Charles's apartment, which was almost three weeks ago now, I asked him what was so special about Debra Mitchell. I guess I was really trying to pick a fight with him. Anyway, he said that he didn't think she was so special anymore, that he was tired of all the demands she was making on him—all that social stuff I mentioned a minute ago. When I asked if he was going to break off with her, he said something like 'Yeah, I think so, but don't get any ideas about you and me. Right now, I'm down on commitment of any kind.' He seemed very depressed. Still, I have to be honest and tell you that gave me a little hope."

"You said earlier that you didn't believe Childress was murdered. That leaves suicide. Got any ideas why he'd want to kill himself?"

She went through a head-shaking routine. "Like I also said before, Charles got depressed about his writing a lot. I picked up on that when he was in Mercer for all those months. I mean, there were periods when days would go by that he'd hardly speak at all. But since I've been living here, he didn't seem particularly mopey. Angry, yes, mainly at me, for bugging him all the time. But depressed—no, I wouldn't say so."

"So you don't have any explanation why he'd be driven to suicide?"

"I really don't. But from what I read in the papers and saw on the TV news, it sounded like that's what it was. Nothing was taken from his apartment, was it?"

"Apparently not. Did Childress indicate to you that anybody was particularly angry with him, or possibly was threatening him?"

"Not really. Oh, he did mention a fight he was having with a book reviewer." She screwed up her face. "And, yeah, he also muttered one time about how ticked off he was at his agent. He'd just been on the phone with the man—Ott, I think his name is— when I got there. And he was fuming. Called the guy all sorts of names and said he was going to fire him and get even with him."

"How was he going to get even?"

"He didn't say. But I just figured it was Charles sounding off. He did that a lot when he was angry. He had a bad temper."

"Did you know he kept a gun in his apartment?"

"No, but I'm not surprised. He told me there'd been some burglaries in his neighborhood."

"Miss Wingfield, can you account for your time on the day Childress was killed? Specifically, up until three in the afternoon?"

Clarice's face froze. She got to her feet without a word. "I have told you all that I am going to," she said tightly, raising her chin. "And I'm warning you, Mr. Goodwin: If you try to follow me back to the gallery, I will phone the police immediately." Her hands shook as she swept her purse from the table and did an about-face, marching out into the sunlight. I made no effort to go after her.

EIGHTEEN

I got back to the brownstone at four-fifty-five, just as the khaki-garbed elevator crew was wrapping it up for the day. "How's it going?" I asked the straw boss, Carl—he was the tall, bald one who had come to the house to make the first inspection after the breakdown.

"Hey, we're movin' right along, nothin' to it," he responded brightly, twitching his shoulders as we stood in the entrance hall. "Should be all done sometime next week, I hope by Thursday." His helpers, including Scarface, nodded. "One thing," Carl added with a lopsided grin, "I guess we really riled up your boss about half an hour ago. We were all working at the top of the shaft, just outside his greenhouse, and he got sore about the noise, the drilling and all. He poked his head into the shaft and gave us what-for." The other two nodded woodenly.

"What did he say?" I asked, raising an eyebrow.

Carl rubbed the back of his neck. "Well, something like 'Gentlemen, will you cease that infernal din? You've long since awakened the dead from their eternal rest.'"

"And your response?"

He made a stab at laughing. "I didn't honestly know what to say—given how famous he is and all. And after all, he is the client. I mainly just told him we knew we were noisy, that we were sorry but some of that was unavoidable, and that we'd try to finish up just as fast as we possibly could."

"Sounds reasonable to me. Don't worry about it; I'll talk to him tonight. He's not big on having a lot of noise around him."

"Hell, we can appreciate that," Carl said. "But there's really no way to get a job like this done without a lot of racket. Usually when we work in a private home, we schedule things when the owner's away on a long vacation, in Florida or Hawaii or someplace like that."

"Believe me, no such option exists around here," I assured him. "Mr. Wolfe is always—repeat, *always*—in residence. So each of us will have to make the best of the situation, himself included." Carl smiled and the three of them trooped out the front entrance, undoubtedly delighted to be away from the wrath of Wolfe until Monday.

I went to the office and checked for phone messages; there were none. Wolfe had written several letters in his precise longhand, however, all of which I entered into the PC and printed out for his signature. There also were three bills. I was writing a check for the last one as Wolfe entered at three minutes after six and got settled behind his desk.

"I saw Clarice Wingfield. Do I report?" I said. He nodded grimly, and I gave him the whole works while he closed his eyes and interlaced his hands over his center mound. Fritz entered silently with the standard refreshments. When I finished, Wolfe came forward in his chair and got to really serious business: pouring beer.

"Your appraisal?" he rumbled. When he poses that question—and he rarely does unless the subject is a woman—he's really asking if I think she is capable of homicide.

"Tough to call," I answered. "The way I see it, Clarice is operating on several levels. Part of her is, or wants to be, urbane and sophisticated. She'd love to kick over the traces of small-town Indiana. But she's also frightened—it doesn't take a genius like you to pick up on that. She's rearing a child alone, on a salary from that art gallery that is probably keeping her just above the poverty level. True, there is that fat trust fund for the kid that Childress set up. And she doesn't want to go back home to the Midwest. God knows what kind of reception she'd get if she did.

"She either was crazy about the guy or desperate that her child have a two-parent home—or some of each. When it became obvious to her that Childress was never going to marry her, did she kill him? I wouldn't rule it out, although somehow, I don't see it. If it's odds you want, make it no more than two in five that Clarice squeezed the trigger."

That brought a scowl. "Meaning there's a sixty-percent chance someone other than Miss Wingfield is the murderer."

"Yeah, although I haven't gotten down to handicapping the others. Do you want me to give you my—"

"No," he snapped. "I will not be able to think clearly until those people are gone for good." He inclined his head a quarter-inch in the direction of the elevator shaft.

"Relax, they won't be back until Monday. I understand you were a little cross with them this afternoon." Archie Goodwin, master of understatement. Maybe Ott was right and I really am urbane.

"The clangor was intolerable."

"Maybe, but it's either that or no vertical transportation for you. They're working as fast as they can, and if you'll just hang on for a few more days . . ."

But I had lost the audience for my sermon. Wolfe ducked behind his current book, causing me to do a double take. I had seen a copy before, in Childress's apartment. A splashy painting on the cover showed a man in coveralls sprawled on his stomach in a field of what appeared to be wheat. A butcher knife was sticking out of his back and very red blood stained his shirt and denims. Looming above the art, menacing crimson letters spelled out *Death in the North Meadow,* and below, in slightly smaller red type, *An Orville Barnstable Mystery by Charles Childress.*

"Good reading?" I inquired.

"*Pfui.* Tolstoy's niche in the pantheon remains secure."

"Thank heavens. When did you get it?"

"In yesterday's delivery from Masterson's. This is not worth a tithe of what I paid."

"How can you judge? You almost never read fiction, or so you have told me more than thrice."

He leaned back in his reinforced chair. "In earlier years, long before I came to appreciate fully the value of each hour of one's existence, I indeed read fiction—on rare occasions even detective fiction. I state that with neither apology nor regret, although my time of course would have been more wisely spent rereading Aristotle and Montaigne. But by any standard, this"—he held up Childress's book and shook it—"is abysmal. As much as it pains me to say so, I must agree with Mr. Hobbs's acerbic assessment. The characterizations are nugatory, the writing sophomoric, the plotting transparent, the outcome already predictable."

"Try not to bottle up your feelings," I said.

"Bah. I am two-thirds through this, and I have no interest whatever in any of its characters, including the fatuous detective, who, the promotional lines on the cover bleat, is 'charmingly eccentric.'"

"Some might term you eccentric as well," I said unwisely.

He grunted. "You already know my feelings about the indiscriminate employment of that word; a moratorium should be placed upon its use. Is Mr. Vinson still in his office?"

"There's one way to find out," I said, reaching for my phone. "Do you want to talk to him?"

"Not particularly. He told us that he was in possession of a disk containing Mr. Childress's final novel. Find out if it has been transcribed. If so, have him send us a copy, preferably by messenger."

"Your capacity for self-flagellation knows no limit," I told him, punching out Vinson's private number. The editor-in-chief himself answered before the first ring had stopped.

"Archie Goodwin here. Mr. Wolfe would like to see a copy of Childress's final manuscript, assuming it has been put on paper."

"Yes, it's been printed out. Is he onto something here that I am missing?"

"If so, I'm missing it, too. Would it be possible to messenger a copy over here tonight?"

"Tonight? Ye gods, I don't even think there's— wait a minute . . . Yes, yes, there is an extra copy, a second one I had made for our editors. By the way, I have just finished reading it, and it is far and away the best work Charles ever did. He finally overcame his problem with plots. God, what a shame it's the last thing we'll ever read by him. . . . I'll get it run over to you as soon as I can find somebody around here to make the delivery. Can we have it back when he's through? I hate having copies of manuscripts floating around unaccounted for prepub."

"Yes. And thanks."

"Actually, I was going to call you before I left," Vinson said. "Have you heard about the set-to last night between Frank Ott and Keith Billings?"

"No, but you've got my attention."

"I only learned of it an hour or so ago myself. Seems they were in the same restaurant, over on Fifty-fourth near Fifth. It's a popular hangout for book people, and both of them apparently had had a few pops. Ott was sitting with his wife at a booth in the bar waiting to get a table for dinner when Keith, who'd already been drinking someplace else, walked in. Frank Ott made some sarcastic comment about how he, Keith, had found the ultimate way to get even with Charles for what happened here at Monarch."

"Interesting. Had there been bad feelings between Ott and Billings?"

"No more than the usual editor-agent friction, at least not as far as I know. Anyway, from what I hear,

Billings lashed back and called Frank a whiner and a second-rate agent. That led Frank to say something else, I'm not sure what, and the upshot was that they started scuffling. Billings, who's at least twenty years younger and twenty pounds heavier, threw one punch—decked Frank, right there in the bar."

"Was Ott hurt?"

"Mainly his pride. The guy who called me is an editor with another house whom I've known for years. He was sitting at the bar and saw the whole silly mess. He said Frank ended up with an ugly bruise on his cheek, and his wife was crying and swearing at Keith —she let loose with a dandy string of those words that give movies the PG rating. The bartender and a couple of patrons broke things up, and as far as my source knows, no charges got filed."

"You literary types certainly live exciting, rough-and-tumble lives," I said. "It's a wonder anybody finds the time to get books written, edited, and published."

"Go ahead, rub it in," Vinson responded, not angrily, but in a weary voice.

"Do you read any particular significance into what happened last night?" I asked.

"I've been sitting here musing ever since I got the call. Honestly, I still have trouble believing either of them could be a killer. I haven't talked to them and don't plan to, but I think what occurred in the restaurant last night was caused by a combination of liquor and the tension of being close to somebody who died violently. Charles's death is all anybody in our business is talking about these days, including people who never even met him."

I thanked Vinson for his time and hung up, turning to face Wolfe. "Keith Billings and Franklin Ott got into a fistfight in a Midtown restaurant last night," I told him. "Billings won on a TKO."

He looked up and frowned. "Archie, in this house, messenger is not, and never will be, a verb."

NINETEEN

After Wolfe had pointed out my latest grammatical faux pas, I filled him in on the Billings-Ott bout, as described by Vinson. He made a face, and after I had finished, he directed me to visit both participants. "Should I call first?" I asked after we had gone over the ground Wolfe wanted covered with each of them.

"No. I am aware that you have plans for this evening; tomorrow is soon enough."

"It is also Saturday, which means I'll have to catch them at home."

"Do so," he replied, returning to the onerous task of reading Childress's book. The plans Wolfe referred to were a dinner date I had with Lily Rowan at Rusterman's, which dishes up the best meals in Manhattan outside of the brownstone. It was founded and operated for many years by Wolfe's best friend, Marko Vukcic, and after Marko was murdered, Wolfe served for a time as executor of the estate, dining there at least monthly and dropping in once or twice a week, unannounced, to check on the kitchen and raise hell if the staff wasn't maintaining the standards for which the eatery had become famed. On the rare occasions when Wolfe dines out today, Rusterman's is still the place—the only place.

Lily ordered the *tournedos Beauharnais* and I had the *squabs à la Moscovite,* and we both showed our approval of the artistry of Felix, the chef and current owner of the establishment, by cleaning our plates before indulging ourselves with the *soufflé Armenonville.*

"You seem a mite preoccupied this evening, Escamillo," Lily said as she eyed me over a cup of steaming espresso, using the nickname she had tagged me with when we first met and I had made the acquaintance of an agitated bull in a pasture.*

"Just musing idly about my agenda for the morrow," I told her. "I need to see a couple of guys who got into a bare-knuckle boxing match in the bar of a restaurant last night."

She arched an eyebrow. "You *do* lead the most interesting life."

"Funny, that's approximately what I told someone else earlier today." I went on to give her a capsule history of the case and all the players.

"Here's my theory," Lily purred. "They all conspired to kill him, and they drew lots as to which one would actually pull the trigger. From the way you describe this Childress person, he can't possibly have had any friends—not even Vinson."

"Surely you are not suggesting that our client himself is a murderer?"

"Why not? I seem to recall that it's happened to Nero Wolfe before."

"Only rarely. Vinson isn't so stupid to try some-

* Rex Stout's *Some Buried Caesar*

thing like that. Besides, he had nothing to gain that I can see by killing Childress.''

She showed me her pearly whites—and they are white. "Okay, scratch him. But I still say all the others are in it together.''

"So noted. I'll pass your theory along to the man who signs my checks,'' I promised. And I did, the next day. He was not impressed.

When I got home, the office was dark, meaning of course that Wolfe had turned in. There were no messages on my desk, and I decided to call it a day myself when I spotted *Death in the North Meadow* on one corner of Wolfe's desk, where he always places a book immediately after he completes it. I figured, what the hell, I should read at least some of Childress's work myself. I already knew what Wolfe thought of the guy's prose, but somewhere in my growing-up process, I fell into the habit of forming my own opinions. The problem is, I've never gotten a crumb's worth of satisfaction out of a novel; to me, they just aren't alive. Give me the newspaper any day.

I took the book upstairs, and I waded through several chapters before turning in. It did nothing to change my mind about fiction in general and detective stories in particular. Sergeant Orville Barnstable was too quirky for my tastes, and I qualify as an expert: After all, I live under the same roof with a world-class eccentric, regardless of how anyone defines the word.

For starters, Barnstable turned out to be an unrelenting bumpkin, even for a cop in a semirural setting. By the fourth chapter, I'd lost track of the number of "gol-durns" and "aw-shuckses" that had escaped the Bull Durham–stained lips of this supposedly lovable curmudgeon, to say nothing of his habits of spouting homespun proverbs (*"The early bird gets Aunt Maude's mince pie and wishes he hadn't"* and *"Never plow the same field twice unless you fell asleep at the wheel of the tractor the first time"*) and consulting his gold pocketwatch with the steam locomotive etched on the back every other chapter. His "solid, stolid, sober" housekeeper-cook, the formidable Edna Louise Rasmussen, nagged him so incessantly and so stridently that any jury in a real-world courtroom would have let good ol' Barnstable off with a justifiable homicide verdict if he'd taken it into his head to silence her forever with his trusty Smith & Wesson.

As far as the story line went—what there was of it —I had fingered the murderer correctly by page forty-six, as a peek at the preposterous and contrived climax later confirmed. I solved the thing not because I'm so clever, but because Childress's plot was as transparent as a used-car salesman's grin. When I told Wolfe the next day that I, too, had sampled Childress's prose, he scowled and turned back to his crossword puzzle. The man doesn't know true sacrifice when he encounters it.

By the time I did talk to Wolfe that Saturday, I already had paid visits to Ott and Billings. Both were listed in the Manhattan directory, and they lived about six blocks apart on the Upper East Side, which was my good fortune.

I called on Franklin Ott first. He and his wife lived in a co-op in the East Seventies just west of First Avenue. The post–World War II red-brick building was easily the newest structure on its block, and from the looks of its black-marble-and-chrome lobby, the literary agent was doing just fine, thank you. I gave the doorman my name.

"Is Mr. Ott expecting you?" he asked, reluctantly putting down the *Daily News* horoscope. He peered over half-glasses with a bored expression on a jowly face that hadn't experienced a razor for at least twenty-four hours.

"No, but we've met, and I think he'll recognize the name. If he doesn't, tell him I'm from the office of Nero Wolfe."

He brightened noticeably. "Oh, the big-time gumshoe, eh? Him I've heard of. Working on a case, are you?"

"As you probably know, Mr. Ott is an author's agent," I answered, stressing the adjective.

"Oh, okay, I get it," he said with a crooked smile. "You guys are doing a book about your work. Make terrific reading, I'll bet. Yes, sir, terrific reading. I'll call Mr. Ott." He picked up the phone and after a few seconds spoke into the receiver. "Mr. Ott? Mr. Goodwin from Nero Wolfe's office is downstairs. What? Yes . . . Goodwin. Yes . . . all right. Thank you, sir." He turned to me. "Go right on up," he said respectfully, his jowls jiggling as he nodded. "Eleventh floor, apartment C. It's to the right when you get off. Good luck with your book. I'll buy a copy."

I thanked him for the vote of confidence and took a nonstop ride in the automatic elevator, which also was done in chrome and something resembling black marble. A slender, mousy, gray-haired woman who hardly looked like the swearing type answered my knock. "Mr. Goodwin, I'm Eleanor Ott," she said softly, making a slight bow, or maybe it was supposed to be a curtsy. "Frank mentioned you to me after

your visit to his office. He's in his study right now."
She leaned closer, as if imparting a secret. "Don't be
surprised when you see him—he's got a bandage on
his face," she whispered, although no one apparently
was within earshot. "He was hit the other night—
maybe you already know about it."

"By Keith Billings, I understand."

"What a vile young man!" she hissed, her pleasant face contorting. "He ought to be arrested and
thrown into jail. I told Frank that he should press
charges, and . . . well, never mind what I think."
She made a feeble attempt at a smile and asked me to
follow her.

As I passed the sunken living room, my initial
impression of the building was reinforced. At least
thirty feet long, the room looked like a prime candi-
date for the cover of one of the slick home-decorating
magazines. I won't attempt to describe the decor,
other than to say I felt for an instant that I was in the
apartment of some very well-off friends of Lily's we
had visited in Paris several years ago.

Eleanor Ott led the way down a long corridor
lined with photographs of writers and gestured me
into a wood-paneled room where Franklin Ott, clad
in an open-collared shirt and yellow cardigan sweater,
sat at a handsome mahogany desk flipping the pages
of what looked like a manuscript. This room was as
neat as his office was messy.

"Oh . . . Goodwin, come in, come in. Pardon
my appearance," he said absentmindedly, rising and
touching a hand lightly to the dressing that covered
most of his left cheek. "I got into a little flare-up two
nights ago. I suppose you've heard about it?"

"I have, and that's why I'm here," I said, taking a

seat facing his desk as he dropped back into his chair and his wife closed the door, leaving us alone. "I'm curious as to how it all came about."

He moved forward and stuck out his chin. "Now don't go trying to make more of this than there is," he cautioned tartly, waggling an index finger. "What happened between Keith Billings and me Thursday night is not going to give you or Nero Wolfe any insight—none whatever—into how Charles Childress met his death. So don't you go getting any ideas." There was menace in his voice.

"Okay, but I still need to satisfy that stubborn curiosity of mine."

"Like a barnacle on a ship's hull, huh? Okay." He sighed. "Here's a play-by-play. I can't say I'm proud of what happened, but I'll give it to you straight." He pushed the manuscript aside and leaned his thin elbows on the desk blotter.

"My wife and I were at Cowley's on Fifty-fourth, maybe you know it. Great ribs, great fish—particularly the coquilles St. Jacques. That's scallops, you know. It's about the only place we ever eat out anymore. We were in the bar waiting for a table to open up in the dining room when Keith Billings swaggered in, or maybe staggered better describes it. Now there's no love lost between us—never has been. I won't say I was instrumental in getting Billings canned as Charles's editor—Charles made a lot of the noise himself—but I had my oar in there with Vinson, too, and Billings knew it, of course. The guy is arrogant, obnoxious, and overrated as an editor. He's also a twenty-four-carat smart-ass, and whenever we meet— which thankfully is not very often—he always gets in a dig at me right at the start. Well, this time I thought I'd beat him to it.''

"And you did?''

He winced and shook his head at the painful memory. "Yeah. Understand, I'd had too much to drink. Hell, so had Billings, for that matter. Anyway, I made a crack about him getting the ultimate revenge against Charles for what I called his 'ignominious departure from Monarch Press.' That was stupid of me, of course. Billings came over to our booth and started spewing obscenities, calling me a 'third-rate peddler of third-rate writers' and a 'disgrace to my profession' in between the four-letter words.

"I replied that his use of profanity was indicative of the paucity of his vocabulary, which in turn was indicative of his lack of ability as an editor, or words to that effect. That's when he said, 'Stand up, you flannel-mouthed son of a bitch.' ''

"And you did?'' I said again.

"Yes. I mean, nobody talks that way in front of my wife," he said angrily. "I'd barely gotten to my feet when the punch came. I never saw it coming, and the next thing I knew, I was on the floor on my back and Eleanor was screaming. The episode won't make a tape of great moments in publishing history.''

"I suppose not. It does strike me you were asking for trouble by baiting Billings," I observed.

"*Mea culpa.* No question about it. As I said before, I'd had too much to drink. But having conceded that, I was still surprised by what happened.''

"How do you interpret his reaction?''

Ott's fingers brushed his bandage and he chuckled. "You'd like me to say that Keith Billings's right to the face indicates to me that he blew Charles away, wouldn't you? Well, I can't honestly do that, as much as I loathe the man. He's a jerk, but sorry, I don't see him as a murderer."

"Is it true you didn't press charges against him?"

"Yeah," he said, waving the thought away with a hand. "Eleanor wanted me to, but I wasn't hurt badly. And besides, what happened was as much my fault as his."

"That's charitable of you," I remarked.

"Charitable, hell!" he said, chuckling again. "Besides, the story has a happy ending of sorts. Keith Billings had been hanging out in Cowley's for years; it's almost a second home for him. When I was still lying on the floor being tended to, I heard Pierre— he's the maître d'—telling Billings in that cultured French voice of his that he wasn't welcome in the place anymore."

I thanked him for his time.

"No problem. I wasn't going anyplace. I was just sitting here thinking about how Billings has been banned from Cowley's." His chuckle had grown to a cackle, and Ott was still cackling when I excused myself and left.

My next stop, at eleven-twenty that Saturday morning, was Billings's place on Eighty-second. His building, a drab, nine-story gray monolith, didn't appear to be in the same ballpark as Ott's. As Billings had told me earlier, there was no doorman. I found the editor's name on the directory in the unadorned, beige lobby and leaned on his buzzer. Nothing. I pushed again, waiting for a half-minute.

I was about to walk out when the intercom

barked a fuzzy sound I took to be a sour and decidedly uncordial "Yes?"

"It's Archie Goodwin," I pronounced carefully into the speaker. I translated the response as "Whaddya want?"

"I'd like to see you for a couple of minutes," I said.

The response was a groan, followed by a four-letter word, and then a pause. "All right, dammit, come on up," he rasped.

Two ceiling lights were out, making the sixth-floor corridor even more dismal than it would have been. Billings's door was ajar, and I rapped my knuckles lightly on it, causing it to swing open. The editor sat slumped on a tired sofa in the small living room, arms crossed and face pouting. "Why don't you do like the TV commercial tells you to and phone first?" he grumped, not bothering to get to his feet.

"A gross lapse in etiquette on my part. Sorry," I told him insincerely as I settled into the nearest chair without waiting for an invitation.

Billings maintained his seat and his pout. "Before you start in, I'll save you some breath. Yes, I popped Frank Ott in Cowley's night before last. No, I'm not sorry I did it. Yes, I'd been drinking. No, our argument had nothing to do with the fact that Charles Childress is dead. Okay, what's next?"

"Thanks for helping me along. Do you often deck people in public places?"

"My, we're hostile today, aren't we? What I do in public places is not really any of your business, is it, Mr. Goodwin? But I'll answer anyway. No, I am not normally given to physical violence. With Frank Ott, I am willing to make an exception, however."

"How does it happen that Mr. Ott is so favored?"

His pout turned to a rigid smile. "We went through this drill once before, when you came to my office. Remember? As I told you then, Ott worked on Vinson to get me canned from Monarch, or at least taken off the editing of the Childress books. Even given that, I probably would have ignored him when I went into Cowley's the other night, except that he started mouthing off, whining loud enough for the whole damn bar to hear, claiming that I had killed Charles in revenge for his part in my—how shall I term it?—*departure* from Monarch.

"He kept it up, so I went over to the booth where he and his wife were sitting, and I chewed on him, told him to get the hell up. He did, and I let him have it. He went down like a rock. His wife got hysterical, the lounge lizards have something to talk about for the next few weeks, and I was told to go away and stay away. End of story." Billings clapped his hands once for emphasis and fell back against the cushions, yawning.

"You told me when we talked last week that you didn't think Childress was murdered. Do you still feel that way?" I asked.

He let his eyes move around the cluttered room —to the bookshelves, to the two-foot-high pile of newspapers stacked in one corner, and to the television set, which rested on a stand and had a layer of dust on its screen. "It's funny, the way things happen," Billings said, interlacing his hands behind his head and looking at the ceiling. "If I hadn't walked into Cowley's Thursday night—and if I hadn't downed a few vodkas earlier—I probably would still

believe beyond any doubt that Charles the Obnoxious
blew his brains out."

"What made you change your mind?"

Billings rolled his eyes. "Oh, come off it, will
you? I thought big-time private eyes were supposed to
be quick on the uptake. And you work with no less
than the great Nero Wolfe. Is it possible that you
don't have a clue?"

"Anything's possible."

"Maybe you really *don't* have a clue," Billings responded with a sneer. "Think for a moment about
what happened at Cowley's: I walk in, obviously tight,
and quiet, sedate Frank Ott, who has never bothered
to acknowledge me—let alone my existence—when
we've met in public before, suddenly goes on the attack with venom, all but accusing me of pulling the
trigger on Childress. He was totally out of character.
Doesn't that tell you something?"

"Help me along," I said with a grin.

Billings actually laughed. "Goodwin, you need
help like Saudi Arabia needs sand. Why do I feel like
I'm being messed with?"

"Beats me. Do you really think Frank Ott has a
strong enough motive for murder?"

"I wouldn't have said so a few days ago, but—
well, dope the thing out for yourself," Billings said
through clenched teeth. "Ott was savaged, albeit un-
fairly, by Childress in that diatribe in *Book Business*. So
was I, of course, but by the time the vicious article ran
—and God, was it vicious—I was already gone from
Monarch and was established in a new job with a new
publisher. Ott, however, did not have the luxury of
changing jobs. He was entrenched in his own literary
agency. Where was he going to go?"

"And you're suggesting that he killed Childress, making it look like suicide?" I asked.

He bounced on the sofa and aimed an index finger at me, firing once. "You said it, Goodwin, I didn't. And I won't. But taking a detached look at the situation, one would be forced to conclude that Frank Ott's best hope for survival as a literary agent was to dramatically take to the offensive and discredit his attacker. And what better way than to point to that attacker's self-destruction as overwhelming evidence of a deranged and unbalanced character?"

"Assuming that you are right, why would Ott, having accomplished his mission of making a murder look like a suicide, then bait you into a fight?"

"Aha!" Billings crowed. "Why indeed? I'll grant you that he didn't know for sure I would be in Cowley's Thursday night, but—and this is a big 'but'—anyone who knows my, shall we say, *habits,* knows that I stop at Cowley's more nights than I don't. So the odds were on his side. Now, Frank Ott already had gotten rid of Childress, but that wasn't enough for him. He also wanted to ruin me if he could. He hated me for pointing out Charles's many deficiencies as a writer."

I snorted. "So he got to his feet and meekly let you punch out his lights?"

Billings stretched both arms above his head and made Vs with the fingers of each hand, in the manner of one R. M. Nixon. "Precisely! He threw out the line, and I took the bait. He *goaded* me, knowing I would lose my temper and do something stupid. He set himself to take the punch, which also was pretty stupid. In the midst of all this stupidity, I did one smart thing, though. I went to my bosses at Westman & Lane the morning after the episode—yesterday—and told them exactly what happened. They're very understanding, I'm happy to report.

"And now, Mr. Goodwin, you'll say good-bye," Billings snarled, finally rising from the sofa to gesture me to the door. I was only too glad to leave.

TWENTY

B y the time I found myself on the sidewalk in front of Keith Billings's building, lunch already was well underway in the brownstone. Rather than disturb Wolfe's digestion by barging in at mid-meal, I ducked into a hole-in-the-wall eatery on First Avenue that dishes up the best hot turkey sandwiches in the city, a fact they proclaim in scarlet capital letters and an exclamation point on a white canvas banner six feet wide that stretches across a wall behind the counter. I straddled a stool, ordering the house specialty—what else?—along with a glass of milk, and I chewed on both the sandwich and our case.

Debra Mitchell assured us that a wildly jealous Patricia Royce had Childress's blood on her hands; Belinda Meeker appeared convinced that her cousin, Clarice Wingfield, did the deed; and now, Keith Billings was pointing his finger at Franklin Ott. So far, nobody had directly accused Billings, Ms. Mitchell, or the arrogant Wilbur Hobbs, but my reading was that with a little encouragement, I could get each of these three also nominated as the killer by one or more of the other suspects.

Every one of this mixed bag seemed to possess a

legitimate reason for having hostility toward the deceased, Charles Childress: Debra Mitchell, Patricia Royce, and Clarice Wingfield all apparently held intense grievances centering on their personal relationships with the man. Keith Billings, Franklin Ott, and Wilbur Hobbs had beefs about how he had beaten them up in the publishing arena—particularly in his diatribes in *Book Business* and the *Manhattan Literary Times.*

Okay, so the guy was hardly a moral paragon—I'll concede that for starters, although I'd never met him. But of these six potential suspects, which—if any—had motives powerful enough to drive them to turn Childress's own pistol on him?

My initial reaction was—none. But as I laid siege to a generous wedge of blueberry pie, I did some reconsidering: An unwed woman rearing her child alone while the father, just across the Hudson, refused even to lay eyes on his offspring; an engagement gone sour, although the woman denied this had occurred and continues to deny it; an apparent love that was not reciprocated; mean-spirited, angry articles that named no names but possessed the power to damage—perhaps even destroy—careers. This was part of the sorry legacy Charles Childress had left. And after all, I told myself, people get eliminated daily in New York as the result of far less-grievous affronts.

Thus persuaded that each of the six had what he or she felt was sufficient reason for terminating Childress's stay on this planet, I began to play "Guess That Murderer." The first time through the list, my mental spinner stopped at Patricia Royce. Why, I'm not sure, except that something about her made me uneasy. I had told Wolfe she was squirrelly, but what bothered me more than her eccentricity was an intangible: The woman was holding something back. Had she indeed been in love with Childress, as Debra Mitchell insisted? I hadn't thought so at first, but there was far more behind those dark blue eyes than I had been able to penetrate during my visit.

I spun through the roster of suspects a second time, and on this round, Wilbur Hobbs came up as my nominee. He's easy to dismiss as an arrogant, supercilious prig, which I had been doing for the last few days, at least subconsciously. But he also is the type—I've seen them before—that is capable of going to extreme lengths to protect their standing. Hobbs had been professionally wounded by what Charles Childress had written about him—not mortally, to be sure—but wounded nonetheless. What was to stop Childress from writing more invective about him? Not legal action, if Hobbs was to be believed. He told us that he had discarded that idea. There was but one way to guarantee that no more damaging articles ran. The more I turned it over in my mind, the more I could visualize Wilbur Hobbs pulling the trigger with his manicured finger—and smirking as he did it.

On the next spin, the arrow pointed at Franklin Ott, maybe because after having seen his apartment, I realized how much the agent had to lose because of Childress's attacks on him. Ott's place of business hadn't looked like much—unimpressive building, dumpy, messy offices, small staff. That had deluded me into viewing the guy as a small-time operator. But he obviously had done very well indeed, and it was conceivable that he, like Hobbs, might take drastic action to maintain his reputation—and his expensive lifestyle.

I started in on the list again, then threw up my hands. At this rate, the half-dozen were going to finish in a dead heat. Maybe Lily really was right. Maybe the whole bunch had conspired to dispatch Childress. I didn't really believe it, but at this point, I was willing to consider any avenue.

Speaking of avenues, I left the diner and leisurely strolled south on First Avenue to Thirty-fifth Street, enjoying the sunny afternoon. I turned west on Thirty-fifth, walking almost the entire width of the island, and by the time I got back to the brownstone, it was three-twenty-five.

The office was empty, which was not normal—at least at this hour. Fritz had left a note on my desk, saying that he had gone out on a grocery run and would be back by four-thirty.

Nothing in the office seemed amiss, except for a two-inch-high stack of $8^1/2$-by-11 sheets on one corner of Wolfe's desk. The top page was blank except for these words in typescript: ONCE MORE WE MEET: AN ORVILLE BARNSTABLE MYSTERY By Charles Childress. So the manuscript had been messengered—make that delivered.

But that did not explain Wolfe's absence. I called the plant rooms, thinking perhaps an emergency had caused him to go up early, but Theodore informed me, in his usual gracious, civilized manner, that "It is three-thirty. Mr. Wolfe is *never* here at three-thirty." He then slammed down his instrument, playful rascal that he is.

I climbed the flight of stairs to Wolfe's bedroom and knocked on his door. No answer. I knocked again with the same result, and I could feel my heart trying to batter its way out of my chest cavity as I eased open the door.

He was in his chair by the window, eyes closed and as still as death, but for one exception: His lips pushed out and in, out and in, with a rhythm as regular as a fine Swiss watch. I stood frozen in the doorway, not moving, not making a sound. Noise wasn't an issue, though; wherever Wolfe was at the moment, he could hear nothing anyway. The lip exercise continued for another fourteen minutes, by my watch. Then he stopped, opened his eyes, and dipped his chin in my direction. If he was surprised to see me standing in the doorway, he didn't show it.

"I see the Childress manuscript arrived. Did you read it?" I asked. He made a motion with his head that I took to be a nod.

"And . . . ?"

"Bah! I have been as blind as Lear himself and deserve a like fate. Get them all here."

"By all, I assume you mean Vinson and the Unholy Six." I thought I detected the corner of Wolfe's mouth twitch slightly at my flippancy, but he managed to control himself.

"Your assumption is correct. We shall discuss this further at six o'clock." He picked up the book from the small table next to his chair and opened it. I considered myself dismissed.

TWENTY-ONE

W hen Nero Wolfe decides to hold one of his show-and-tell sessions—Inspector Cramer sneeringly refers to them as "charades"—he never bothers himself with the petty details. Such as, how do I, Archie, round up all these people and persuade them to come to the brownstone and sit patiently in the office while he, Wolfe, painstakingly, and some might say arrogantly, explains why one among them should be a permanent house guest of the State of New York?

And that's the way it was Saturday at six when he came down from the plant rooms on foot and settled in behind his desk, ringing for beer.

I was filled with questions, as Wolfe knew I would be. He poured beer and patiently answered them, peeling back the layers of the onion. I saw where he was headed before he got to the end, but just barely.

"I suppose it's unnecessary for me to state I would never have doped it out," I told him. "One last question: Why were you doing your noodling in your room, rather than down here?"

He scowled. "I could not face the entire climb to the plant rooms at once."

"So you broke the trek into two parts, eh? Very smart. Okay, when do you want to gather them?"

"I suppose tonight is out of the question?"

"You suppose right. I know it may shock you, but many New Yorkers actually leave the sanctuary of their homes, particularly on Saturday nights, to sample some diversion or another in this great metropolis."

"Sarcasm does not become you, Archie. You wield a broadsword when a rapier is called for." He sighed. "But I suppose that is but one of the many prices I must pay for having a man of action on the premises. Tomorrow night, then."

"Any idea how I can lure Clarice Wingfield across the Hudson?"

Wolfe sniffed. "You will find a way."

Easy for him to say. We agreed on nine o'clock Sunday, which gave me twenty-seven hours to assemble the entire cast. I tackled the easiest one first, calling Vinson at home.

"Wolfe knows the murderer?" the publisher said tensely. "Who is it?"

"Sorry, but this is like a raffle—you've got to be present to be a winner," I told him. "It's a long-standing house rule here." Vinson muttered something about this being a fine way to treat a client, but not for long, and not with any real conviction. He asked who would be present, and I reeled off the guest list, not bothering to mention that none of them had yet been invited. "Well, it should make for a damned interesting evening," he conceded. "I wouldn't miss it."

I also got Franklin Ott and Debra Mitchell at home on the first try, telling each of them only that

Wolfe had some important information pertaining to the death of Childress. Both squawked a bit before agreeing to show up, and, like Vinson, both wanted to know who else was on the guest list, which I told them. "I don't know why you would possibly want me there," Ott sputtered. "But I admit to a morbid curiosity. Deal me in."

Debra Mitchell kept asking if Wolfe was going to expose the murderer. "That's how he usually does these things," she insisted. "I do read the papers, you know."

I refused to tell her in so many words that names were going to be named, but I did toss out some broad hints that Wolfe might get specific, which satisfied her to the point where she grudgingly said she'd join the party.

I got no answer from Keith Billings, Patricia Royce, or Wilbur Hobbs on Saturday night, but I nailed all of them on Sunday morning. For the sake of brevity, put it down that on a hostility scale with ten as the tops, Billings was a nine, Hobbs a seven-plus, and Ms. Royce a four. But they all said they would show after learning who else would be in attendance.

Now to backtrack briefly to Saturday night: Clarice Wingfield was a special case, and I handled it accordingly by phoning Saul Panzer. "You were so successful in locating our missing Hoosier lassie that we've got another project," I told him.

"Fire away," came the reply. Saul has never been big on lengthy phone conversations.

"Mr. Wolfe is hosting a love-in with all of the Childress murder suspects, and I'm going to have my hands full orchestrating it. Would it be asking too much to have you deliver Clarice Wingfield to the brownstone tomorrow at, say, eight-forty-five in the evening? Without using undue force, of course? And at your usual rates, of course?"

"Consider it done."

When Saul says that, I don't need to hear anything else.

Sundays in the brownstone are pretty much free-form. The rigid weekday schedule sails out the window, and Wolfe may or may not play with his orchids. He normally spends much of the day at his desk plowing through the Sunday papers before vanquishing the *Times Magazine* crossword puzzle.

He was working his way through the *Times* at eleven-forty-five in the morning when I hung up from verbally sparring with Keith Billings. "That's it, they're all coming," I told him, swinging around in my chair. "What about Cramer?"

He filled in another word, set down the puzzle, and drew in air, expelling it slowly. "Get him."

Heaven forbid that Wolfe should have to punch out a telephone number himself. I called Homicide and was told that the inspector would not be in at all that day, so I looked up his home number in my address book. Mrs. Cramer answered and sounded reluctant to put her husband on. She muffled the speaker, but I could hear her saying "It's Nero Wolfe's office. Do you want to take it?"

I nodded for Wolfe to pick up his instrument while I stayed on the line, and the next thing I heard was the familiar, gruff "Yeah?"

"This is Nero Wolfe, Mr. Cramer. I regret disturbing you at home, but I felt you should be aware that I will be divulging the identity of Charles Childress's murderer tonight.''

That brought one of Cramer's most frequently used epithets, one you will never read in these pages. He repeated it, presumably to make sure Wolfe knew precisely how he felt. ''Is this on the level?'' he then snorted.

''It is, sir. You would do well to be here at nine o'clock. Will you be bringing Sergeant Stebbins?''

Cramer spat a yes and the line went dead. ''He never even bothered to say good-bye, that barbarian,'' I commented.

Wolfe scowled. ''You know how to reach those people who were here?''

''The members of PROBE? Yes, I have telephone numbers and addresses for all of them, as you instructed.''

''Call the woman, Wilma Race,'' he said, proceeding to give me brief instructions that were so surprising I made him repeat them. ''Why her?'' I then asked.

''She is clearly the most intelligent and perceptive of the three,'' was his reply, which was good enough for me.

Fritz and I got the office set up with extra chairs from the dining room, and we converted the small table in the corner into a bar, stocking it with scotch, rye, gin, vodka, mixers, and a carafe of a good French white wine. The doorbell rang at precisely eight-forty-five, and I bet myself it was Saul and Clarice Wingfield. I won the bet.

As I opened the front door, Clarice glared at me from the stoop, her expression an interesting blend of anger and terror. "This is a disgrace, an absolute disgrace," she hissed as Saul ushered her into the hall.

"She's not a happy camper, Arch," he said. "A neighbor's taking care of the baby, that wasn't a problem. But she—"

Clarice wheeled on Saul, eyes afire. "I am quite capable of speaking for myself, thank you," she snapped. Turning to me: "Mr. Goodwin, this stops just short of kidnapping. The only reason I finally consented to come is that Mr. Panzer here guaranteed that your great Nero Wolfe is going to tell us all who killed Charles. Why he insists on a group meeting is beyond me, however."

"Well, your presence is most appreciated," I responded, flashing a smile that failed to alter her dour expression. As per our plan, Saul steered her to the front room, where they both would stay until everyone else was seated. Clarice complained mildly and curtly declined my offer of liquid refreshments, but she went along with the program. I closed the front room door behind me and reentered the hall just as the bell rang again. It was Cramer and Sergeant Purley Stebbins.

"All right, you got us here," Cramer wheezed, stating the obvious and barreling by me with the sergeant in his wake. A word about Purley Stebbins: He has worked for Cramer at least as long as I've worked for Wolfe. He's got a long, bony face with a square jaw at the south end, and if he has a sense of humor, he manages to keep it out of sight. He's tough, he's honest, and he doesn't waste words. Purley and I have what I would term grudging respect for each other; Purley doesn't completely trust me—or Wolfe—and never will, figuring that anybody who earns his keep as a private detective is questionable by definition and will during any case eventually be at cross-purposes with the machinery of law enforcement. And while I appreciate many of Purley's qualities, I would not put it past the good sergeant to withhold even nonessential information from us, for no other reason than to be contrary.

I didn't bother to follow the homicide team to the office because I knew they would find their usual chairs in the back of the room without an usher. The next ring of the doorbell brought Vinson and Debra Mitchell, who had shared a cab south. Vinson gave a tight smile and a nod, while she whispered to me that "This is a stupid way to do business, you know, wasting a lot of people's time."

I replied that I hoped she wouldn't find the trip a total waste and led them to the office, casting an admiring glance at Debra's beige outfit, which looked like it cost somewhere in the neighborhood of my weekly salary, if not more. The woman knew how to dress, I gave her that. Vinson, as our client, merited the red leather chair, while I placed Debra three places to his right in the front row. They both looked quizzically at Cramer and Stebbins, who already were seated, but I didn't offer introductions.

The next arrival was Franklin Ott. The agent looked angry enough actually to throw a punch himself this time. His face was still bandaged. He was followed in quick succession by a pale, somber Patricia Royce, a surly Keith Billings, and an arrogant, offended Wilbur Hobbs.

"I want to make it clear that I am here as a member of the press and not as some suspect in a sordid so-called murder,'' Hobbs pronounced as though he were reading from a script. I smiled, nodded, and escorted him to the office, where the critic surveyed the gathering, sniffed in condescension, and settled into the chair I indicated as though he were doing me a favor.

"Where the hell is Wolfe?'' Billings demanded.

"He'll be here shortly,'' I told the editor. "Would anyone care for drinks? Help yourselves. We've got a wide selection on that table, and if you don't see what you want, ask for it.''

"This wasn't billed as a cocktail party, but I have a feeling we're all going to need a bracer before it's over,'' Ott said, getting up. "I'm going to have a scotch. Can I get something for anyone else?''

There were no takers, only hostile muttering, so I went to the front room, opening the door. "They are all in place,'' I told Saul, who was reading an old copy of *Smithsonian*. He and Clarice rose, she reluctantly, and we proceeded down the hall to the office, where I seated her next to Vinson. Her entrance brought looks of puzzlement from around the room.

Saul took a chair in the back row next to Stebbins while I went around Wolfe's desk and pressed his beer buzzer. It rings in the kitchen, where he was waiting with Fritz until all were in place.

A half-minute later he appeared at the door, looked at each of his guests in turn, and walked in, skirting the desk and settling into his chair. "Good evening,'' he rumbled. "Thank you for adjusting your schedules. Your time here—''

"We don't need some meandering preamble,'' Billings snarled. "You asked us to come here, and we're here. Get on with it.''

"Sir, I never meander," Wolfe replied coldly. "And I do not indulge in the careless or unnecessary use of verbiage. As I started to say, your time here will be brief—assuming I am allowed to proceed without incessant and needless interruptions. First, I realize that many of you do not know the identity of others in the room, a condition I will rectify."

Even though the door to the hall was now closed, I could detect the faint ring of the doorbell, although none of the others in the room appeared to notice. That would be Wilma Race, whom Fritz was instructed to admit to the house. Wolfe continued: "The gentleman in the red chair is Horace Vinson, editor-in-chief of Monarch Press, the publisher of the late Charles Childress's books. He has hired me to identify Mr. Childress's murderer, which I am prepared to do. On his right, and likely a stranger to you all, is Clarice Wingfield, a cousin of Mr. Childress. On her right, Franklin Ott, a literary agent who formerly represented Mr. Childress, and next to him, Debra Mitchell, who had been engaged to Mr. Childress."

"I was *still* engaged to him when he was—when he died," the television executive protested.

"I did not mean to suggest otherwise," Wolfe said evenly. "In the second row, behind Mr. Vinson, is Keith Billings, an editor, formerly with Monarch Press and now employed by Westman & Lane. On his right is Patricia Royce, a novelist and friend of Mr. Childress's. And next to her is Wilbur Hobbs, a book reviewer for the *Gazette*."

"Who are they?" Ott stabbed a thumb toward Cramer and Stebbins.

Wolfe glared at him. "I was getting to that, sir. The gentleman in the brown suit is Inspector Cramer, head of Homicide for the New York City Police Department. Next to him is his associate, Sergeant Stebbins."

"And just what might *they* be doing here?" Wilbur Hobbs demanded shrilly. "I was not informed this was to be a police investigation."

"As indeed it is not," Wolfe replied, ringing for beer. "They are here at my invitation, and they remain at my sufferance. They may be of use before we adjourn, however."

"Meaning?" Patricia Royce asked tightly. It was the first word she had spoken since she had entered the brownstone.

"Meaning that as I said a moment ago, I intend to name Mr. Childress's murderer."

"Well, do so, man!" Billings barked. "Or are you being paid by the hour?"

"Dammit, you're making a mistake to slow him down," Cramer put in gruffly. "I've been to these sessions before, and he does them his way. He's as stubborn as a Missouri mule."

"As a police officer of high rank, I should think you would want to know immediately what's going on," Hobbs interjected loudly.

"If I can spend a few minutes here, so can you," Cramer shot back, the color rising in his cheeks.

"Thank you," Wolfe replied dryly, pouring beer from one of the bottles Fritz had brought in silently. "Mr. Vinson approached me shortly after Mr. Childress's death. He requested that I conduct an investigation. He was not satisfied with the verdict of suicide, and soon I concurred.

"It quickly became apparent that, metaphorically, there was a missing chapter in the story of Mr.

Childress's life and death. To begin with, a number of people harbored varying degrees of animus toward the dead man. To my knowledge, they all are in this room.''

Patricia Royce shuddered.

"Those who harbor what you term as animus don't necessarily go around shooting people," Franklin Ott snapped.

Wolfe dismissed the comment with a sniff. "Early in my investigation, an acquaintance of Mr. Goodwin's suggested, perhaps in jest, that all of you here, excepting Mr. Vinson, had conspired to dispatch Mr. Childress. I briefly—"

"That is . . . outrageous!" Clarice Wingfield huffed, leaning forward and clenching both fists. Her eyes blazed. The woman clearly possessed her late cousin's temper.

"Capricious, perhaps, but not outrageous, Miss Wingfield. I confess to you all that I briefly considered the possibility of a conspiracy before I discarded it. I then turned to the motives each of you, individually, possessed for wishing Charles Childress dead."

"*What* motives?" Patricia Royce snapped. She seemed to have regained control of herself.

Wolfe drank beer and set down his glass. "Madam, I am aware of three people in this room who have been accused of murdering Mr. Childress. And two of the accusers are present."

"I don't believe it."

Wolfe flipped a hand. "I mention that only to underscore that there are many conceivable motives for murder."

"And what was *my* motive?" Patricia persisted.

"That will come later. I weighed what I perceived

to be the various motives and the degree of stimulus behind each, considered the accusations that had been made, either to me or to Mr. Goodwin, and proceeded."

"Let's speed this up, dammit!" It was Keith Billings again, whom I had seated well beyond the reach of his old sparring partner, Franklin Ott. Debra Mitchell watched all of this exchange with cold interest. Maybe she was casting an episode of *Entre Nous*.

"All right, I shall begin with you," Wolfe told Billings. "Your dislike for Mr. Childress was manifest and widely known. From the beginning, the editor-writer relationship was extremely fractious. He was hostile to your suggestions and your attempts to strengthen his prose—particularly his plot structures. His friendship with your superior, Mr. Vinson, exacerbated the situation. Finally, the writer demanded a new editor, and that demand was met by Mr. Vinson. You resigned in anger from Monarch. Your hostility toward Mr. Childress increased when he excoriated you in an article that was read throughout the publishing community. Your career had been seriously damaged. Many would consider that series of events an adequate motive for murder."

"Bunk," Billings howled. "I landed on my feet after I left Monarch. My career has been doing just fine."

"Has it?" Wolfe raised his eyebrows. "Mr. Hobbs, you are a presumably disinterested observer of the publishing universe. Is Mr. Billings's current position of equal status to his former one?"

Hobbs chuckled smugly, a chilling sound. "By no means. In the first place, Monarch is an infinitely more prestigious house than Westman & Lane. Second, Mr. Billings has far less responsibility now than he had at Monarch. Also, you should know that the rumor on the street is that Westman is getting ready to dump him."

"That's a goddamn lie!" Billings screeched, lunging across Patricia Royce toward Hobbs. Purley Stebbins neatly grabbed the editor from the rear by his belt and forced him down into his chair with a thud. "Don't get up again," Purley said in a tone that left no doubt that he was in charge of maintaining order. Billings glowered at a spot on the floor between his feet, his face and neck a fiery red.

Wolfe finished his first bottle of beer and started on the second. "Miss Wingfield, you had known Mr. Childress longer than anyone else here. That relationship—a blood relationship—was renewed when Mr. Childress returned to his home in Indiana for a protracted period to attend to his mother during her final illness. While he was there, certain events transpired that pointed to the possibility of a permanent liaison between you."

Debra Mitchell twitched. This news had clearly penetrated her impassive facade. "And what events would those be?" she demanded shrilly.

"They are not germane at present," Wolfe replied crisply. "But Mr. Childress eschewed such a relationship with his cousin, which was a bitter pill for her—one that might be deemed a goad to violence."

"Bull. You don't even know me!" Clarice protested.

Wolfe lifted his shoulders a fraction of an inch and let them drop. "Did you not visit Mr. Childress at his domicile in Greenwich Village on numerous occasions, pleading, sometimes angrily, for a reconciliation?''

She toyed with a silver bracelet on her wrist, then looked up, her face anguished. ''That doesn't mean I shot him. I loved him,'' she said hoarsely.

''That's the first I've ever heard any of this,'' Debra Mitchell told Clarice in an accusing tone. ''In fact, I've never even *heard* of you. Charles never mentioned you—not once.''

''I'm not surprised to hear that,'' Clarice replied, still subdued. ''He was the father of my baby girl, and he didn't want anything to do with her—or with me.''

''I don't believe it,'' Debra said loudly as everyone else started jabbering excitedly. Wolfe scowled, waiting for the din to subside. When it did, he said, ''Miss Wingfield, you chose to divulge information that I was content to omit from this discussion. But since you have divulged it, I will only say that my knowledge of it intensified my interest in you as a suspect.''

''I'm not ashamed of what happened in Indiana between me and Charles.'' Both her tone and her expression were fiercely defiant.

''So noted.'' Wolfe turned toward Wilbur Hobbs. ''Sir, you incurred the anger of Charles Childress with your acerbic reviews of his books.''

Hobbs chuckled again. ''Not the first writer who's gotten mad at me, and likely not the last.''

''Indeed. But few if any authors have lashed back as did Mr. Childress. His denunciation of you in print was scathing.''

''And defamatory,'' Hobbs added without rancor, stroking his mustache.

''Perhaps. And prisons are filled with inmates

whose motives for murder were far less compelling than yours.''

The reviewer's smug expression did not change. ''Huh! Childress's diatribe did not harm me in the slightest. It's true that I didn't think much of him as a writer, but I wished him no ill.''

''So you now say,'' Wolfe replied impassively. ''You were not so mellow when you sat in this room previously and spoke of your anger toward Mr. Childress and your contemplation of a lawsuit.''

''I have had time to reflect,'' Hobbs said amiably.

Wolfe glowered, turning his attention toward the agent. ''Mr. Ott, you, too, suffered in print at the hands of Mr. Childress and his acid-tipped pen. He impugned you and your professional capabilities, and as an apparent result, you lost other writers that you had represented.''

''You can't prove that,'' Ott argued, shifting in his chair and gingerly touching his bandage.

''I believe I can, sir,'' Wolfe retorted. ''Further, there is the curious episode of the fracas in the restaurant between you and Mr. Billings. One might be tempted to surmise that you baited the man so that he would strike you and thus appear outraged—and by extension, guilty—of the incendiary accusation you leveled: that he had murdered Mr. Childress.''

''I had too much to drink.'' Ott waved away Wolfe's statement with a hand. ''I'm not proud of the way I mouthed off, but it was the liquor talking.''

''Or perhaps it was a stratagem on your part, the tactic of one who seeks to shift suspicion elsewhere.''

''Nonsense. That's the kind of logic that crops up in bad detective novels.''

''The novels of writers you represent, perhaps?''

Wolfe posed, raising his eyebrows. "Miss Mitchell, you had been affianced to Charles Childress for—what—six months?"

"Almost, yes," she said. "We were to be married in September."

"Yet Miss Royce insists that he was about to terminate your engagement."

Debra Mitchell turned and looked over her left shoulder at Patricia, who was in the row of chairs behind her. "In your dreams," she sneered at the other woman. "You always wanted him yourself—don't deny it. And you probably used every opportunity to turn him against me, you bitch."

"That's a lie," Patricia retorted. "I didn't have to say anything. He finally saw you for what you are, a—"

"Silence!" Wolfe roared. It was hard enough on him, having three women under his roof at once, but feminine bickering stretches him to the limit of his tolerance. "Miss Mitchell, at least one other person—someone who is not acquainted with Miss Royce—also reported that Mr. Childress was about to end your relationship—and perhaps already had." He was referring to the conversation I'd had with Clarice over coffee in Hoboken.

"So you say. Maybe . . . maybe Charles and I were having some, well . . . differences. Some differences, differences . . ." She seemed to crumble, burying her head in her hands. It was not pretty to behold.

For a moment, I thought Wolfe was going to get up and flee, but he courageously held his ground as Debra's sobbing gradually subsided. He drained the beer from his glass and forged on. "From the first, I felt it most probable that one of the women in this room was the killer. For starters, would Mr. Childress likely allow any of the three men—Messrs. Ott, Billings, or Hobbs—entrance to his apartment without a struggle? I think not, particularly given his current relationship with each of them. And there was no sign of a struggle, was there, Inspector?"

Cramer shook his head.

"But Mr. Childress would have readily admitted any of the women, even Miss Wingfield. They had feuded, but he continued to tolerate her presence in his abode."

"Tolerate! Is that what you call it, you pathetic male chauvinist?" Clarice shrieked, throwing up both arms and almost striking Vinson and Ott. "The man who fathers my child and then refuses to have anything to do with either of us deigns to tolerate *me*?" I thought she was going to dive at Wolfe, and I came halfway out of my chair before she slumped back, her chin against her chest, as she muttered about chauvinism and injustice.

Wolfe considered her through lidded eyes. "Madam, I confess to an unfortunate selection of words; you have my apology. Is it true that despite fractiousness between you, Mr. Childress did not bar your entry to his apartment?"

She looked up. "Yes. But that doesn't mean I killed him. That doesn't—"

Wolfe held up a palm, which, to my surprise, silenced her. "Mr. Childress's ownership of a handgun was widely known. Indeed, he crowed about it. This, as it turned out, was fatal braggadocio. It would have been relatively simple for any of these women to secure the pistol when Mr. Childress was otherwise occupied, to come upon him unawares, and to fire a single lethal shot at close range. After all, he felt no physical peril from their presence. Miss Wingfield's assaults—at least so far—had been verbal ones.''

''Meaning?'' interjected Cramer.

Wolfe ignored the bark of the NYPD and shifted his attention. ''Miss Mitchell, when you came to this office several days ago, you accused Patricia Royce of murdering Charles Childress.''

''And you said *I* was trying to shift suspicion to someone else,'' Franklin Ott snapped. ''Now there's your prime example.'' He pointed at Debra, who was still pale and shuddering from her earlier crying jag.

''I was misled,'' Wolfe conceded. ''Miss Mitchell behaved in such a fatuous manner when she was here that I discounted virtually all of her prattling. That was my mistake. I sit before you chagrined.''

''Wha-a-a-t?'' Ott bleated. ''What is it you're telling us?''

Debra Mitchell dabbed her eyes with a handkerchief and jerked upright. ''He's telling you that Patricia Royce *did* murder Charles. She loved him, but she couldn't have him. So she shot him.''

''Miss Royce *never* had amorous longings for Mr. Childress,'' Wolfe stated firmly. ''They were good friends until she learned he was a thief—in her eyes a thief of the worst sort.''

That set everybody off again, until Cramer silenced them with a bellowed ''Shut up!''

''Okay, Wolfe,'' the inspector growled, getting to his feet. ''Now I have to agree with Billings that this has dragged on too long. Are you accusing this woman''—he stabbed a finger at Patricia Royce—''of Childress's murder?''

250 · ROBERT GOLDSBOROUGH

"I am." Wolfe looked at Patricia. She met his gaze steadily. "Miss Royce had been working on Mr. Childress's personal computer to compose a novel because her computer had malfunctioned. Concurrently, he was writing a new Barnstable mystery. It is widely agreed, and I concur on the basis of reading one book, that his greatest weakness—although by no means his sole one—was a debilitating ineptness at constructing plots. Wilbur Hobbs had recently crucified Mr. Childress in his review of *Death in the North Meadow* for that very failing. That criticism rankled deeply. I surmise that one day, while at his computer, Charles Childress looked at Miss Royce's work-in-progress, perhaps out of simple curiosity. And he found some—or perhaps all—of its plot to his liking. He quickly saw a way out of his own dilemma and he seized it. He plagiarized. Very likely, he took only a little of Miss Royce's structure at first, but like so many thieves, he grew increasingly bold, and soon he had co-opted much of her book's structure, altering it of course to fit his characters and locale."

"That sounds incredibly farfetched." Horace Vinson was shaking his head.

"So it does," Wolfe conceded. "But how else do you explain his latest manuscript being described by you, sir, as far superior to the previous efforts? A description with which I concur. Miss Royce undoubtedly looked at *his* work in the computer—also driven by curiosity—and what she saw enraged her. They had been friends and mutual supporters in their chosen vocations for years, and now she found that he was duplicitous. He had stolen something very precious to a writer—her creation."

Cramer snorted. "Where's your proof?"

"I have none," Wolfe said, turning both palms up. "But is it not noteworthy that Miss Royce destroyed everything she had drafted for a novel that was reportedly nearing completion? Mr. Vinson, am I correct in stating that most authors preserve virtually everything they write?"

"Yes," he said. "Even if a manuscript is rejected by a dozen publishers or if the writer is deeply dissatisfied with it, he or she will almost always squirrel it away, whether on paper or, more recently, on a computer disk. The material may get reworked at a later time. And sometimes portions are cannibalized and used as part of another opus—this occurs more frequently than most readers realize. There's no question—authors are pack rats when it comes to their own prose. Nothing ever gets pitched."

"Just so. Yet Miss Royce carelessly mentioned to Mr. Goodwin that she had destroyed a nearly completed manuscript. That was her fatal error. And why had she destroyed it? Because she realized that if Mr. Childress's novel, much of which already was in the hands of his publisher, was to be posthumously published, hers never could be; the similarities would be so striking as to attract comparison. This in turn would raise cries of plagiarism—and probably also would cause speculation as to how Mr. Childress came to die. There was no question in Miss Royce's mind: Her book had to go. It was a price she must pay because she had murdered him."

"So I was right all the time!" Debra Mitchell crowed, turning again and smirking at Patricia as Purley moved in behind her.

"You were right about very little," the writer replied mildly. "First, I had no romantic interest whatever in Charles at any time. Mr. Wolfe is quite correct; we were friends and supporters of each other's work —until the end, that is. Second, Charles had absolutely no intention of marrying you. He couldn't stomach your social pretensions and your shallowness. He told me he wanted to stop seeing you, but hadn't worked up the courage to tell you."

"That is a lie—the lie of a murderer!" Debra keened, her beautiful face grotesquely contorted into a mask of rage. "Charles wouldn't have done that to me—he was a wonderful man!"

Patricia Royce smiled thinly. "You are wrong again. Charles was a twenty-four-karat bastard."

She was still smiling as Purley Stebbins read her the Miranda warning.

TWENTY-TWO

P atricia Royce got a life term in a brief trial and now resides in one of the state institutions. Her attorney tried to make the case that she shot Childress in a rage, but the prosecution's contention that the murder was premeditated held sway, as it should have.

Childress's last book never did get published. After Horace Vinson heard Wolfe's revelation, he lost all interest. Presumably, we have read the last of the exploits of one Sergeant Orville Barnstable of the Commonwealth of Pennsylvania.

As far as I am aware, Franklin Ott still toils as a Manhattan literary agent, although I have no insight as to his success in that Byzantine vineyard. Both Keith Billings and Wilbur Hobbs were unemployed at last report. Billings did indeed lose his job at Westman & Lane, reportedly because of his chronic inability to get along with his writers. And Hobbs "retired" as a *Gazette* book critic, although I happen to know from Lon Cohen that the departure was instigated by the paper's management. Lon, who did not appear heartbroken by the news, told me that Hobbs had accepted one too many gifts from a publisher.

Debra Mitchell, who still was screaming at Patricia Royce when she left the brownstone that Sunday night, did not immediately disappear from our lives. In the days following, Ms. Mitchell telephoned Wolfe six times, trying again to get him to appear on her network's *Entre Nous* TV show. The first time she called, he told her, politely but plainly, that he had no interest whatever in participating in any television program, now or ever. Damned if she didn't make another stab two days later, saying on that occasion that public interest in both his life and work was so intense that he had an "obligation" to appear.

"Indeed?" he replied with as much surprise as his voice ever conveys. "Madam, I know of no such obligation. My life is simple and my work is straightforward. The former is of no concern to anyone other than my immediate circle, and the latter already is well-chronicled in the press when such airing is merited. Please do not make this request again. Good day."

He didn't respond to her other four calls.

Wolfe's rebuff may or may not have been a contributing factor to her leaving town. About a month after her last call, Debra Mitchell took a job with a television station in Miami, according to an item I read in the *Times*. It said she was "leaving network public relations to fulfill her longtime dream of anchoring an evening news show." God help them in South Florida.

As for Clarice, she, too, is fulfilling a dream. I saw an ad in the Sunday arts section of the *Gazette* for an exhibit at a Village gallery of "Watercolors by Clarice Wingfield." I toyed briefly with going, but decided my appearance would bring only bad memories to a woman who already had more than her share of them.

The case had yet another postscript: Two days after the office gathering in which Patricia Royce had been nailed, we were paid a visit by the PROBE threesome, who had asked for ten minutes of Wolfe's time. As on their earlier visit, Claude Pemberton took the role as spokesman: "Mr. Wolfe, we appreciate your allowing Wilma to sit in on your denouement," he began after they all had been served coffee by Fritz.

"*Stand* in, you mean!" Wilma Race said with a good-natured laugh. "I was out in the hall the whole time—peering through the hole in that picture." She turned and gestured toward our waterfall painting. "Mr. Brenner was kind enough to supply me a footstool. That peephole of yours is built for a six-footer, not somebody five-three like me." She was beaming.

"She gave us a wonderfully complete description of what transpired," Pemberton went on. "We can't thank you enough."

"Yeah," Daniel McClellan put in. Today his sweater was pale yellow. "It was a hell of a lot more complete than the version in the *Gazette*."

"It should have been," Wilma chirped. "After all, it *was* an eyewitness report. The only nervous moment was when I had to jump off the stool and run into the kitchen as people started leaving the office. But nobody saw me."

"As to the money we raised to help pay you," Pemberton said to Wolfe, "we made another canvass of the donors, and they agreed with us that it be used to seed a trust fund for Clarice Wingfield's and Charles Childress's child. We haven't told any of our members her identity of course—we in this room are the only ones who know her name, and it will remain sacred within the confines of this room. But our donors were unanimous in saying that was an ideal use for the money."

Wolfe dipped his head a quarter of an inch, which for him is enthusiastic affirmation.

And yes, the new elevator finally got installed. I even rode in it the first day it was operational, and it's a dandy: dark, mahogany-look paneling, chrome trim, and indirect lighting. And it's as quiet as a Trappist monk. Never again will I be able to write that "the rumble of the elevator signaled Wolfe's descent from the plant rooms."

Too bad. I've grown fond of that phrase.

About the Author

ROBERT GOLDSBOROUGH, award-winning author of *Silver Spire, Murder in E Minor, Death on Deadline, The Bloodied Ivy, The Last Coincidence,* and *Fade to Black,* is a long-time Nero Wolfe fan and expert. Formerly an editor with the *Chicago Tribune,* he is now an editor with *Advertising Age* and *Business Marketing.* He lives in Wheaton, Illinois.

REX STOUT'S NERO WOLFE

A grand master of the form, Rex Stout is one of America's greatest mystery writers. Now, in this ongoing program dedicated to making available the complete set of Nero Wolfe mysteries, these special collector's editions will feature new introductions by today's best writers and never-before-published memorabilia from the life of Rex Stout.

❑	Fer-de-Lance	27819-3	$4.99/$5.99 in Canada
❑	The League of Frightened Men	25933-4	$4.99/$5.99 in Canada
❑	Where There's a Will	29591-8	$4.99/$5.99 in Canada
❑	Murder by the Book	27733-2	$4.99/$5.99 in Canada
❑	Not Quite Dead Enough	26109-6	$4.99/$5.99 in Canada
❑	Triple Jeopardy	23591-5	$4.99/$5.99 in Canada
❑	The Mother Hunt	24737-9	$4.99/$5.99 in Canada
❑	The Father Hunt	24728-X	$4.99/$5.99 in Canada
❑	Trouble in Triplicate	24247-4	$4.99/$5.99 in Canada
❑	Homicide Trinity	23446-3	$4.99/$5.99 in Canada
❑	The Black Mountain	27291-8	$4.99/$5.99 in Canada
❑	If Death Ever Slept	23649-0	$4.99/$5.99 in Canada
❑	Too Many Cooks	27290-X	$4.99/$5.99 in Canada
❑	Before Midnight	25291-7	$4.99/$5.99 in Canada
❑	The Mountain Cat Murders	25879-6	$4.99/$5.99 in Canada
❑	Over My Dead Body	23116-2	$4.99/$5.99 in Canada
❑	The Silent Speaker	23497-8	$4.99/$5.99 in Canada
❑	And Be A Villain	23931-7	$4.99/$5.99 in Canada
❑	Too Many Clients	25423-5	$4.99/$5.99 in Canada
❑	Three Men Out	24547-3	$4.99/$5.99 in Canada
❑	Some Buried Caesar	25464-2	$4.99/$5.99 in Canada
❑	Plot It Yourself	25363-8	$4.99/$5.99 in Canada

BANTAM MYSTERY COLLECTION